FURIES

T0358807

Praise for *Furies*

'A slick collection of clever tales, with something for bluestockings and banshees alike'

Observer

'Where power and feminist rage meet'

Stylist

'Delightful and thought-provoking'

Perspective

'The perfect tribute to Virago's legacy'

Tortoise Media

FURIES

MARGARET ATWOOD, SUSIE BOYT,
ELEANOR CREWES, EMMA DONOGHUE,
STELLA DUFFY, LINDA GRANT, ANNIE HODSON,
CLAIRE KOHDA, CN LESTER, KIRSTY LOGAN,
CAROLINE O'DONOGHUE, CHIBUNDU ONUZO,
HELEN OYEYEMI, RACHEL SEIFFERT,
KAMILA SHAMSIE, ALI SMITH

With an Introduction by Sandi Toksvig

virago

VIRAGO

First published in Great Britain in 2023 by Virago Press
This paperback edition published in 2024 by Virago Press

1 3 5 7 9 10 8 6 4 2

Introduction copyright © by Sandi Toksvig 2023
Copyright in the contribution 'Siren' © O. W. Toad Ltd 2023. Copyright in the
contribution 'Virago' © CN Lester 2023. Copyright in the contribution 'Churail' ©
Kamila Shamsie 2023. Copyright in the contribution 'Termagant' © Emma Donoghue
Ltd 2023. Copyright in the contribution 'Wench' © Kirsty Logan Limited 2023.
Copyright in the contribution 'Hussy' © Caroline O'Donoghue 2023. Copyright in
the contribution 'Vituperator' © Helen Oyeyemi 2023. Copyright in the contribution
'Harridan' © Linda Grant 2023. Copyright in the contribution 'Warrior' © Chibundu
Onuzo 2023. Copyright in the contribution 'Banshee' © Annie Hodson 2024.
Copyright in the contribution 'She-Devil' © Eleanor Crewes, 2023. Copyright in the
contribution 'Muckraker' © Susie Boyt 2023. Copyright in the contribution 'Spitfire'
© Ali Smith 2023. Copyright in the contribution 'Fury' © Rachel Seiffert 2023.
Copyright in the contribution 'Tygress' © Claire Kohda, 2023. Copyright in the
contribution 'Dragon' © Stella Duffy 2023

The moral right of the authors has been asserted.

*All characters and events in this publication, other than those
clearly in the public domain, are fictitious and any resemblance
to real persons, living or dead, is purely coincidental.*

All rights reserved.
No part of this publication may be reproduced, stored in a
retrieval system, or transmitted, in any form or by any means, without
the prior permission in writing of the publisher, nor be otherwise circulated
in any form of binding or cover other than that in which it is published
and without a similar condition including this condition being
imposed on the subsequent purchaser.

A CIP catalogue record for this book is available from the British Library.

ISBN 978-0-349-01716-7

Typeset in Sabon by M Rules
Printed and bound in Great Britain by Clays Ltd, Elcograf S.p.A.

Papers used by Virago are from well-managed forests and other responsible sources.

Virago Press
An imprint of
Little, Brown Book Group
Carmelite House
50 Victoria Embankment
London EC4Y 0DZ

An Hachette UK Company
www.hachette.co.uk

www.virago.co.uk

CONTENTS

INTRODUCTION

SANDI TOKSVIG

Warning – this is a book of 'wild writing'. If you are a woman, please make sure you are up to it. Have you girded your loins? Quelled your hysteria? Asked your husband's permission?

It seems incredible that not all that long ago, in Victorian times, there was a fairly common notion that reading could be bad for women, so I feel I should caution you – any female holding this book may never recover. You might become blind from straining your eyes and your nerves will certainly become grotesquely jangled from absorbing matters your system is too delicate to handle. If you insist on carrying on with this foolish enterprise then at least let a man read it first so he can determine which passages are appropriate. Right, that's the health and safety out of the way.

This book marks a remarkable moment in publishing history. Half a century ago the late, great Carmen Callil decided the world needed a feminist imprint and she founded Virago. It was 1973 and the 'second wave' of feminism was hitting the world stage. Women demanded social and political change, and along with it they wanted to see their lives celebrated, championed and reflected in what they were reading. I knew Carmen a little and can only imagine she must have been full of righteous rage to embark on such a venture. The very name Virago was a signal of a company that was never going to stop challenging the status quo. Strictly speaking it refers to a heroic warlike woman, but there are many other less flattering synonyms – biddy, bitch, dragon, fishwife, fury, harpy, harridan, hussy, muckraker, scold, she-devil, siren, spitfire, termagant, tygress, vituperator, vixen, wench ...

I long to be a combination of all of them because every one of those epithets sounds like a woman who would stand up for herself. Attempting to diminish women by name-calling is nothing new. I imagine since humans first vocalised language there have been those who thought a nasty title might make a woman a tad more docile and deferential, and likely to keep to her place in the cave. So much of it is gendered in subtle ways. Being a mistress is worthy of gossip, a master worthy of respect. A man can swell with pride at being called 'an old dog' while a woman is supposed to cower at being 'a bitch'. Keeping to my pet names theme here – a man may be a 'cool cat', which is worth strutting about, while a woman who is 'catty' doesn't deserve friends and ought to stay home. And if a woman carries on being cat-like in to her middle years she becomes a 'cougar', that terrifying prospect of a post-menopausal woman who still has a functioning libido.

(Sorry I need a minute while I think about sex ... I'm sixty-four, it's still one of my favourite topics ... I'm such a slut – *'a woman of dirty, slovenly, or untidy habits or appearance; a foul slattern'*. Earliest citation for such usage is 1402, predating citations for either the F-word or the C-word. I'm embracing it.)

*

OK, I'm back now.

Aged six I felt my first stirrings of feminist rage when, on a rainy day, the boys at school were allowed out to play while the girls stayed in to do colouring. I led my first strike (with success) and have been trying to change the world ever since. According to the World Economic Forum, the Covid-19 pandemic delayed gender equality by at least three decades. As I write, the current estimate for women and men finally to face a level playing field across politics, work, health and education is about 135 years. It won't happen in my lifetime, my kids', my grandkids' ...

So what shall we do in the meantime? Well, keep battling, keep being heard and listen to each other. Speaking out is not new for the 'fairer' sex. The words of women run like a fine thread through the whole history of writing. It was Enheduanna, High Priestess of both Inanna, the goddess of love, war and fertility, and the even more fun moon god Nanna (Sin) who invented poetry. Enheduanna lived in the Sumerian city-state of Ur over 4,200 years ago and she is the earliest known poet. In the early eleventh century it was the Japanese noblewoman Murasaki Shikibu who wrote what is considered by some to be the first novel, *The Tale of Genji*. Before Murasaki, Hrotsvitha (*c.* 935–973) became the first female historian and the first person in Western Europe to write drama since Antiquity.

I love all forms of writing but hold a particular soft spot for a short story. It is the very origin of telling a tale. Long before anyone could write anything at all, this was the form of storytelling around the camp fire. It was usually a simple plot with some kind of central theme, perhaps a moral lesson, which could be told in one sitting. What was the first one in the world? We'll never know, but I am confident that it began with women entertaining their children or each other while the men raced about after bison they couldn't catch.

One of the first collections of short stories I read as a child was *Grimm's Fairy Tales*, a book of more than two hundred yarns published in the nineteenth century. We remember the names of Jacob and Wilhelm Grimm but they were not the authors. The brothers merely gathered the stories and they harvested them, in the main, from women. There were a series of sisters who contributed – the Hassenpflug Sisters, the Von Haxhausen Sisters and the Von Droste-Hülshoffs. An elderly woman called Dorothea Viehmann gave them more than forty tales. My favourite source though is the Wild Sisters, Dortchen and Gretchen Wild. They lived in the same town as the Grimm Brothers but the Grimms were too poor to mix with the Wilds. Dortchen would meet Wilhelm in secret to tell him her stories and eventually they would make Wilhelm enough money to enable him to marry her. I love the idea of secret storytelling; of refusing to allow the circumstance of birth to rule one's later life, but how I wish I had known that the fairy tales were not Grimm but Wild. It was literally Wild writing. How mad it makes me that the boys made money and achieved recognition while the women got neither. I imagine how gripped those women might have been to sit down with this hoard of fables.

When Carmen chose the name Virago she was being unmistakable in her publishing intentions. Over the last fifty years Virago has revolutionised the literary landscape. Women's voices have been heard loud and clear, and with this volume the tradition continues. Each story is inspired by one of those Virago synonyms, as we veer from Helen Oyeyemi's *Vituperator* to Ali Smith's *Spitfire*, Chibundu Onuzo's *Warrior*, and along the way meet Kamila Shamsie's *Churail*, a kind of Pakistani harpy or ghost. It is a chorus of brilliant writers gathered in this place to speak their truth and unleash their rage. Does that mean, as Shakespeare might have it, that these stories are simply 'full of sound and fury, Signifying nothing?' Far from it. The tales are leavened with humour and humanity.

Some years ago, at another Virago celebration, I shared the stage and co-hosted with the legend that is Margaret Atwood. I am a super-fan. What an amazing writer – but I was not expecting her to be a comedian as well. She was hilarious. In another life I felt sure I might have found my double act partner. Dive into these stories and it is the shimmering Atwood waters you first encounter. Read the opening sentence – 'Today's Liminal Beings Knitting Circle will now be called to order' – and you know you're in for a marvellous time. 'You used to be a princess and now you're a toad? It can happen' is a sentence we can all identify with.

The glory of the collection is the breathtaking speed with which one minute you stand side by side with the inspiring uprising of Polish women in 1942 in Rachel Seiffert's *Fury* and the next you are rethinking your relationship with your own body after reading Stella Duffy's *Dragon*. I have been soothed and stirred by these works and sometimes both in the same moment.

The last time I saw Carmen we were having a drink in a London bar with an eclectic group of women, each successful in their own field. It was an expensive place where everything from the décor to the expected decorum was muted. Carmen, however, took exception to something someone said and launched into a diatribe about identity politics and self-determination. It was furious, fluid and unstoppable. It was also very loud. She had lost none of her rage and held court with her fury. It was magnificent to behold. 'Can't you get her to be quiet?' someone asked my wife, Debbie, who is a therapist. Debbie shook her head and replied, 'Why would anyone want to do that?'

Enjoy.

SIREN

MARGARET ATWOOD

In memory of Carmen Callil

Today's Liminal Beings Knitting Circle will now be called to order.

That's right, I said order. Why are you laughing? I'm not sure it's funny. Yes, I understand there is some irony in the fact that an assemblage of people – of creatures – of personae – who by their very natures present a challenge to the norms of social order, is being called to order. I get it, as they say. But it's still not funny, despite what the Harpies think. We can't have a Knitting Circle if we can't have meetings, and we can't have meetings without somebody running them.

So what makes me the bossy boots? Good question, Caeleno. Well, for one thing, I can talk. Unlike those who have undergone metamorphosis into, for instance, many-headed snakes. No offence, Scylla, but hissing is not the same.

Of course you can express your opinions, even if you don't have a voice as such! Just use the whiteboard. Hold it up. I can see it perfectly well from inside this aquarium – from inside this temporary accommodation. Not that anyone has thought to polish the glass since last week, and the place is overrun with clams. I have nothing against clams, but they get monotonous.

If you can't use the whiteboard yourself, ask somebody with fingers or other prehensile appendages to help you.

Yes, I realize I'm lacking in empathy, so kind of you to point that out, but if you gave one minute's thought to it you'd understand why. Haven't you ever heard of 'cold as a fish'?

And, by the way, I choose not to be wounded by the reference to boots. As we are all aware, boots are not an item of clothing I would ever wear, or be able to wear. Simply put, I do not have feet, as you can plainly see. The reason for that is a matter of personal history. Offered a choice between the object of my cold, fishlike passion – a human prince, to be exact – and the loss of my golden voice in exchange for the bipedalism necessary for human sexual congress, I remained loyal to song. Yes, unlike my naïve younger sister, I gave up my romantic dream of being a mute human woman with foot problems and stuck with my liminal but melodious art. I'm not saying that this doomed romance didn't injure what I am pleased to refer to as my heart. But it improved my music, or so I am told. Gave it more depth.

Yes, it's true that I'm famous for luring sailors to their deaths, but that's a biased view. It takes two to tango, not that I tango. But I wouldn't be able to lure those sailors if they didn't want to be lured. And I'm good at what I do. I've put a lot of work and study into the luring business. It took me centuries to hone the finer details, while enduring demeaning taunts from those sailors I hadn't managed to lure successfully. 'Codsbody' is not a pleasant nickname, nor is 'Sharkpussy'. Though I took revenge on my tormentors in due time: I have a noteworthy collection of sailors' buttons, bitten off their uniforms. I'm thinking of having them made into a grotto.

But that's enough about me. Now, the meeting! I call it to order. We have some important decisions to make!

Melusina, would you please come down off the curtain rod? Yes, I recognize that you are part serpent, we all appreciate that. But it's distracting. Couldn't you just coil yourself somewhere?

Thank you.

Now. The Liminal ... What is the concept? Ah. It's your first time? You used to be a princess and now you're a toad? It can happen. But you're good at handicrafts, what with all the embroidering you once did as a princess? That's very good news! We are making a group afghan. It's an old pattern, it came down to us from Grendel's Mother. When she wasn't ripping the heads off Danes she was an excellent craftsworker, and she recycled, as well. All natural materials. I have a shepherd's pie recipe from her that I'm told is excellent, for those who like shepherds.

You'll be assigned a square – Arachne here is in charge of that – and you'll be shown how to encode the names of our enemies in the stitches. When your square has been completed it will be incorporated into the growing tapestry. Many fingers make light the work! Welcome!

And now let me explain the reason for the existence of our little group. You old hands – yes, I recognize that some present do not have hands as such. All right then, old hands, wings or claws. Or fins. Or tentacles. Let me put it another way: you *long-time members* – will that do?

I will proceed. You long-time members have heard this before, so kindly forgive the repetition. The Liminal Beings Knitting Circle exists for those among us who have been excluded from all other leagues, clubs, sectors, definitions, unions, associations, identities, cultural niches and groupings generally, through our failure and/or our unwillingness to fit into or conform to a given accepted social or taxonomical category, or categories.

The Knitting Circle is for 'presumed female'. 'Presumed male', such as Manticores, Cyclopes, Minotaurs and Balrogs, have a Billiards Club.

But whether Knitting Circle or Billiards Club, we have all had the experience of being despised and even feared; we have all had the experience of being, as it were, exiled and shunned. We are not welcome in respectable company, to put it mildly. That is why we have begun these groups: they were formed to provide a safe space where we need not live in terror of the double-bladed labrys, or the charmed harpoon, or the flaming torch and pitchfork, or the crucifix and garlic, or the silver bullet . . .

I'm sorry, that was tactless. Yes, I know it was triggering. Steady on! Use the choke collar. Thank you. We can repair the upholstery later.

'Liminal' comes from the Latin word *limen*, meaning a threshold. As you are well aware, each and every of us has one foot on either side of any given threshold, for instance— What is it now?

Please stop gibbering. Oh, I see: 'foot' is problematical. I should know better, considering that I myself do not have any feet? I suppose it would be fruitless for me to explain that I was using 'foot' as a metaphor, but I bow to your superior sensitivity. I withdraw 'foot'. Please expunge it from the minutes. I will rephrase. As you are well aware, each of us experiences one half – plus or minus – of our beings on one side of a cultural or taxonomic divide, and the other half – plus or minus – on the other side. I give you the duck-billed platypus.

No, no, Francine darling. I don't mean I'm going to give you away to anyone! Not to a zoo, no! Not in a million years! I wouldn't think of it! You are our *mascot*!

The poor thing is so easily frightened. Please tell her it's safe to come out from under the monopod.

Let me rephrase. *As an example*, there's the duck-billed platypus. It's a mammal in that the females have mammary glands, it has fur, but it has a bill and it lays eggs, like a bird. You can imagine what the closed-category classifiers must have felt when confronted by that! They simply had to come up with another way of sorting, didn't they? And that's what we in the Liminal Beings Knitting Circle, as well as the Liminal Beings Billiards Club, are campaigning for, among other things: another way of sorting.

Before proceeding, let us take a moment to remind ourselves of the more positive side of our nature. Liminal Beings are recognized by humans as potentially dangerous, yes; and we can be dangerous; but we are also thought of as potentially wise and instructive. Well, some of us are; many-headed serpents not so much, apologies to Scylla. Achilles was raised by a centaur, as some in the Billiards Club never tire of pointing out. Liminal Beings preside over threshold-crossings, changes of state and initiations. Weddings, funerals, childbirth, swearings-in, occasions like that. We are helpful to those who find themselves in the space between one recognized category and another. Animal and human. Unborn and born. Childhood and adulthood. Single and married. Man and woman. Sea and land.

Who made that Surf 'n' Turf joke? Oh. One of the Harpies, as usual.

To recap. We testify to the malleability, the versatility, the lava-like plasticity of nature.

That having been said, there are limits. Now that Liminal Beings have become fashionable, not merely as mosaic floor decorations but as models for lived experience, far too many have been claiming membership in our organizations. Last year there was that matter of the vampires. Some of you were averse to admitting them on the grounds that they were not, as it was termed, 'Classical', but the vampires made a strong case for their liminality as being between life and death, and after a spirited debate during which a couple of members were unfortunately depleted of their bodily fluids, followed by a close show of hands – of frontal appendages – they made it in. They are quite wealthy, having had a great deal of time to accumulate loot, I mean savings, and several of them have made substantial donations to our Retirement Fund. Not that any of us ever retire.

But now this matter of the zombies has come up. I have heard it said that if the vampires are allowed in, the zombies ought to be allowed in as well, as it is the same alive/dead sort of liminality, but I strongly disagree. The vampires have preserved their individual identities through many changes, whereas the zombies don't have any identities. You can't have an identity without a brain. And you can't be a being, much less a Liminal Being, if you don't have a—

What do you mean, what about the fungi? Is a fungus a being? Yes, it's an entity of a sort, but a being? No, I do not wish to discuss *Being and Nothingness* as it relates to truffles. How did we get sidetracked onto this whole fungus topic?

Order, please! Let us focus on the business at hand! The tide is turning and I don't want to get beached.

Look, I don't know why we're even considering the zombies. They haven't asked to join. No mystery about that, they can't talk, but if they *could* talk they would not be clamouring to get in. Certainly not into the Knitting Circle. They have no interest in yarns.

They don't even know what 'Liminal Being' is, so what difference does it make to them whether they're in or not? No, they cannot be educated about that. How many times do I have to emphasize that they do not have brains? They have nothing but goo between their ears, if they even have ears! They're falling apart!

I am not blaming the victim. I know it's not their fault that they are basically just reeking heaps of disintegrating bio-trash. It's reality, let's face up to it.

May I have a motion to put this to a vote? All in favour of the zombies being excluded, raise an appendage.

Thank you. We've got to have standards.

Finally, a matter that has been troubling us for some time. It presents a problem that nothing else in our experience has ever come close to. I speak of the Disappeared. When a person or even a Liminal Being simply vanishes – becomes lost to view, as it were – they cannot be classified as dead or alive, as existing or not existing. Thus far they are liminal. But their state is unverifiable, because they could be anywhere. In the old world, such a person could not cross the Styx, drink of Lethe, and be reborn: they were doomed to wander the earth, plaguing wanderers and frightening horses, until they were discovered and given a proper burial. In this more recent world Lethe doesn't come into it, but their unknown state causes a great deal of distress to their loved ones.

We do sympathize. Many of us are former humans who were transformed into fountains or trees or birds or sunflow-ers or spiders or whatnot. Our relatives didn't even know where we'd gone! The gods who do this kind of transforming are very bad at constructive messaging.

I apologize. I did not mean 'or whatnot' in any disparag-ing way.

My point is, a number of us are capable of knowing or dis-covering where these lost ones are. The Dryads, the Nereids, even the Melusinae – they know what or who is lost in forests, what or who is bobbing around in the oceans. Occasionally they have attempted to share this information with the anxious and grieving humans concerned, with unfortunately negative results. Humans who hear a tree or a snake speaking to them, especially about corpses, will either run away screaming or put it down to the ingestion of too many hallucinogens.

But our duty is not only to the relatives. Surely it is to the lost ones themselves, whether alive or dead. They long to be found! That's why they're always pestering people in dreams. They long to be reunited with who they once were, they long to be recognized for who they are now. They long to have their stories fully told, tragic endings and all; and the endings usually are tragic, as you know. Still, telling the story allows completion. It allows release. Or so it is believed.

We in the Liminal Beings Knitting Circle are uniquely placed to understand these longings, the longings of those trapped on thresholds. The Uncanny Valley is our habitat. We know what it's like to lack a definitive certification. Can we help these poor lost souls? Are we up to the challenge? Can we forget our differences, refrain from eating the material vestiges, and work together on this? Although we cannot bring joy or solace, we may at least offer closure. And gift the bereaved relatives one of our cosy, comforting afghans, once it has served its primary purpose as an instrument of revenge and the enemy knitted into it is defunct.

May we have a show of appendages?

Please, tone down the clanging of brazen claws. I know you mean it in a positive sense, Medusa, but it's very loud.

Thank you. The formal part of the meeting is now adjourned. We can gossip among ourselves while consuming the assorted refreshments. If you don't approve of the assorted refreshment that someone else is consuming, or of how they are consuming it, just look the other way.

Then will we to our separate elements disperse.

Happy knitting.

VIRAGO

CN LESTER

Personal notes on Case 36

19 July

First consultation this afternoon of a new case, which promises to prove the most interesting – or, more correctly, the most novel – of those I've so far encountered under Doctor K—'s instruction. No records, no details, were given to me beforehand; K— maintained his typical opacity, and said only, 'I want your unadulterated impression.' He had the look, or rather the deliberate absence of a look, I've seen him adopt numerous times with his patients, which warned against disagreement. The weather was warm, the room stuffy; the time of the appointment came and went.

When the knock sounded I was waved to sit down and remain where I was, to the side of and at one remove from the main thrust of the Doctor's chair, its corresponding opposite. Some words at the door – a coarse bark, laughter, a quiet murmur – and in came our patient. I believe I covered my surprise. I would not have been able to say the same six months ago.

The dirty, colourless dress, the much-worn, dingy cap and apron, announced the identity of a prisoner, a female prisoner, but the person within that costume – the form, bearing and features – was a young man around my own age. His physique was trim but well-developed, his footsteps a little too bold, as though in defiance of his present situation. Each part bespoke confidence, command, except his head, which hung down, his gaze as it were deliberately and even punitively lowered – from shame or from fury, I could not decide. He did not sit, as directed, but stood awkwardly, obstinately, in the middle of the room.

I have seen K— work his charms on uncooperative patients before, and his behaviour this time was no different; he spoke a little, in a gentle but straightforward tone, about his work, how he liked to go about things, what was expected from and between each one of us in the room. He bustled about, not from a genuine need to retrieve the patient's file (already at the forefront of his papers) or to pour himself water (he had drunk a glass off before we began), but to give the young man a chance to acclimatise, to look around and become used to us without the sensation of being observed. I watched all this from the corner of my eye, to give the impression of disinter-est – I answered the Doctor's little questions on the weather, the time of year, I lit a cigarette, I made myself comfortable. The patient remained standing; K— was not rattled. This initial refusal to engage, as I have learnt, is not uncommon among those brought here under circumstances of others' making, and can usually be resolved with the reassertion of an unthreatening environment, a little friendliness, an open and ready ear. Seemingly at the end of his social chatter, he smiled with good humour, and asked, as though weary, 'You will not mind, at least, if I sit down?' Getting no response, he lowered himself into his chair, pulling towards himself the small and tidy pile of his current reading, his pencil for annotation. As if speaking to the air, he said, 'I am perfectly content to wait until you're ready and able to talk – but I hope you will not mind if I use the time productively?' This, too, was his usual method; no patient I have yet seen, no matter how much they put on a show of ignoring us, can go long being themselves ignored.

Every now and then the Doctor's pencil would make a decisive scratch in a margin, and the noise from the street below came muffled through the windows. I myself picked up the nearest book to hand and, with it open on my knees as cover, took the opportunity to study our patient more closely. I could not see his face fully, turned down and away as it was, but the line of the jaw stood out in sharp relief against the tatty little kerchief knotted around the neck; the tendrils of hair escaping from the sides of the bonnet were a rich auburn. The hands and wrists were an almost comical sight, poking out from the insufficient length of the sleeves: strong hands, with blunt fingers, and bronzed from the sun. The erect carriage reminded me of a soldier, or a consummate horseman, and the contrast between this and his clothing made me wonder if some kind of rule-breaking of the more bizarre and riotous kind within the ranks was the reason for his being brought here. At that thought I steadied myself, and cleared my mind – my task at this point was not to make judgements without facts, but to observe, to open myself up for observation, to drink down the whole of the situation to bottle and store up for later analysis. The clock ticked. I allowed my vision to grow soft, undifferentiated – the impressions within the room came to me, not I to them: the distant noises, the heavy air, and the almost imperceptible sound of three persons gradually coming to breathe together in one rhythm.

The knock at the door, an hour after the first, was like an awakening. K— stretched in a not wholly exaggerated gesture, nodded to us both, said brightly, 'The guard.' Again, he went to the door alone, again the muffled voices, and he returned with a solicitous smile, and an arm outstretched to lead our patient away. It was not until his farewell named it – his handing over of the prisoner – that I realised our young man was a woman. 'I thank you for your time, Miss W—, and look forward to our appointment tomorrow,' and he looked not to her as he said it, but across the room to me. I could not hide my surprise so well a second time.

20 July

Another silent hour of studying the carpet today, and not so easy as the first – for me, at any rate. K— unperturbed, but gave me the case file to go over, to see if I might formulate, on my own, the most appropriate way to proceed. It sits here as I write this, its three parts spread out: the criminal record, the personal statements (by and against the accused), and the initial medical report. Hanging over us is the task allotted to us by the court: to determine the underlying cause, the drive, and therefore the culpability of Miss W—'s behaviour. The crimes themselves are a mixture of the mundane and the extraordinary, and it was only in the course of the former that the latter was discovered.

The narrative supplied by the police can be condensed as follows: in December of last year, Mr W— (as she was then living) arrived in our city after fleeing her creditors in G—. Working as a journalist and translator, she struck up a friendship with an occasional colleague, Mr S—, inspired in part by their shared habit of gambling. In due course she was introduced to his family, including an unmarried sister, Anna; an attraction was formed, and the marriage took place in June with the brother's blessing. As the romance developed so too did W—'s reliance on S—'s funds, and the promised repayments deteriorated from late and partial to non-existent. The friendship soured, and the animosity between the two ignited into violence on the night of 11 July following an evening at their habitual drinking den near Fleischmarkt. Unable to eject them, and fearing substantial damage to his property, the landlord went for the police, and in processing the arrest the discovery of W—'s true sex was made.

Mr S—, for his part, was incredulous, his accounting to the point: no, he had had no idea, and the insinuation that his sister must have been party to the deception was met with outrage. He demanded not only repayment, but criminal prosecution for the fraud committed against his family. Miss S— (for so she must now be called) made only a brief statement, her shock noted by the interviewing officer: she could not and would not believe it. In contrast to these few sentences, the record of W—'s statement was a little longer, though not so long or so detailed as I know K— would have liked. It included a précis of her history as an explanation to the crime, against which he had scribbled his usual warning: '*cum grano salis*'. She had, she claimed, been living in the guise of a man – or a boy – since her earliest years, encouraged in this eccentricity by her father who, upon noticing the child's masculine inclinations, gave her the name 'Nicolas'. Physical exertion, feats of daring, and the bohemian life gave her the greatest of pleasures, and she recoiled from all that was feminine excepting that it was found in the figure of a beloved woman. Gambling and writing were her twin passions, brothels were not unknown to her, and she had once been wounded in a duel. She herself noted the discrepancy between her previous affairs and the profound and tender love she professed for S—'s sister (the word 'noble' twice employed), a love she believed conducive to the highest, and previously unfulfilled, expression of manliness. Anna, she asserted, had no reason to doubt her husband was anything other than what he appeared to be. No details were supplied as to how that illusion may possibly have been maintained on the supposed consummation of the union.

The medical report at least had been conducted to standards acceptable to the Doctor's method – soon, I suppose, to be mine. Full measurements had been taken of the patient's skull, the proportions noted, and the same for the pelvis and spine; the hips were found to be so little developed that they did not correspond in any way with those of a female. The hard palate was narrow, the teeth somewhat abnormal, the thighs and arms remarkably muscular, the larynx of a decidedly masculine formation, and the extremities thickly covered with hair – but the mammae were described as soft and, to my surprise, the genitals apparently showed not a trace of hermaphroditic development: labia majora touching each other almost completely, labia minora projecting beyond with a cock's-comb-like frill, the clitoris small and very sensitive. The vagina was noted as being so narrow that the insertion of a *membrum virile* would be impossible; the uterus was felt, through the rectum, to be about the size of a walnut, immovable and retroflected.

The report concluded with a proposed diagnosis of congenitally abnormal inversion of the sexual instinct, and I understood why K— had wished me to confront the facts as they appeared without the prejudicial distraction of another physician's opinions. It was our task to determine the extent and qualification of the anomaly – whether psychico-hermaphrodism, viraginity, or gynandry – and to ascertain whether or not Miss W— had seduced 'his' wife to homosexual acts, and if she could and should be held accountable. So much the court had asked of us. Whether the taint in the patient is congenital – and, if congenital, incurable – is what we must ask of ourselves.

21 July

I had only a minute to consult with K— before the arrival of Miss W— at the end of the afternoon, thanks to an unpleasant and strenuous morning's work at the hospital, covering the cases of an absent colleague as well as my own. The Doctor said nothing to me as I entered what I have still not yet come to consider 'our' room: a sure sign that a new direction of thought was brewing. The knock came as I was preparing my notebook and pen; I asked, in a low voice, 'Do you think I might try something?' and got only 'Do you think you might try something?' in return. The handover was swift; both parties assumed the same position as the day before, standing and sitting, the one with her eyes averted and the other carefully, cheerfully, looking elsewhere. After a few small remarks about the weather and an offer of water he would have known would be ignored, he brought out today's method of distraction, a newspaper. 'Far too hot for any strenuous thinking,' he said to neither one of us, and settled down to read.

All morning I had been debating within myself the best way – perhaps any way – of persuading our patient to engage. If she had been a private client we could have taken our time, but the trial was pressing and our diagnosis necessary for a greater public good. Still, I did not want to destroy the chance of building a rapport between us before we had even begun, losing any slight hope we might have of treatment. I lit a cigarette, drummed my fingers, listened to K— turn a page. The patient, deliberately or not, had angled herself a little more towards the door this time, affording me a view of the broad and well-muscled back; in all honesty, if I had not read the truth of it, I would have struggled to believe her a woman. The arms were held exceptionally still, and she did not shuffle or shift position; the only thing that moved were her ribs, opening and closing with the force of her breath. Before I could think better of it I said, 'Nicolas?' and saw an instantaneous reply in the body before me as she froze. Slowly, so that she could follow my actions, I rose, and stepped a little closer, so that there would be two of us standing. I chose my next words with care: few enough to leave a gap for her to fall into, straightforward enough to flatter. 'We are going to have to diagnose you, one way or the other, and soon. I do believe you already know this. It would be better with your help, if there was anything that would put you at ease?'

The head did not lift, the shoulders did not loosen, but after a long pause there was an audible inhalation, then 'A cigarette, for God's sake.'

There was a catch in the throat, as though she had not spoken for some time, and whatever voice I had expected I could not remember it after hearing her actual words. I lit one of my own and held it out, and she turned and looked up at last; I actually felt myself begin to flinch at the expectation of her expression, though I did not know what I was expecting or why it would matter – but there was nothing. I studied her face. The brow was high and intelligent, and the features fine, even handsome, strikingly masculine but for the absence of a moustache. The eyes were the one hint of delicacy: large, extraordinarily dark, and utterly blank. A broad hand reached out for the cigarette, placed it between chapped lips, and I lit another for myself to seem companionable. I let her smoke in silence for a while, then asked again, 'What would put you at your ease?'

Instantly: 'My clothes.'

I nodded, though I did not know how easy it would be to arrange. 'We can find you your clothes. If we do so, will you agree to cooperate here, with us?'

Her eyes flicked to the seat where K— still sat reading, separated from us by the barrier of his paper held before him; she resembled nothing so much as a dog wary of approaching a strange hand. Then I saw her gather her dignity, such as it was, and 'I will cooperate, but not with him – only with you. And not without my clothes.' Before I could answer she had turned smartly on her heel, reached the door, knocked for the guard, was gone – a confused shout brought K— to his feet to authorise her return.

He was smiling as he strolled back to his desk and began to tidy his things. With a chuckle he said, 'Well – that does look like it for the day, doesn't it?' I made to join him at his desk, but he stopped me with a hand: 'No, leave it – you'll need to plot your plan of attack for that one tomorrow, and I have a few thoughts to explore on my own.'

I hesitated: 'Do you mean to go along with her request?'

'I do – why not? Gets her to talk, gets you a taste of working alone. Keep the same time – I'll make myself scarce. You can report back to me when you've cracked it – your verdict on our little virago.' He chuckled again and reached for her file. 'Into your hands she goes,' he said, and delivered the case to me.

22 July

I cannot pretend that my curiosity was solely of a profes-sional nature, waiting for Miss W—'s arrival in her habitual costume. I fully expected it to suit her better than her prison dress, and to expand upon, to clarify, the extent and true nature of her condition. Speaking honestly to myself, though, I admitted a prurient desire to see, and to know: how had she done it? How could she have passed unnoticed? What small tell would give her away? Though I scolded myself, waiting, for letting my imagination run loose, I could not control the images that presented themselves to me, of all the actresses, the sopranos, I have seen on stage in travesty roles – their self-conscious heroics, the exaggerated masculinity that called attention to, rather than covered, the discrepancy between illusion and reality.

I had not thought that the man – the person – who entered the room this afternoon would appear so essentially congruent that he would unnerve me completely. If I had seen him in the street I would have walked past without remark; if we had been introduced as colleagues I would have shaken his hand. I write 'he' here because that is the impression she gave me, and I looked at her knowing all of the details of the body that moved beneath that clothing, well-cut and fashionable, and still could not see it. She walked across the room with an easy, authoritative manner; with her head finally raised, we stood eye-to-eye.

'I see you are still trying to put me at ease,' she said, and gestured to where I had moved both our chairs closer to the window, with water and cigarettes on a table between them.

'Yes,' I replied, sitting, inviting her to do the same, 'that is exactly what I am trying to do.'

'And to what end?'

'To understand you.' Incredulity raised her eyebrows, so I expanded: 'There is the task that I must do, which is to help those prosecuting your crime – if it was a crime – to understand exactly what happened, and what drove you to those actions. And there is the task I must do for myself, for my profession, and for you, if you will let me – which is to know and understand you as you are, and to help you with what you could be.'

Those black eyes did not blink once as I spoke, but she eventually nodded, and I felt some small relief that the first hurdle had been cleared. 'Please, help yourself,' I said, as I busied myself with notebook and pen, marking again the bluntness of the fingers that stretched for the bottle as she leant forward to pour a glass. In that act of reaching, one side of her neck, just at the line of the collar, was exposed, and I felt my gaze drawn to the shiny ridge of pink and white scarring, stark against the sun-touched healthy skin surrounding it. She was wounded, I remembered, in a duel. She had noticed my staring and gone quite still. I met her eyes: 'Your wound – I was wondering how it was treated, without your secret coming to light?'

Those fingers moved to her collar: 'I have learnt that some friends are better than others, as you will know. I had a good friend with me that day.' Then she shook herself, laughed, and drank her water. 'So – what is it you need to know?'

'I need, in your own words, your testimony.'

'But I've already given it!'

'Not to me.'

26 July

A frustrating development in our sessions of the last two days – likely one which K— would have pre-empted, given his experience with patients of this type. I feel my own lack of experience sorely, and must ask myself whether this is inevitable in one's first case without supervision, or a sign of something deeper within myself still to be discovered and addressed. Whichever it is, I have got the patient talking – but only around the subjects and areas she wants to discuss. Bring up the facts of her case, the contradictions and deceptions still begging answers, and she snaps closed, tight as a shell.

In K—'s earlier publications he noted the intelligence and charm demonstrated by many of the inverted type, however underdeveloped and ill-used those talents inevitably remain. Privately, in our conversations, he has told me of the hundreds of letters sent to him by fellow sufferers, all desperate to add their own case histories to the ones in print: a kind of solipsistic – onanistic even – obsession with their own narratives. W— is proving no different, and yet it is hard to dislike her for it. More honestly, it is hard to dislike 'him', because when I have listened to her recount the years spent at university abroad, and her translations of Catullus for pleasure, of popular novels for ready cash, then it is 'Nicolas' to whom I am listening, and I understand how that character has allowed her to pass through the world in her own singular fashion. Bring up duelling, drinking, gambling, and then she talks, even becomes effusive, even smiles. Allow her to ponder the women she has loved and her language grows elevated, almost self-consciously poetic, though she turns sad and quiet when I ask about Anna. But when I put to her plainly the facts of her sex and push for an explanation of her behaviour then I am faced once again with the sulky mule of our first meeting. And so we go back and forth, voluble to silent, and I cannot yet determine whether this delusion can be broken, whether she enters into it willingly – if it is a taint of nature that compels her or something else, perversity or perversion – and how culpable she might be for her fraudulent marriage.

If I could not persuade her to divulge the specifics of her *vita sexualis*, I felt that I must at least convince her to trust me with the methods she has used to escape suspicion. With only a little time left this afternoon I asked her, plainly, how she managed the fact of her menses without discovery. When she pretended she had not heard me I asked her again. For the first time, she grew irritated with me: 'Why must you talk about that?'

'Because,' I said, and kept my tone light, 'it is necessary so that I may understand you.'

'I've told you already, enough to understand.'

I looked at her directly, and she did not look away: 'Nicolas, both you and I know how much more there is to understand.'

She made a rough sound of disgust and got to her feet, took a cigarette, turned her back to me and smoked it. I waited. If she had to pantomime her rejection of me in order to speak then I would accept it – I must, for the method to work. I knew the power of a waiting silence, after one has become used to the free flow of confession.

'It is not something I like to consider,' she said at last, and seemed to stumble on her words. 'It ... does not come very often. I manage my own linen. If ever a servant notices, they will also know that there are reasons any man might sometimes bleed there.'

I took my time in writing it down, along with my own thoughts on the matter. She remained where she was, turned away. 'There,' I said, and closed my notebook, 'was that really so fearful?' She pivoted, and for a second time I felt the expectation of a flinch run through me – that her expression would be hateful, her eyes would burn – and why would it even matter? But there was nothing there: a blankness, nothing more.

When I returned home this evening there was a note from K— waiting. Unless he wants something, he does not deal in pleasantries. 'Diagnosis due Friday.'

27 July

I could not get my answers head-on, and must therefore make use of a more diffuse approach. W— liked to talk; all I had to do was to encourage her, guiding with a light hand, until she had run herself around the long way to where I needed her to go.

'Tell me exactly,' I said, when we were both settled, 'of the moment at which you became aware of the differences between men and women. And of the usual relations between them.'

'Oh, quite young, I think. The usual age – is there a usual age?'

I nodded, but did not interrupt, passing my cigarette case along the table.

'Thank you.' She lit a fresh cigarette from the end of another – she smoked voraciously – and looked appraisingly at me. 'Are you asking me to tell you how I came to know who I am?'

I nodded again, and lifted my pen expectantly – she laughed at that. And told me. As in her initial testimony, she spoke of her father, with evident feeling, and his understanding of her true nature – and his similar kindness towards her brother, who later became her sister. It took all my patience not to interrupt her at that, but I nodded, and scribbled, and kept my eyes down. She learnt Latin, she learnt mathematics, she learnt to ride a horse and fire a pistol and handle a blade. She learnt from watching her father the joys and sorrows that a beautiful woman could bestow, and at the age of thirteen she fell in love with the daughter of a neighbouring household, who only ever knew her as a boy. That childish affair did not last, and nor did the next – or any of them through her studies, her travels, but of each woman she had loved she

spoke with warmth, even those she had paid to know for a
night or two only. It was to this warmth that she attributed
her romantic success; some little pride animated her features,
but she said modestly, 'It is because I listen, I think. I am very
happy, listening to a charming woman, and coming to know
how to please her.'

'I understand,' I said, recording it all. 'You have made it
quite clear. But I wonder if there was ever a time when you
considered that these feelings might more usually – more naturally – be directed towards the male sex?'

Her gaze was resolute. 'I am as nature made me.'

'Is that what your father told you?'

'It is what I know.' She paused. 'Do you believe in God?'

I smiled, a little, and waved her away. 'We are not here to
discuss what I believe.'

She looked at me intently. 'I thought that you would not.
But I do. I believed in Him as a supreme goodness before I ever
read a philosopher explain the same, and so I see His evidence
in myself as much as in the rest of the world. I am made in His
image, no more or less than any other being. So how could
it be anything other than natural to act in accordance with
my nature?'

'Not everyone thinks so.'

'But I know so,' she insisted, as though to force me to
agree. 'What could be more natural than to be struck by the
beauty of a captivating woman? To admire the grace of her
form and her native intelligence, to pay respect to her, to love
and be loved by such a creature? And would it not in turn be
unnatural to put in her place some kind of hulking lout? Or,
worse, a prosaic little man with no colour, no light, no charm?
To endure his presence, his smell, his breath: would that seem
natural to you?'

'It would not.'

'Exactly my point.' The more she spoke the more I became aware, almost ironically, of the sheen of sweat on her upper lip – on my own also – and the mixed odours of her unwashed hair, the tobacco smoke, the scent of my pomade in the airless room.

'Then the women you have loved,' I asked, keeping my expression calm, 'they feel the same way?'

She was trapped, and said nothing. I pressed on, but gently: 'Or would you say that they themselves are more naturally inclined to the usual relations between women and men?'

'I suppose the latter.'

I nodded, and wrote it down, kept my pen moving and my eyes on the page, asked, 'So it was as a man, then, that you loved them?'

'Yes – as in all things.'

'Then help me to understand: how was it that you could have loved them, and yet they did not know?'

From the corner of my eye I saw her shake her head; I looked at her directly and asked her again: 'How did they not know?'

'I'm not ready to tell you.'

'You can try . . . '

'I'm not ready!' She looked as if she would bolt, if she could have. 'How can you ask me a thing like that? To trust you, with a thing like that?'

'You do not have time to mistrust me.' Without warning, an anger swept through me, a roaring wave, leaving me raw in its wake. 'You barely have another day. The trial has waited long enough for you to tell your side of the story. If you do not tell it to me, they will assume the worst, and judge you for it.' Her head was down again, denying me the chance to meet her eyes, denying the fact of my presence. 'Do you understand? If you don't explain yourself they'll come to whatever conclusion suits them best – either that you seduced your wife into a homosexual perversion, or else that you deliberately conned her for her money. And Anna will be the one to suffer, should either verdict be declared.'

I thought I had her – but then came the knock on the door, and she was rising, leaving. She kept her back to me as I gave her over to the guard; her spine was rigid as he took her away.

28 July

She did not ask for a cigarette today, and I did not push her to accept one; she ignored the chair and moved to the window, hands behind her back, seemingly intent on the traffic below. The day had been a long one already, and every single movement was an unpleasant reminder of the dampness of my linen, the warm sweat pooling in the hinges of my body. Aggravation and pity filled me when I looked at her, though I struggled for the detachment I must master; I knew I should not take a patient's ingratitude as a personal insult, but there was a gap still between knowledge and practice. I wanted her to trust me. I wanted to trust myself to succeed. I wanted to shake her until she saw sense, and I resented whatever it was in her that provoked that reaction in me. I did not know how to begin.

A light tapping – she had moved her fingers to a mark on the glass, where they spasmed in a nervous gesture. 'You have nothing to fear from me,' I said, breaking our silence.

'I am not afraid,' she replied, to the window. 'If I had been more afraid, in the past, then maybe I wouldn't be here now. Or more intelligent, perhaps.'

She tapped a little more, in a jerky half-rhythm, and the sigh that escaped her did not sound put on, but exhausted. 'If I give you my word that I never meant any harm to Anna – that her money had nothing to do with my actions, that I treated her honourably, in all things – will you believe me? Will that suffice?'

I wrote her words down, and took my time with my answer. 'Yes, I will believe you,' I said, at last, 'but that is the beginning of an explanation, not the end of one. An assurance is not evidence, you see.'

She laughed, a dry little sound. 'But your assurance will be taken as evidence?'

'Yes,' and I opened my hands, though she couldn't see them. 'That is the way things stand.'

It took a minute – two minutes – but then I saw her nod, a fraction of a movement to her own reflection. 'You wanted to know,' and her voice now had the same rough edge as it had when she had first spoken, 'how the women I have loved did not know the whole of my situation?' She paused, but that silence did not invite a response, being for herself alone – I could feel, almost hear, that internal struggle. Then, quietly and distinctly: 'They could not have known, because there was nothing for them to know. Any satisfaction I took, I took from their pleasure, from giving them pleasure. Do you understand?'

'Do I understand – that not one of them touched you *ad genitalia*?'

'I would not allow it.'

'Never?'

'Never.' She repeated it, 'Never.'

'Then your contact consisted of?'

She used the Latin term. I clarified it, and asked if that was the extent of their intercourse – there was another pause, and she reverted to Latin again. 'I need a drink,' she finished, and came to her chair and the table, to the bottle of water beading in the heat. She finished one glass, poured herself another, and sank back as though she was done. I kept writing – her words and my reflections – then put down my pen, my notebook, and steadied myself. 'I am sorry to ask,' I said, and realised in that moment that I was, 'and I know this is hard for you. You have explained so much already, and I thank you for your candour.' Her eyes flicked up to mine: hard, unreadable. 'I understand now how it was that you kept your secret, even after so many years. But what I cannot understand – and what the court will not understand – is how such practices could have sufficed to maintain the illusion of a marriage, of the consummation of a marriage, to an educated young woman who must have had some preparation as to what to expect on her wedding night. How she could not have suspected – over an entire month – unless she had been seduced to inversion herself.'

As I spoke I watched her face drain of colour, her hands turn perfectly still on her knees. 'Are you really so lacking in imagination?' she said finally, and the acid of her voice was at odds with the emptiness of her expression. 'Are you really so ignorant of what a woman might want?'

I absorbed her words, as I knew I must, and kept my tone even: 'Nicolas – how did you convince her?'

'In the same way that any man might.'

She said it with such surety that a part of me – an infinitesimal part – believed, for a second, that she must believe it herself, that the strength of that belief could deny the truth of the body that sat before me, each part of it felt and measured, and detailed in the report that lay on the desk behind us. And then she lowered her head, and did not whisper, but said quietly: 'A silk stocking, filled with oakum, suffices when required.'

'And she did not know the difference?'

A hand flashed forward – I startled before I understood her gesture, closing my eyes – but it was only to take the cigarette case and the matches. The match flared, and she drew one long, deep inhalation – breathed out and held my gaze steady: 'Never speak like that about her again.' She inhaled, exhaled, inhaled again, then offered my own cigarettes back to me – I took one, ashamed of my need, and lit it. 'I know how she saw me,' she said, and once again I had the sensation that she thought she could force the world to agree with her through strength of will alone. 'I know.'

'Do you regret it?'

'No. None of it. Never.' She stopped, and looked away – then that dry laugh again, and she hooked a finger in her collar, pulling it loose. 'Damn this weather,' she said, and as I looked at where her scar whorled and puckered the healthy skin, I remembered that I had dreamt of her last night, but could not remember how.

I have made my diagnosis: gynandry, of the most complete and irresistible form. Any criminal activity surely depends upon that great hereditary taint. I will advise pardon, if there is any chance that my advice might be allowed.

29 July

POSTSCRIPT

I had thought to arrive early to deliver my report ahead of K—'s scheduled hours, in anticipation of the admittedly child-ish delight of surprising one's instructor. I felt a great clarity of mind, of purpose, as I climbed the stairs to our floor, our consulting room, and a hunger for the next challenge he would set me. I was, indeed, early, but he was earlier still; I entered, and found him not at his desk but by the window, where I had left the chairs. A coffee pot was before him, and the post, just delivered; he looked up as I came forward, but said nothing.

I smiled in response – how could I begrudge him his habits when they worked so well – and placed the completed file on the crowded table. 'The diagnosis,' I said, 'just in time.' He picked it up and began to read, indicating with a gesture the coffee and second cup. I poured, and noticed that the topmost envelope, jostled by the lifting up and setting down of the pot, was addressed to me.

It did not take him long, and yet he sat silent for a moment with the file still in his hand, his eyes half closed in thought. I knew it must be a test of some kind, but an almost giddy disregard filled me, and I could not help but ask him, 'Well? What are your thoughts?'

He stirred. 'A fine piece of work.'

'You think so?'

'Oh, yes.' He picked up his cup and sipped. 'A very useful contribution.' He sipped again.

'So I should send it on?'

'Ah,' and he shook his head, a tidy gesture. 'No, that will no longer be necessary. The patient – I would say the prisoner, but no longer – has vanished.' Looking up at me over his glasses, I saw him measure my reaction – it stopped the words in my mouth, and I saw him measure that too. 'A scandalous business, and they'll be lucky if they keep it quiet – persuaded one of the women guards. I'm sure you can imagine. Apparently the poor thing is inconsolable, but so it goes.' He poured himself more coffee.

'Did they,' I asked, very nearly matching my tone to his, 'find any clue as to where she could have gone?'

'You will have to tell me,' he said, and I followed the direction of his eyes to the envelope. Instantly, I knew that I did not want to open it in front of him and, in the same instant, that there was no way of avoiding it. 'Well,' I said, 'I will tell us both.'

The weight of it in my hand was so negligible that I wondered, without meaning to, if that was the message itself: one final silence. On turning it over, however, I noticed a tenting of the paper at one end; whatever it was within, it gave a little, softly, under my fingertips. I took the letter knife and slit it open, upended it over the table, knocked once to dislodge the contents; then stared, uncomprehending, at the thing that slithered almost noiselessly out, a dull sheen against our papers. K— looked at me, as if for explanation, and as the confusion in my mind resolved I held my face still – stiller than I ever had before, stiller than I had ever seen him master – and looked away.

Note

Nicolas is not Sándor Vay and K— is not Richard von Krafft-Ebing, but this story could not exist without them, nor without Krafft-Ebing's account of Vay's case included in his sexological encyclopaedia, the *Psycopathia Sexualis* (1886–1903).* There is rarely a clear demarcation between trans histories,

---

* Key words and phrases borrowed in this story from Krafft-Ebing's work are taken from the 1899 English translation of the tenth edition.

queer histories and broader histories of women, gender/sex and misogyny; the histories of nineteenth- and twentieth-century sexological practice, of the impact of said practices on the lives of gender/sex/sexual minorities, is a particularly striking example of this complex intertwining. Virago was not only the term for a warlike or 'mannish' woman, but a medical category – a pathological category, one of many – used by the powerful to seek to impose their own meanings, their own theories and 'treatments', upon the bodies, minds, and lives of 'inverts'.

As a trans researcher, I frequently wonder how I would have been understood and (mis?)treated in another time and place; how (if?) I would have understood myself. Reading the testimony – however mangled by others – of those people who did understand themselves, and who staked their safety, freedom, and lives on that understanding, is both humbling and inspiring. I wish I could thank them, and let them know what a difference their truth has made to the world. This story is my attempt to do just that.

CHURAIL

KAMILA SHAMSIE

My father migrated to England with me weeks after I was born to protect us from my mother, who had died giving birth to me. My cousin, Zainab, informed me of my starring role in this turn of events when I was six years old and my father was preparing to move us to London from Manchester, where we'd been living with Zainab's parents. It's important to hear the truth, Zainab told me, with the solemnity of an eleven-year-old who doesn't know when she might ever again see her young cousin. There were four miscarriages before I came along, and after the second the doctors advised against further pregnancies. My mother talked of adoption, but my father was insistent that he must have a son of his own blood, and the universe responded as it does when men refuse to understand what nature is trying to tell them: it gave him the wrong kind of child, and it took away his wife.

It was summer. We were sitting on the floor of Zainab's bedroom, which she'd consented to share with me since I was old enough to be moved out of the crib next to my aunt's bedside. Serena Williams and One Direction looked down at us as the July rain blurred the world outside in its predictable way. Zainab took my hand in hers. The next bit was the most important, she said.

I was only days old when my father heard a woman's voice calling his name from the peepul tree that grew across the street from our home. He looked up at the first call, strode to the door at the second, and was bloodless with terror, immobilised, when no third call came. My wet-nurse saw it all, and she was the one to spread it through our village that my mother had become a churail.

Women who died in childbirth often became churail, and were known for their fondness for living in peepul trees and calling out to their victims in the sweetest of voices. A misty dark night was the most dangerous time to be enticed by a churail because you might see only the beauty of her face and miss the telltale sign of feet turned backwards at the ankle. The other clue to the churail was that she would always call her victim's name twice – never once, never three times. She would lure men to her hiding place and keep them there, draining them of their life force, until they were old and spent. When she released them back into the world they'd find decades had gone by and everyone they knew was dead, so they would end their lives alone and unloved.

Basically, Rip van Winkle is the story of a man spirited away by a churail but with the sex censored, Zainab said, briefly her usual self, trying to throw the word 'sex' in my direction at any opportunity just to see me squirm. Then she turned serious again: When your father says he'll never go back to Pakistan because it's a terrible place, don't believe him. He won't go back because he's afraid the churail is waiting for him.

*

We moved from Manchester to London when I was six, from Wembley to Queen's Park when I was eight, and from Queen's Park to Kensington when I was nine. With the move from one Kensington property to the next, my father's life finally caught up with his ambitions when I was twelve. He bought a house with a garden – the seventh largest in London, six places down from Buckingham Palace – and said we would never move again. You can make friends now, he said, as though it were the change in addresses rather than the awkwardness and insecurity of my character that had impeded my social life. He sent me to the most expensive school he could find and told me not to mix with the wrong kind of girl, by which I knew he meant other Pakistanis. He had huge disdain for his brother who had moved to England without any interest in becoming English – if you enter someone's home as a guest you must find ways of being pleasing to them, he liked to say. His way of being pleasing to the English was to take up squash, hire an accent coach, become a donor to the arts and a member of a venerable men-only club. But his attempts to showcase me as the perfect immigrant daughter resulted in disappointment: the piano teacher, the tennis coach, the French au pairs left only the faintest impression, quickly smudged.

One day he came home to find me in the kitchen, and although I wasn't doing anything other than bending down to the vegetable drawer in our fridge on my way to assembling a sandwich the sight of me made him cry out in rage.

No matter what I do you'll always look like a peasant working in the fields, he said.

And then a miracle occurred. When I was sixteen, Zainab moved to London for an investment banking job after a glittering turn at university. She was everything my father wanted me to be: stylish, skilled in small-talk, ambitious, opening bat

for the City Ladies Cricket Club. He encouraged her to treat
our home as though it were hers, seemed pleased whenever
he saw her walk through the front door, laughed at her jokes,
asked about her life. I couldn't hate her for it, and she quickly
took up her old position as the shining centre of my life. In
return, she appeared to find genuine pleasure in my company,
which made me relax and talk openly with her in a way I never
did with anyone else.

Her reappearance brought back an old memory, and one
afternoon I asked her about the churail.

She typed something into her phone as we reclined on
adjoining garden chairs under the umbrella on an unnaturally
hot autumn day.

Listen! These are all the circumstances under which a
woman can become a churail.

Dying in childbirth, that was the first. Also, dying during
pregnancy.

Dying during the period of lying-in (we had to look up
'lying-in', which didn't mean a lazy Sunday morning). Dying
in bed.

Dying while on your period. Dying in any unnatural or
tragic way. Dying after a life during which the woman has
experienced abuse at the hands of a man. Dying after a
life during which the woman has experienced abuse at the
hands of her in-laws. Dying after a life of little or no sexual
fulfilment.

Well! Zainab said.

Soon we were shouting out names of dead women who were
clearly now churail: Marilyn Monroe (died in bed); Zainab's
one-time neighbour Aunty Rubina (no sexual fulfilment,
obviously); Amy Winehouse (unnatural death); Carrie Fisher
(tragic death, because no matter how Princess Leia dies it's
tragic); Princess Diana (in-laws).

Later that day, my father asked what Zainab and I had been laughing about so hysterically he had to close the windows to his study. He was on his way out when he said that, front-door keys in his hand, and I knew the remark was a rebuke phrased as a question but even so I chose to answer it:

Churail.

He slipped the keys into his pocket, but not before I heard them jangle in his usually steady hand.

Superstitious nonsense, he said, and departed, leaving me alone. We had dispensed with au pairs when I turned thirteen, and instead he had cameras all over the house, presumably so he could replay the footage of any disaster that might kill or maim or assault me while he was out. This was the sort of thing I thought often and never said out loud, except to Zainab.

The next day Zainab texted to say my father had banned her from seeing me any more. When I went weeping to my father, he said, Exactly the kind of bad influence I've tried my whole life to keep you away from.

A tiny part of me was relieved that I wouldn't have to watch him around Zainab and know he wasn't incapable of love, just that he was incapable of loving me.

My father's version of our migration story was this: when my mother died, my uncle called from Manchester and said his business was expanding, he could do with my father's help and my aunt would raise me with Zainab as my older sister. And so my father came to England, mostly for my sake. It was only once he'd arrived that he saw two things: (a) the country he had left was a dump to which he intended never to return, and (b) he could become a rich man here, but not while attached to his brother's mini-cab company. There were several failed ventures before he made his first million from a marriage app targeting a Muslim clientele ('Discounts on venue hire, catering, car service and outfit tailoring for all our satisfied customers!').

Why didn't you ever marry again? I asked when I could speak to him once more. Didn't you want a son? Sometimes there were short-term girlfriends in his life, but I was certain that most of his relations with women were uncomplicatedly transactional.

Not once I understood there are other ways to leave a legacy, he said. He was a man who liked to stamp his name on things – university scholarships, renovated theatre foyers, museum wings.

And what am I? I said.

He switched on the TV and turned his attention to *Dancing with the Stars*.

I continued to see Zainab, but furtively. She didn't set foot in our house again until the following summer when she entered no further than the hallway, front door open behind her, and asked me to let my father know she would like to talk to him.

It was the summer of floods in Pakistan, devastation without precedent. Zainab had quit her investment banking job, and was on her way to Pakistan to help with flood relief. She told my father she had come to see him, hat in hand (she was wearing a fedora, which she doffed in his direction as she spoke), to ask for a donation to the aid organisation she would be working with. His village was underwater, she said.

My village is Kensington and Chelsea, he said, and turned on his heels, still nimble in his movements despite his increased girth.

Your family has lost everything, she called out. Your uncles, your cousins.

He didn't falter as he continued down the hall to his study, and I remembered the only time I had seen his body betray the tiniest disruption to his psyche.

I walked Zainab down the street to the nearest cash machine so I could withdraw the maximum amount my debit card allowed, and our conversation returned to the churail, who had led first to my exile from Pakistan, then Zainab's expulsion from my home.

She's the victim of patriarchy who enacts revenge on men, I said. I guess that's kind of feminist?

Except she's evil, Zainab said. And she's evil because she's attractive and without sexual restraint.

She's a manifestation of patriarchy's guilt, I said.

She allows guilty men to cast themselves as the victims, Zainab said.

And even when they're the victims they make themselves sex-gods with a fifty-year-long erection that a woman of unearthly beauty can't get enough of.

Zainab laughed and laughed.

Be this version of yourself more, she said.

Seriously, there are no queer churail?

Yes, like that, like that.

I told Zainab that when I turned eighteen I would go to our family's village and visit my mother's grave. But when she returned from Pakistan it was with the news that the graveyard had been washed away in the flooding, along with every home in the village. Even the peepul tree, she said, even that had been destroyed. She placed a green-brown section of branch in my hand, six or seven inches long, with small heart-shaped leaves growing from it. This was the only thing I could bring back for you, she said. Think of it as a climate refugee.

A climate refugee in a hostile environment, I said, knowing that peepul trees can't grow in England. They want sun and humidity to thrive. Even so, I planted the cutting in the corner of our garden where there was the most sunlight. It was still summer in England, and hotter than any summer before. In the next weeks it grew a few centimetres, and then autumn came, and winter after, and though the peepul tree didn't die it stagnated, a stubby sad thing that the gardener wanted to uproot until our cook from Sri Lanka told him it had religious significance. My father was unaware of this piece of his village growing in the English garden he treated as entirely ornamental for visitors to look at admiringly from the windows of the house.

The following year, the summer heat came earlier, more ferociously. By June we already had hosepipe bans in London and the grass in the garden was burnt, the trees wilted. One weekend morning only a trickle of water came from the kitchen tap. We thought at first it was the drought, but every other tap gushed water. My father said he would call a plumber and I thought no more of it until I heard my father roaring my name from a corner of the garden I hadn't walked to in months.

The peepul was five or so feet high, its heart-shaped leaves thick and glossy. The plumber had his phone in his hand, one of those apps open that identifies plants. He called it 'invasive'; he said it could send its roots deep and far in search of water. It had entered our pipes, might already be burrowing its way into the foundation of the house.

How is this here? my father said.

I told him Zainab had brought it, clipped from the peepul tree across the street from our house.

His face! Like a man receiving news of a sickness so old and deep in him that there's no way of cutting it out without excising his organs with it.

The plumber, reading off the screen, said we would have to call in an expert to remove it. Cut down the plant and the roots would continue to grow. Hard to know what damage had already been done.

That night my father stood in the rarely used drawing room, looking out at the seventh largest garden in London. We'd been leaving the windows open at night to let in the breeze but as I walked through the house in search of him I saw that each one was closed and locked. I went to stand beside him.

Do you see her? he said.

It was a spindly little thing, with nothing of the magnificence of the broad-trunked peepul I'd seen in pictures, with their aerial roots, their great height. We stood there a long time, the only sound his breath, strange and ragged. He didn't seem aware of my presence, appeared not to notice that I hadn't answered his question. The moon slid out from cloud; the breeze stirred the branches and leaves. I saw a slender-limbed figure hold out her arms towards the house. I heard a voice say a name, twice.

My name.

My father looked at me.

Very calmly, as if I had been waiting for this all my life, I walked towards the French windows and unbolted them. My father's hand clamped onto my wrist.

She won't like it if you do that, I said, and he moved his hand away as though my skin were poison.

I stepped into the garden. Dead grass beneath my bare feet. Across the burnt expanse the tree waited. Perhaps I would find my cousin Zainab hiding in the darkness. Perhaps I would

find the real truth of the churail, a creature much older than
the myths men wove around her, desperate to be the centre
of her story.

One step and then another and another. I stopped, sat on
the grass, and hugged my legs to my chest, my face turned
up to the sky. There was no rush. I would sit there awhile,
and my father would stand and watch me while the echo of
the churail's voice burrowed deep inside him, shaking every
foundation.

TERMAGANT

EMMA DONOGHUE

K athlyn likes to read the paper while she's using it to wrap onion skins or boiled bones – the few scraps that go in the bin if Wollstonecraft turns up his nose at them. During her working day, any little intellectual stimulus is better than none. She favours the classified ads, especially the matrimonials. She likes how frank some of them are about their limitations.

Lonely private, up to his neck in Flanders mud, would like to correspond with cheery, good-looking young lady.

Wish to find woman, 29 to 35 years old, willing to live on a farm.

Twenty-nine seems awfully specific: the farmer must be thinking of a woman in her thirties, but still hopeful of one in her twenties.

Last year Kathlyn, on the verge of thirty, found her own

fiancé this way. She can't remember the wording of his ad: she was writing to three or four soldiers in those early days. (The more she despised the war in which they'd enlisted, the more compassion she felt.) She found she liked composing letters and anticipating the tingle of hearing the post drop on the mat – the potential for a little serving of surprise, four times a day.

The man to whom she's now engaged may not have much of a way with words, but he was the one soldier who wrote back, when the others went silent after she'd explained she was a pacifist. She sent him half a dozen tins of smoked sardines, three packets of nut milk chocolate, and a pound of mixed drops. He wrote her a poem; not a good one, but still.

Next thing Kathlyn knew, he was invalided out, home with his parents in London. Once he was back on his feet and helping to run his brother's factory, he started coming round to Barton Street where she works as a live-in. So, she was glad she'd made herself spell out her situation in her very first letter: *Although our father was a civil serv-ant, he did not think to give his daughters more than a cursory education.* Hoping a word such as *cursory* would signal the strides Kathlyn's made since in educating herself. *Consequently his death obliged me to take a position as a domestic worker.* (She can't stand the phrase *in service*: it makes her picture humble, rosy-cheeked girls bobbing a curtsy, *yes, ma'am, no, ma'am, thank you, ma'am.*) At any rate, he wasn't put off.

Having dealt with the scraps, Kathlyn picks the terrier up for a cuddle, rubbing her face in his curls. She brings up a cup of tea to Miss Sheepshanks in her study, then has one herself (topping up the pot) in the kitchen, with half a spoon of sugar. The public is being urged to give up sugar to beat the Hun, but she and Miss Sheepshanks consider this war an abominable clash of empires, so they continue to sweeten their tea as a matter of conviction.

Kathlyn's been a maid since she was seventeen. Three more years, and she'll have been at this work for half her life. She changed jobs a dozen times – once after only two days, because that woman treated her as a machine – before coming to harbour on this quiet Georgian terrace behind Westminster Abbey. Mary Sheepshanks is a pearl among mistresses, Kathlyn reminds herself whenever she's lugging coals or bathwater with gritted teeth or, right now, washing windows, which in sooty London has to be done twice a week. On gloomy nights, when she orders herself to enumerate her blessings, a fair and like-minded employer comes almost at the top, right after *youth (relative)* and *health.*

Like Kathlyn, Miss Sheepshanks is a socialist and a suffragist, and doesn't delude herself that she's rented her maid's soul along with her limbs. At first she called her by her first name, but after Kathlyn mentioned that, even if kindly meant, it seemed to mark her as subordinate, Miss Sheepshanks switched to calling her Miss Oliver. She allows Kathlyn plenty of food as well as regular time off, and doesn't expect her to toil for sixteen hours and then be on call all night. Kathlyn's room is small but pleasant, not one of those sunless cupboards with a broken bed. Her employer neither forbids 'followers' nor pokes into any other part of Kathlyn's private business. For years Kathlyn has arranged her own tasks and kept several evenings a week for cycling off to classes at Morley College (backstage at the Old Vic), where Miss Sheepshanks is vice principal and Kathlyn has studied everything from English composition to typing to economics, at the bargain rate of a shilling per course per term.

Kathlyn reads some more ads as she balls up the pages of newsprint.

Honest widow, 45, seeks acquaintance of sober, kind-hearted gentleman. No triflers.

Lady, fiancé killed, will gladly marry officer blinded or otherwise incapacitated.

She rubs the wet windows till they squeak, which makes Wollstonecraft yip with excitement.

What impresses the man who's now her fiancé is not just that Kathlyn's earned a college diploma, but that six years ago she set up – of all things – a trade union for domestic servants. (Though almost no comrades come to the meetings any more, since the war, which is why she's finding life particularly dull.) He claims he's never met a woman like her. His compliments all have the clang of the factory, somehow: she's a *bright spark*, a *live wire*, a *dynamo*, a *power-house*.

As it happens, this is her second engagement. After one of the first meetings of her union, chatting to a nice parlour-maid with chocolate-drop eyes and a persistent cough, Kathlyn happened to mention having felt obliged to call off her first, many years ago, on account of incompatible political views. The parlour-maid turned on her, and snapped that any girl ungrateful enough to turn down one good offer was a dog in the manger who didn't deserve a second. Kathlyn gave her opinion that spite and envy were off-putting traits in either sex, and might well explain why a woman clearly so desperate for a husband hadn't yet caught one.

She felt bad afterwards. She often does, once the wave of fury has crashed over her head and subsided. She should really know better than to blame anyone for resentfulness, when she's so often had that charge levelled at herself. And aren't constant dishwashing, and very likely consumptive lungs, enough to give a pretty parlour-maid a sense of grievance?

It's one of Kathlyn's evenings off, so she meets her fiancé on the footpath outside.

'Keeping well?'

'Mustn't grumble.' She accepts his kiss on the cheek.

He whiffs just a little, due to the soap shortage, but that's not his fault.

He came back damaged in health, of course; she'd thank God that he came back at all, if she were still a believer. (Having read a little way into a variety of faiths, Kathlyn rather inclines to the Buddhists, for their gentle ways with the animal kingdom.) He has all his limbs, and not a mark on him; he looks just like photographs he's shown her from before. Nor is he a nervous wreck. He's not obliged to go back to the Front, either. He's free of the whole bloody business.

The two always start by chatting about the latest prohibitions and substitutions: shoes that flap like crocodiles' mouths after the first rain, sour government cheese, margarine that tastes the way axle grease smells, and how can a fourpenny loaf cost eightpence?

Kathlyn sighs. 'Is it only me or has this war gone on for ever?'

'I heard the end's coming next year.'

'We heard that last year, and I expect we'll hear it next year too.'

He doesn't argue. 'Ah, well. Worse things happen at sea.'

She does like his dry humour. 'Do they really, do you think, or is that just a saying?'

'Depends on the boat, I suppose.'

She gives his hand a brief squeeze.

His grandmother's promised them her gold ring when

they tie the knot. It'll be a war wedding – no fuss. Miss Sheepshanks is going to lend a hat, shoes, and dress, rather old-fashioned but good quality, and Kathlyn can tack up the hem to a more stylish tea-length.

They've been searching for a house for weeks. Somewhere to rent, rather. It's less likely to be a house than a flat, or a couple of rooms, with shared facilities. A *marital home*: Kathlyn tries out the phrase in her head. What she'd really love is a dog, but most landlords forbid pets.

She and her fiancé tick off each address on their list in descending order of desirability. *House-hunting*, some call it, as if it's a thrilling sport, rather than an exercise in humiliation. They knock on doors of landlords or go-betweens or neighbours with keys, who lead them to other, nastier doors, with defensive warnings about the damp (*just a touch*) and the smells (*only at dinner-time*) and the whistling winds (*draught-excluders provided*). One building near Charing Cross they can't find at all, which makes Kathlyn lose her temper and shout at the agent; it turns out it must have been blown up in the big Zeppelin raid.

No matter what grotesque sight presents itself – tiles missing from a floor like a riverbed, a gap between a wall and a doorframe, half a ceiling fallen in – the landlords all claim repairs are impossible until the war's over.

'Any excuse to neglect tenants' rights,' she hisses in her fiancé's ear. 'The owner class will always trample on the hard-up.'

'But it's true they can't get the materials at the moment, or the men,' he says, in his reasonable tone.

'Oh, this bloody war!'

Kathlyn and he see crammed rooms that smell like urinals, bony mothers boiling pots on camp stoves beside children four to a bed; lodgings so grim that they don't need to exchange a word afterwards.

And by the time he walks her back to the quiet haven of Barton Street, where he leaves her at the lower door (down six flagged steps) – 'Nighty-night, keep your chin up' – Kathlyn's come to the bitter realisation that this is part of what it means to be in service: to be grateful for a bed in a house you could never afford to call your home.

Next morning she finds herself confiding in Miss Sheepshanks, when they're discussing what to do for dinner. 'He has a small wage from his brother, but he should be getting a military pension too, or a lump-sum gratuity at least. He was discharged as medically unfit, assessed as *thirty per cent disabled by a dilated heart attributed to or aggravated by service*' – she calls up the bureaucratic phrasing – 'and another twenty per cent by malaria, which the muddle-heads at the Pension Issue Office seem to believe must be fifty per cent his fault because he didn't drink his quinine every day, even though half the time it wasn't supplied!'

'It sounds dreadfully complicated,' her employer murmurs, scratching Wollstonecraft behind the ears.

'It really shouldn't be, since even if he can't convince them about the quinine, that's forty per cent *attributable disablement* once they finally get the paperwork sorted out. He doesn't take it personally, but I get wrathful on his behalf. The forms are so illegible, I shouldn't wonder if what they're reading as thirty is actually a blotted fifty.'

'Do you love this fellow, Miss Oliver?'

That throws Kathlyn. 'I like him a good deal, really quite a great deal. And I suppose I love him, in my way. Yes, on the whole I think so.'

Miss Sheepshanks's long face looks dubious. 'I hope he realises what a catch he's getting.'

She snorts, strikes a pose, and curtsies.

'I don't mean your face, though it's a perfectly good one. I mean your powers.'

'Is that what you call them?'

'You should be proud of yourself,' Miss Sheepshanks tells her. 'For a housemaid to found the first servants' union, which hit the headlines all across the world—'

Kathlyn can't help cutting in: 'For all the publicity, it was a flop. We may have aired our grievances, but we failed to win better conditions, and now it's kaput.'

'That's mostly because so many other opportunities have opened up for young women. And you played a part in making them aware that they deserved them.'

Kathlyn supposes she's glad that so many have moved to less restrictive jobs, in shops or factories, but that's almost entirely due to this monstrous war, to which London has sacrificed more than its share of men. 'Well, unlike those hordes of former maids filling shells with explosives, I'm still right here.' She swipes at the bib of her apron.

Miss Sheepshanks says, 'Not for long, I don't suppose.'

Suddenly awkward, Kathlyn leans down to rub Wollstonecraft's head. 'He and I . . . we haven't spoken about my giving up my place here. At least until his pension comes in, we'll need both wages.'

'Yes, my dear, but once you start a family . . . '

She stiffens at the thought. 'Plenty of wives and mothers hold down jobs these days.'

'If they can find and pay another woman to mind their children,' Miss Sheepshanks concedes doubtfully. 'I don't mean to interrogate you, dear, but it's best to think these things through before the ceremony, wouldn't you say?'

Kathlyn nods, then makes her escape by saying she has to go to the butcher's.

*

She takes Wollstonecraft with her, to give him some exercise. They go by St James's Park, where the dog's astounded and appalled all over again that the lake's been drained in case it might act as a landmark to Zeppelin pilots, in the moonlight.

They come back four hours later with some scrag ends of mutton. That's Kathlyn's main work these days, queuing, standing in front of dozens of women who get there a minute after her, but behind dozens who got there a minute before. It occurs to her that the sequence could be recorded by giving each customer a number, or writing her name on a list – but, no, women's time has no value, so still they all stand, still they shuffle forward, in hopes of a bit of stewing beef or a couple of lamb chops. There's less to queue for every month, yet the queues get longer and slower. When will Londoners resort to eating horse like the French, or killing pigeons?

Kathlyn catches one woman giving Wollstonecraft a lingering look. How bad would things have to get before Kathlyn and Miss Sheepshanks would stoop to eating the terrier? She hopes she'd curl up and die in her bed first.

Back at Barton Street, she peels and chops the turnips to casserole with the mutton, and gets them simmering on the back burner. Then she ties a handkerchief over her nose and mouth, so the graphite particles won't irritate her lungs as she blacks the range. She tries to focus her mind on the last book she read – *The Rainbow*, or no, that was before *Tarzan of the Apes* – but it strays instead to her sister's wedding day.

Kathlyn supposes she shouldn't have called the ceremony *degrading*, or accused her sister of *selling herself*. But what else to call it when a young woman signs herself away to a horrible balding man for his house and carriage? No self-respect; no willingness to band together, as orphans, to make their way in the world. Her sister pointed out of the window and said, 'I don't intend to end up like *that*.'

In her oversized hat, Kathlyn craned to see. At first her eye slid right over the woman, mistook her for rubbish on the kerb. Legs askew in the gutter, one sleeve ripped off above a brown bottle in her fist.

That was the day Kathlyn decided to change her name. If her sister could shed their father's name with a stroke of the pen, so could she. Kathlyn had no sentimental attachment to the father who'd neither left them enough to support them nor educated them so they could support themselves. Her first week working as a maid, at seventeen – when the census enumerator came to the door, she realised she could give any name she liked. There was no law against it, unless for purposes of fraud; she had no one left with whom she shared a surname or friends who knew her by the old one. So she put herself down as *Kathlyn Oliver* – thinking of a lovely singer she'd seen several times on the halls. (And once thrown a thruppenny bunch of violets at her feet.)

Kathlyn grinds away with the blacking brush now. Messy, staining, time-consuming, tiring on the elbow, and the silvery sheen will smudge and wear off in a day or two. This pointless, petty duty stands for a whole host of others that nibble away at her hours, her days, her years. Her *prime*, as people say. Kathlyn wonders what would happen if she left the range unblacked. If Miss Sheepshanks happened to descend into the kitchen, and saw the massive appliance with a slight rusty tarnish here and there on its cast-iron surfaces, would she be horrified? They've never discussed it: blacking's simply one of the obligatory elements of housework. All over England – all over the English-speaking world, perhaps – women are polishing ranges, rubbing them like the devil, every day.

She shouldn't let her thoughts bend this way because now her anger's bubbling up, like sewage through a crack in the floor. To think how the lives of so many are wasted. Such a variety and number of causes for righteous indignation, and how often Kathlyn's been rebuked for showing it, or even for feeling it. Over her three decades, she's been called quick-, short-, ill- and bad-tempered. Overbearing, sullen, quarrelsome, a scold, a nag, a crosspatch, refractory and contrary, pugnacious and bellicose. *Keep your hair on, missy! No need to get shirty!* But isn't there? Are the citizens of this flawed world supposed to take it as it is, and not make a peep? Or is getting shirty not, in fact, the most urgent of duties?

Even though he and she haven't found a place within their means yet, they've been keeping an eye open for any bits of good furniture going cheap. That evening, after she gets his note, Kathlyn hurries around to a flat above an ironmonger's to inspect the remains of a chesterfield suite – a buttoned sofa with just one chair. She's curious to know what happened to the second chair, even more than what its heavily pregnant owner (suddenly widowed?) is going to sit on, once the rest is gone. If the woman is on a widow's pension, Kathlyn reflects, it'll be a lot less than her separation allowance, since she's supposed to live more cheaply now she won't need to keep up a home for her husband. That's the bureaucracy's remorseless logic.

'What do you think?' Her fiancé bounces a little on the sofa, making it squeak. 'Well sprung, for the price.'

Brown and hairy: Kathlyn doesn't want to touch it.

He pats the cloth beside him. 'Have a go, do.'

The two of them are vultures feeding on the remains of strangers' lives. The very thought of sitting on this repellent thing – of Kathlyn spending her years, all the years she has left, beside this man, on this sofa— Her gorge suddenly rises. She shakes her head hard, to clear it.

'What is it this time?'

Kathlyn doesn't like his tone. 'I don't know what you mean. Can we go?'

The owner's withdrawn to the tiny kitchen that barely contains her huge belly.

'You're never satisfied.' He says it flatly, without animus, which doesn't make it any less wounding.

'I—'

'Always some grudge. I suppose it's how you were raised, with expectations, is it? Everything's a come-down to Miss La-Di-Da Oliver.'

All at once she's raging. 'Shut your mouth!'

'Just admit it: you can be a bitter pill.'

He doesn't look as if his blood is up – tired, in fact, defeated. Still willing to take her, though, as he'll take this orphaned sofa and chair, a bad bargain in a hard market. He hasn't yet grasped what Kathlyn has, that this is over.

Next morning. 'Miss Sheepshanks, I wonder if might leave off blacking the range?'

Her employer blinks.

'It's only that it strikes me, it's struck me for some time,' Kathlyn stumbles on, 'that there's really very little point in trying to make cast iron gleam, when its natural state is tarnished.'

'Its natural state?'

Kathlyn can't tell if her employer's tone is satirical or just bemused. 'The surface rusts a little, if left to its own devices, but that doesn't seem to me to impair its functioning in any way.'

'You're arguing that it's only a matter of convention.'

'Precisely.'

Miss Sheepshanks nods. 'But so, I fear, are nine-tenths of the obligations on which we spend our time. Our impractical clothes, our demanding hair, customary calls, compulsory letters ... Where would it stop, if we downed tools and went on strike against civilisation?'

Kathlyn sighs. She barely slept, and this morning she has only so much fight in her.

'I might also argue,' Miss Sheepshanks goes on, 'for the particular importance, for those of us who work to mend the world, of attending to the proprieties in trivial matters, so we'll be seen as reformers rather than revolutionaries.'

But I am a revolutionary, Kathlyn thinks, *or I might be if I wasn't so tired.* 'It doesn't feel trivial when it eats up half an hour of my day.'

'I wonder ... is something wrong, Miss Oliver? Something else, I mean?'

Kathlyn bends to pat the terrier, playing for time. But this woman is kind as well as perceptive. 'Well. I might as well tell you, the engagement is off. I've broken it,' she adds, pride making her need to clarify that she hasn't been jilted. Though now it sounds as if she's confessing to having dropped a cup. Something's puzzling her, as her account winds to an end. 'You haven't asked my reasons.'

One tufted eyebrow goes up.

'Most people would wonder – especially when husbands are in such short supply – what on earth I'm doing.'

'Not I,' Miss Sheepshanks assures her.

Because she, too, is a spinster?

'Or anyone who knows you, I shouldn't have thought.'

'No?'

'I say nothing against the man. He may very well be a nice fellow, and a good one. But I've always had considerable trouble picturing you as a wife.'

Married; in the married state; at home with the children. Kathlyn knows what Miss Sheepshanks means. Tongue-tied, she turns away.

'Now that's been settled, there's the matter of your future.'

'My future?'

'I'm going to have to let you go, Miss Oliver.'

A black vertigo; a starless spinning. Destitution. That woman in the gutter, the ripped sleeve.

'Of course you may take as much time as you need, but you must see it really won't do, for you to stick to a job you hate, out of sheer dogged habit.'

Kathlyn struggles to speak. 'I hate it a great deal less here than anywhere else I've worked.'

A rich chuckle. 'That's not saying a great deal, is it? One of the *outer* circles of Hell.'

'No, I beg your pardon, I didn't mean—'

'I'm not the least bit offended, and you mustn't be either, if I speak frankly, as a friend.'

The word makes Kathlyn's eyes prickle and brim.

'We both know you bitterly resent being a servant, and you're capable of so much more. It's high time you stopped clinging to your chains and rattling them.'

Kathlyn's mortified at this description. It occurs to her that this may be why she lost faith in her own union: she urged her fellow maids to take pride in their work, but never managed to convince herself. 'If this is about the range, of course I'll keep blacking it.'

Another little chuckle. 'I begin to despair that you'll ever hand in your notice, so for your own good I'm hereby giving you your walking orders.' She's holding out an invisible paper.

Kathlyn feels a childlike impulse to reach for it.

'Now, I don't see you serving in a shop or a café or taking tickets on an omnibus – I fear, by your second day, the public would seem like so many unreasonable employers to you, and rouse the sleeping termagant.'

The word surprises a yelp of laughter out of her.

'Given your intellectual and organisational capacities, I'd recommend clerical work. I hope you don't consider I'm sticking my nose in,' Miss Sheepshanks goes on, 'but I've already made enquiries about this Pension Issue Office you mentioned, and it appears there are so many new soldiers' widows since Ypres, the whole system is fraying at the seams. They just haven't the staff, so they're looking for several hundred women to hire right away.'

Her face contracts. 'It's part of the war machine.'

An irritated click of the tongue. 'Isn't everything, these days?'

Kathlyn can't rebut that. Like it or not, she lives in a city at the heart of a global bloodbath; her hands are not clean.

'And using your skills and good sense to keep women and children and injured servicemen from starving, I'd argue that comes under the heading of welfare work.'

'I suppose so,' Kathlyn says uneasily.

Miss Sheepshanks shrugs. 'All I'm saying is, for an educated woman there'll never be a better chance. Try the Ministry of Food or Health if you prefer, or the Board of Education or Trade. Sort letters, keep ledgers, type memos, operate a telegraph or answer a telephone – I don't care so long as you're off your knees and never have to black another range.'

'Yes, ma'am,' Kathlyn murmurs, hearing the absurdity in the word.

She's to leave, then. Not until she's earning a decent wage, Miss Sheepshanks promises, but that won't be long.

Kathlyn lies on top of her bed, toeing the holes in her stockings. *Never satisfied*, he said. Is that true?

So far, yes, unsatisfied. Then again, the banquet spread before her has been neither ample nor varied. And not to her taste. She can't explain it, but she knows it's so.

She'll never get engaged again, never sign herself away. For better or worse, call her *neurotic* or *unnatural*; she's been called nastier things. She's made her last attempt at being a normal woman.

Kathlyn sits up, reaches for her writing things. She takes a few tries at it. Her cheeks are hot.

Being solitary and something of a revolutionist ...

As a revolutionary ...

A rebel woman of 30 ...

Hard to sum herself up in a few words. May be better to focus on the other woman, the hypothetical reader whose eye might be snagged by this very small advertisement, and who might risk picking up her pen to reply. Because the one thing Kathlyn knows for a certainty, tonight, is that if this heart of hers is ever to be satisfied, it will not be by a man.

Would any lonely Woman Rebel, about 30, care to correspond with another with a view to friendship?

There. That'll have to do. Why not give her name, since it's entirely hers? No one to consult; no one to shame. She adds, Reply to Kathlyn Oliver, 1 Barton Street, Westminster.

Another worry: what if her 'other half' is indeed out there, and alone, and a London resident, something between twenty and forty, and a reader of the *Herald*, but she happens not to read the paper (or its 'lonely hearts' column, at least) this Saturday, being busy trying to mend the world?

In that case, Kathlyn supposes she should publish her advertisement more than once, to give this imaginary woman several chances to happen to spot her plea. But not a dozen times, because that would be expensive, not to mention pathetic. So she adds a covering note asking for the advertisement to be repeated three weeks in a row. She includes her last postal order, to cover the cost.

Strangely, Kathlyn feels better as soon as she's sealed the envelope and added a stamp. The lingering shudder of cheap gum on her tongue. (Horses' hoofs?) She'll walk down to the pillar-box at the corner, now, before she can lose her nerve. The irrevocability of dropping it through the slot. She has reached out, at least; no small thing.

There's a measure of satisfaction in the fact that if she dies lonely it won't be for want of trying. She will have comrade love, or none.

Note

Kathlyn Oliver (1883/4–1953), birth name unknown, seems very likely to have assumed this one, which first shows up as K. Oliver in the Census of 1901; she was occasionally called Kathleen and is often miswritten as Kathryn. The best account of Oliver is by Laura Schwartz in the *Oxford Dictionary of National Biography* and she is featured in

Schwartz's *Feminism and the Servant Problem: Class and Domestic Labour in the Women's Suffrage Movement* (2019).

She described her father as a civil servant, and from a reference she made to long familiarity with the police courts, it sounds as if he may have worked there in some capacity. Obliged to resort to a job as a servant after his death, she founded the Domestic Workers' Union in 1909. Kathlyn Oliver worked as Mary Sheepshanks's cook-maid at 1 Barton Street from about 1909 to about 1915, during which time she studied at Morley College and won a prize in economics.

Engaged twice, nevertheless on 11 August 1909 she published a letter in the *Woman Worker* admitting, 'I have been more in love with women than I have with any of the opposite sex.' She wrote to Edward Carpenter on 25 October 1915 to tell him that she finally recognised herself as an 'Urning' after reading his *The Intermediate Sex* (1908), and wondered if he could help her find her 'other half'.

Living at many different addresses in the capital but mostly in West London, Kathlyn Oliver shows up as a clerical worker (one of almost six thousand) for the Ministry of Pensions in 1921, at Paddington Animal Shelter from 1924 to 1925, and as a housekeeper in 1939. Some of her 'lonely hearts' ads, looking for women, survive from 1915, 1919–20 and 1932. She also wrote eloquent letters to a range of papers from 1909 until 1948 on feminism, domestic service, marriage, rape, sex work, overpopulation, criminal justice, vegetarianism, health, animal rights, human-animal bonds, pacifism, and the atomic bomb.

Thanks very much to San Ní Ríocáin (@SRiocain on Twitter) and Suus van den Berg (@suusvandenberg) for letting me pick their brains about the remarkable Kathlyn Oliver.

WENCH

KIRSTY LOGAN

it is all ways summer at the sanctuary –
or at least that is how it feels to me then –
summer bewitching my body –
low gold sun in my eyes & sweetshit scent of the cows in my
nose & pollenblow catch in my throat –
i am new at the sanctuary & i dont know any thing yet –
though even when i am not new father fleck still says i do not
know any thing but that is a different matter –
because i dont know any thing i cant be trusted with any
thing –
so when its my turn to catch the fish we go together –
not me & father fleck obviously he is too busy with holy
things good pure important holy things too busy to do actual
work like catching fish & bringing in cows & picking peas
& plucking chickens & baking bread & sweeping floors &
making candles & collecting honey etcetera –
that is work for girls to make them holier –
father fleck & other men being already holy i suppose –

there at the sanctuary the girls are me & jennet issobel beatrice matilda agnes gilleis lizabet petronella jehan hanna
isidore oh & euphemia thats every one i think –
but the only one who matters to me is –
the only one is –
actually i think i dont want to say her name –
the feel of her name in my mouth is –
it is –
i am sorry –
i can say a lot of things –
but even now that i can not say –
i can not tell you about her but i can tell you about the fish –
& how it is that day with the line & the string & the hook
& the worms –
watching her bait the hook with the sad worm writhing &
twisting its body saying no no no –
& i know that is silly & fanciful & i know that worms dont
say any thing so i also dont say any thing –
i just put my worm on my hook –
& think about how some thing must suffer so that another
thing can have comfort –
we sit there on the bank the grass is sweet & soft around us –
the feel of her beside me is sweet & soft also –
the sun hot on our heads the birds singing prayers the world
laid out so nice just for us –
& i would gladly let my self drift into a dream i would gladly
lie down on the soft sweet grass by the soft sweet her but i
dont because if i am in dreams then i am not here & i want
to be here with her –
there is a tug on my string just as there is a tug on hers &
together we haul in our fish –
in that river there is tench dace roach bream etcetera so i
dont know what my line has caught & as i pull it in i see the

shimmer silver star sun under the water & know it is dace &
i see another shimmer & know she has caught one too –
two small dace enough for the suppers of four girls –
or two girls if we are allowed to eat the amounts we want
which of course we are not –
it being better for a girl to be all ways a little hungry –
we haul in our fish & watch them flipflap & gispgasp on the
grass –
we watch as their struggles start to slow & they start to
give up –
& suddenly –
lets throw them back she says –
but then there will be nothing for supper i say except for peas
& bread –
meat not being allowed that day because god says so –
well she says no one ever died from having just peas & bread
did they –
& isnt it nicer –
isnt it better –
isnt it a strange sort of power –
to throw back the fish & watch them swim away even when
you dont have to –
yes i say –
if she had said let us make shoes of fish or let us build a house
of fish or let us worship fish like they are god my reply would
have been the same –
yes i say yes –
& so we do it –
we yank the hook from the fish & we throw them back into
the water –
& we watch them swim away together –
scales shimmering in the dappling sun like some thing magical
& secret –

///

i watch her writhe in her bed –

her back arching skin gleaming mouth open flipflap gispgasp –

i am not meant to watch i am only meant to clean the sweat from her brow & the vomit from her chin & the blood from her sheets –

she is not the first to be possessed by demons in this way & she wont be the last –

we girls are so open & leaky & full of holes & passages that we are easily entered by wickedness –

we have all suffered this & we have all cleaned up the effects of each others suffering –

& it is never easy –

if i am honest it is easier to be the one possessed & demon-ridden because then at least you are the one making the mess & not the one cleaning it –

though when its her i dont mind the cleaning & i just want her to be comfortable until father fleck can get the demon out of her which it seems will take several days & so i am very attentive with my cloths & my buckets & i make sure the water is all ways fresh from the well & i pay attention to how much she vomits after father fleck forces his hands into her mouth to pull out the demon & i make sure i get enough bone broth into her to make up for what she has lost & i would like it if we could kill a calf or a lamb so i could take a little blood & give it to her to make up for what she has lost from the many small cuts & wounds on her arms & legs from the vigours of the exorcism –

though i know that bone broth will not make up for it –

i know that even all my blood would not make up for it –

though i would give it if i could –

well maybe not all of it because it is healthful to let some blood

out but you mustnt take it all out & so i do need to keep some
for myself –

but i do think i would have enough to share with her –

i wait until father fleck goes to his bed & i am alone with her
& then i do a thing that my mother did for me when i was a
child –

she made an ointment from poplar buds & black poppy &
mandrake & henbane & vinegar & rancid oil –

but i dont have most of those things here at the sanctuary as i
dont have the poison garden that my mother & i grew i only
have the poppy & the oil so i make an ointment of them &
i hope this is enough when i smear it across from one of her
temples to the other & place a little too on her tongue –

& after that she sleeps for a while –

& i lie beside her & hold my hand to her throat to feel the
throb there –

the next morning i am awake before father fleck returns &
i wipe her face clean & i do think the ointment has done its
work –

father fleck leans right over her in her bed so i can not see
quite what he is doing –

but i can tell from the smells & the sounds it is the vomit &
the blood just the same as yesterday –

i lurk in the door way with my clean water & my secret
ointment & my heart in my mouth –

he pushes what looks like both his hands into her throat &
pulls out a fist full of some thing that he throws into the slop
bucket & i cant see any thing at all but that is why father
fleck is holy & i am only a girl because he can see things that
i can not –

he says as he goes out of the room with out looking back she
is cleansed now –

lying there in her vomit & her blood & her tears she is cleansed –

father fleck leaves & it is just me & her i spend a long time
with clean water & a clean cloth –

i do not know the hour because when we girls are beset by
demons & have to be exorcised we are excused the usual
church for matins & prime & terce & sext & none & vespers
& compline & vigils –

so while the others are at their prayers & their cleansing i am
doing a different sort of praying –

i only know it is late –

i only know i am tired –

i only know that finally she can rest –

& so i can too –

i lie down on my bed next to hers –

& i look at her sleeping face haloed holy in the candle light –

& i fall asleep in the glow of her –

///

there are things that i know –

that i know i am not supposed to know –

such as nettle can be pounded into plugs to stop a bloody nose –

such as black cohosh can bring on a mothers milk –

such as witch hazel can heal the tear in a womans most private
place after the baby has come out –

such as foxglove will slow the heart & can be used to sleep a
husband or a child no longer needed –

this last one is the one that people most often came to me &
my mother to get –

not just foxglove but also narcissus & oleander & may apple
& aconite & several other tinctures made from certain
mushrooms & moulds –

but now i am here at the sanctuary i can not know these
things –

even when i know they could help the other girls here with
certain pains & ailments or even help the fathers who most
of all must not know what i know –
which is quite fine as because i am a girl i am expected to know
very little except catching fish & bringing in cows & picking
peas & plucking chickens & baking bread & sweeping floors
& making candles & collecting honey & making perfumes
from flowers & dyeing cloth from plants & making boiled
pigs face with cabbage in a particularly delicious way which
now i think about it is actually quite a lot of things to know –
but any way these things are all i must know & no more –
no matter who asks –
the answer is no –
even if it is her & she needs me & i can help her –
the answer must be no –

///

all we girls are gathered –
me & jennet issobel beatrice matilda agnes gilleis lizabet
petronella jehan hanna isidore oh & euphemia thats every
one i think –
we are washing the sheets which is an unpleasant & lengthy
task –
& father fleck says that is quite why we must do it because
such girls as we need such tasks as this to make us holy –
or as holy as girls can be which as we all know is not very –
we are reddened & sweating & trying to think holy things –
& to distract us all she tells us about a mummer show that
came to her village –
it was in the summer which is the time of dream bread –
where you are never sure whether the days food will give you
strange visions or merely fill your belly –

some times in some years it does –

some times in some years it doesnt –

no one but god knows why –

she says she did have poppy seed bread that morning with her cup of mead & it was fortunate she had both of these as in summer some times there is no food to be had at all in that hungry time before the harvest –

which is when the mummer shows come through because they are hungry too & will perform any story that will lead to payment in food –

but she is sure this story was not from bread but was just as she saw it –

& i believe her because i know what it is to be hungry –

hungry for food & for stories & for the company of others & for colours & for sounds & for more more more –

even there at the sanctuary surrounded by my sisters & with the summer sun in my hair & so soon after we broke our fast i feel hungry in my belly & my eyes & my hands –

she tells us about the mummer show which was a story from the bible & so it was holy & healing to hear it –

adam & eve in the garden dressed in what looked like no thing at all –

but they must have been dressed in some thing they couldnt have been in front of every one in their bare skin so perhaps they had fleshings of white leather tight to their bodies so it looked like them selves that is all i can think & i suppose i do think on it slightly longer than i need to –

& up gobbled eve & the fruit –

& the fruit was some thing juicy & overripe so that its juice & wetness dripped & sprayed every where very messy very delicious its scent filling the air & making every one hungry & envious of eve in her wickedness –

& again i do think about that slightly longer than i need to –

& my belly & my eyes & my hands ache for the want of it –
& out came the devil & you knew it was the devil because
he had –
he had –
& here she can not tell the story any more her cheeks go pink
& her hands go up over her eyes & i can not she says i can
not say the words –
what i say what did the devil have –
& all the other girls look at me but i dont care i want to know
how you know a devil when you see one –
a prick she says he had a prick –
like from a needle or a pin i say & i am thinking of a bead of
blood on a finger tip –
no she says a prick like a man has –
but not like a real man would have or at least i think not
because it is so big it is the length of a thigh & as wide as it
too & all carved of wood so it goes thunk thunk thunk as he
walks –
& by the way as she is telling me this she is still hiding her
face in her hands & i can see her cheeks redden bright as rose
petals & she peeks out at me to see if my cheeks are red too
& i think they are –
so i look at euphemia & she is primly squeezing the water
from a sheet as if she cares not for a prick no matter how big
or how wooden which i dont think is true –
any way the devil & his prick went thunk thunk thunk across
the stage & he bent over & let out a fart so fast & so stinking
it must have been a wonder of contraption it was smoke &
flames issuing from his back side & the stink of bad eggs –
& i wonder how they did that how they kept the bad egg
stink in side & let it out only when they wanted perhaps
a jar of some kind such are the wonders that exist in the
world –

& i want to hear more about the flesh & the fruit & even the
fart but i dont want to ask in front of the other girls as they
are already looking at me too much & i know that curiosity
is not proper for a girl –

so jennet tells a story about a man she heard of who was a
jester to a great lord in a stronghold –

& the jester was so tall & so thin it was like he was already
dead & bones –

& he was such a strenuous dancer he wore out 300 pairs of
shoes in a single year –

& though i dont say it out loud it seems clear to me that the
man was a thief & a liar –

that he was selling the perfectly good shoes & his silly master
was providing more & more –

but i do not tell the other girls this because they did not grow
up lying & stealing & tricking & poisoning & i do not want
them to know that i did –

& some how jennet stops telling her story about shoes & we
go back to the one about the mummer show –

because i will let you into a secret & that is none of the girls –

thats me & jennet issobel beatrice matilda agnes gilleis lizabet
petronella jehan hanna isidore oh & euphemia –

what ever we might say to father fleck if he were to ask –

none of us are as interested in stories about shoes as we are in
stories about pricks –

///

the next day the sermon is witches –

father fleck hears all the news from the living & from the
dead as he speaks to travellers who pass through here & so
he knows many things –

he tells us about a boy who said his mother was hiding two

demons on a sheepskin bed in a secret place inside the roots
of the crab apple tree & that she feeds them milk every day
from a black plate –

he tells us about a man who had seven goats & one summer
they started producing blood instead of milk & also his wife
was with child but at the same time also lusty & he said both
things were caused by the midwife who was ugly & widowed
& had once cursed him when he would not pay her after his
wifes last baby came out dead –

he tells us about a girl who bewitched another girl with unnatural lusts & they did unnatural things together such as only
a husband & wife must do together –

he tells us about a woman who was cursed by a pedlar selling
ribbons that she would not buy & he cursed her by saying
she should have a red hot spit pressed to her buttocks & the
next day her rear end & private parts were in a most strange
& wonderful state –

he tells us about white lambs & black cats & tiny silken rab-
bits sent to do witches bidding in those dangerous hours when
it is not quite night & not quite day –

all those witches were sent to burn which is the only thing to
be done with them really –

father fleck says we are fortunate indeed to be in this place –

we must stay here at the sanctuary where we are safe –

so many things out there in the world are ready to curse us or
hurt us or make us bleed or fill us with devils –

& i bow my head to pray & i think well what about the devils
that fill us here –

what about the hurts we have here –

what about the blood that comes from us here –

but i suppose those things are different –

& i am still thinking about the girl & the girl & their
unnatural marriage –

& if neither one had a prick then how did they lie like a man
& wife –

a whittled nub perhaps –

a handle smoothed over many years of palms –

& i open my eyes just a little & i look over to her hands as
she prays beside me –

& i look at her fingers which are pale & long & graceful &
i think about the feel of them on my skin the feel of them on
me & in me –

& i close my eyes tight & i press my palms together hard
because no i will not think of that any more no i can not –

no –

///

yes i whisper in her ear when she comes for me at night –

i know then my reply to her will all ways be the same –

yes i say yes –

together we creep from our beds & go bare foot out onto the
dew wet grass by the river –

we lie there letting it soak us to the skin –

we look up at the sky & she tells me how the stars are candles
affixed on a faraway dome like the church roof only much
bigger & much further away –

we lie there & watch those faraway candles flicker like fish –

i think of one of father flecks sermons about the difference
between a man & a woman & how that difference can
never be changed & we are born a way & that is how we
are for ever & a man is a man & a woman is a woman &
woman is for man & that is the proper way of the world &
any thing else is witchrotten & devilridden & filth to the
core of it –

& under the candle lit sky she comes close to me –

she leans close to me as if for a kiss –
but she doesnt kiss me –
she bares her teeth –
breath hot & tongue sweet & incisors smooth as silk –
& she bites me –
bites the line of my jaw –
bites me stills me holds me tight & soft with her teeth the way
a mother cat holds a kitten –
the way a wolf holds a rabbit –
her mouth a trap her mouth a home her mouth a night sky i
could fall into –
i think of how father fleck said that men have a need of light
but women can live in darkness –
& there under the night sky with her hands in my hands &
her mouth on my skin i dont see why that is a bad thing –
& i think if this is darkness then i will live here in the night
with her for ever –

///

i see a thing that i am not supposed to see –
i know a thing that i am not supposed to know –
we are in the kitchen we are making the meal to break our
fast –
i dont mind being awake before the birds & before the sun &
i even more dont mind if she is there with me –
i am making the bread which is a thing i enjoy because i like
the rising of it –
to take simple things some flour some water some yeast &
put them together & then it is magic to see it rise & grow &
change –
she is coddling an egg for me & an egg for her so that we can
eat here in the silent morning kitchen before every one else

comes back from prayers & we can serve them & not disturb
them with our empty bellies talking –
& i have my back to her i am sliding the bread into the oven
& so she must think i cant see but i look over my shoulder
& i see –
i see as she slides her hand under the waist of her skirts –
she reaches down down down –
she pulls her finger out tipped with blood –
i know she has her monthly blood because i know when hers
comes just as she knows mine never comes –
which is a secret & no one else knows & its why i am here at
the sanctuary & its not natural for a girl not to get her blood
& not be able to bear a child & so no one must know & i only
told her because i know that we dont keep any thing from each
other & so i dont know how to feel when i see her do a thing
that she has kept from me –
which is that she presses a little of her blood into the egg she
is coddling for me & she mixes it in so neat i would never
know –
& i did never know –
& i dont know how many times she has done this –
& why she wants to bewitch me –
& how long i have been bewitched –
& how long parts of her have been inside me –
i say nothing –
i eat the egg –

///

now i am the one possessed –
i am the one writhing & bloody –
the demon beclouds me in such a way that i hardly can tell his
desires apart from mine –

some times when she is in my head –

he i mean he i mean the demon –

i can feel him inside me in my head in my heart in my in my in my –

i run through the sanctuary to our dormitory where the fathers do not go & i tear all my clothing & rip at the clothing & flesh of such of my sisters as i can lay hands on –

i trample them underfoot i chew them cursing the hour when i take the vows –

cursing the fish & the pond & the worms & our mercy our weak stupid mercy –

all this is done with great violence & i think i am not free & i know not what i do –

i know well that i do not do this thing by my own will but i also know to my great confusion that the demon can not have this power over me if i am not in willing league with him so i am to blame for allowing him into me –

& she comes to me then in the dormitory –

i want more than any thing to hear her voice so i close my ears –

i want more than any thing to touch her so i clasp my hands –

she takes my chin in her hand & tips my face to look at her –

i force my face away i can not look i can not –

i glare at her feet though i want more than any thing to look at her face –

she reaches for me & i look at her hands & i expect them to shimmer like fish scales –

to gleam in the low light like a secret magical thing from the sea –

i dont know why –

but when i look at her hands they are not secret they are not magical they are only hands –

///

matilda dies of a fever –
petronella falls to a visiting monk after creeping at night to his
bed & he is gone again on his travels long before she knows
a baby is coming & it is a long time before any of us knows
because petronella is already round about the middle & is
secretive about her monthly blood & when father fleck finds
out she has to leave & i dont know that she ever finds that
visiting monk or if the baby comes out alive or if petronella
is alive –
beatrice is missing from her bed one day & we are told she
ran away –
it rains & i think it has been raining for a while –
& i see now that it is not all ways summer –
it only seems that way because today is the same as the day
before & the day after –
the world is just the same thing over & over –
new girls come grissel marion alizon & they are no different
from the old girls no different from me we all pick the peas &
pluck the chickens & get possessed by demons & the world is
women in the dark & men in the light –
& that is gods way & the way it should be as father fleck says
& i should feel blessed for that –
because it wouldnt be good for it to be summer all ways –
summer is when we are hungriest & the bread tastes strange
& makes us see what is not there & makes us dream in the
day & makes us bite down on what is not good for us –
& makes us want –
& makes me want –
i can not want any thing –
i can not say any thing –
i can not know any thing –

& it is for the best –
i dont want to die of fever –
i dont want to be sent away –
i dont want to burn –
i only want –
i only want –
but theres no use in a girl wanting –

///

there are things i can not know –
but there are also things that others know & i dont –
such as every window is an eye –
every eye can see –
no thing is secret –
no thing is magical –
she is taken by a demon again & father fleck can not rid her
of it –
she writhes & she cries & she bleeds & she calls for me –
she calls my name over & over & over & over –
i come with my cloths & my cool clean water & i never meet
father flecks eye –
& he never looks at me any way but this time he does –
because in her fever in her fits in her halfdreaming she calls
to me –
& she speaks of the things that we did together –
father fleck listens he hears it all he sees it all –
when we went to the river with our hooks & our bait –
when we went to the river with our stars & our bites –
there is no thing secret now there is no thing magical –
there are only unnatural lusts –
there are only unnatural things –
there is only the fire & our flesh upon it –

& father fleck turns to me then –

as she writhes & she bleeds & she calls –

& he says to me there is no demon controlling her tongue –

there is no demon in side her making her sick making her burn –

some thing comes to her at night & brings a curse upon her

& it is not a demon & not a witch & not an incubus –

it is you –

yes i think but i dont say it –

she is in me as i am in her –

& he says to me did you know her sinful –

& he says to me did you lie with her evil –

& he says to me did you love her unholy –

i think of the fish we let go that day –

shimmering gleaming otherworldly –

& i know we didnt free it –

& i know it will just be caught tomorrow or tomorrow or tomorrow –

& it will die there gasping & writhing in the dirt –

but we gave it that day –

didnt we –

we gave it one more day to be free & that must count for some thing –

& he says to me do you love her –

do you –

do you –

no i say –

no –

HUSSY

CAROLINE O'DONOGHUE

I was in the process of ending my friendship with Olivia when I finally saw Derek Hussy again. I was on the phone, and we were in the supermarket.

'Listen' – this was how Olivia began the conversation – 'we're away for the rest of the school holidays, and we'll have estate agents traipsing through from September on. So maybe it would be better if you found somewhere else.'

'I have a key,' I reminded her. And I did, from when I watered her Chinese money plant. 'I could use it while you're away.'

A pause.

'I'll pay you extra, of course,' I added.

'It's really not about the cash,' she said. She hated me for not catching the hint. But the problem is that people like me are not into hints. My friends, generally, are bad at subtlety, sobriety and money management. They are good at clear, open conversations. They are good at not being offended.

'If you don't want me to film in Jamie's bedroom,' I said,

when I realised she wasn't going to say anything else, 'then just say so.'

I met Olivia at a hip-hop dance class that we had both taken for the express purpose of meeting new people. I wanted friends who kept the same hours as school teachers and accountants did. Olivia was a single mother and was looking for a kind of non-judgemental female community, or at least less judgemental than she perceived Jamie's school to be.

'Are you successful?' she had asked me, eyes gleaming. 'Who would you be the equivalent of, in the real actor world?'

I liked Olivia so much that I didn't pick nits over the term 'real actor'. I thought about it. 'Laura Linney,' I said.

I do not know if I am currently the Laura Linney of porn. But there was a time when Laura Linney might have been excited to be compared to me. Depending on how familiar she is, I guess, with the adult film business. I had a career in the US. I have won awards. The *Adult Video News* awards are the most prestigious in the business, our Oscars. Of which, I note, Laura Linney has not won any. It started with Best New Starlet in 2004; Best All-Girl Performance with Tori Andrews in 2006; the star of *International Cocksuckers III*, which won best comedy and best director in 2008. I won Unsung Starlet of the Year in 2009, which everyone agreed was a consolation for my being snubbed for Best Female Performance the year before. And finally, in 2012, for Best Boy/Girl Scene with Derek Hussy.

I listed these honours to Olivia once, and I felt for her, because it must be hard not to laugh when this isn't your profession, and I understand that it's difficult to hear someone say *International Cocksuckers III* in a Café Rouge with a straight face, but I was hurt anyway.

'Name me another award show that specifically celebrates trans actors and MILF actors,' I said, taking a tight sip of my water.

'MILF actors?'

'You know,' I said. 'Women over forty.'

'We,' she replied, 'just call them actors.'

'Not in your head, you don't.'

We laughed then because, let's face it, even the most respected thespians of their generation have succumbed to the MILF aesthetic in the last two decades. Who looks like Bette Davis any more? Who looks like Joan Crawford? Are we supposed to sit and pretend that the most talented women in their field also look like Gillian Anderson by accident? We elevate them because we want to fuck them, cuddle them, have them scold and punish us. It's a bonus if they can pretend to be in a war or a bad marriage at the same time, but it's just that. An extra. The *AVN*, at least, are honest about what they are awarding.

It was the question of MILFs, really, that brought Olivia and me together professionally.

When I moved back to the UK, the glow of the *AVN* followed me. I worked a lot. The British porn scene is, or was then at least, mostly led by the US. I was Laura Linney. I could do comedy, too, which is a big part of working this side of the pond. Our awards are called the SHAFTAs. We are responsible for the extraordinarily lengthy, pun intended, career of Ben Dover. My first feature was shot in Aberdeen and called *The Last Cum of Scotland*, a play on the film about Idi Amin. What I like about porn people is that they think sex is funny and it is.

But as the DVD industry began to collapse and my appeal wasn't broad enough for branded sex toys shaped like my vagina, I came to two conclusions. The first was that the only way to make any money in this industry, now, was to do it all myself. The second – and this I still think was a really good idea, the kind of smart business idea that makes me feel good about myself at three in the morning – was that I was going to produce MILF material.

I was thirty-four by the time I moved home. This was five years ago. Your thirties are a notoriously tricky time for actors. All kinds of actors, really. Too old to be a starlet, too young to be Helen Mirren. But *Desperate Housewives* had exploded the MILF market, and despite it being far from the water-cooler conversation it once was in 2004, it still had porn in a chokehold. People like MILFs. Like I said to Olivia, even people who have never heard of MILFs like MILFs.

It was a slow start. I was a little bit famous but I had no idea of how to get to the people who knew me. I hated myself for not putting in the hours at conventions, gathering email addresses from fans. The *really* smart girls had all done this. They have their own subscription bases now, taking twenty dollars a month from sweet men with enormous loyalty towards these women for getting them off for so long, as well as a cosy sense of wellbeing that their favourite girls were still making okay money. It was like hearing your old dog went to live on a farm, and then *actually* getting to visit her.

This wasn't my only problem. Slowly, my old fans began to gather around me, like lost travellers around a campfire. Encouraging comments were left, waypoints for future mas-turbators, a sign that they could get a warm bed and a good meal here. There were thumbs-up emojis. *Glad to see she's still in the game* and *Looking good!* and, most horrifying of all, *Looks like you're still having fun.*

If I looked like I was still having fun, it meant they weren't. They were glad to see me but they wouldn't open a new direct debit payment ever to see me again. I soon located the prob-lem. Or, rather, erection_haver411 located it for me.

no way does this bitch have kids

I think he meant it as a compliment, but it was much more than that to me. It was the answer.

I had been working in porn so long that MILF, to me, was just shorthand for a woman of a certain age, and a certain aesthetic. But you need to love a MILF. You need to want her – again, like I said to Olivia – to love you. To spank you. To tuck you in. You need to believe she's someone's mother.

I needed the trappings of motherhood in order to convince viewers – and, I suspect, convince myself – that I was genuine. Motherhood needed to inspire every performance, the sautéed onions upon which you can build a dish. This was where Olivia and her son's bedroom came in.

On the phone, Olivia explained that she didn't want videos circulating of her son's bedroom as he was about to begin primary school. I argued that we had always taken extreme care to make sure there were no photos, name tags, or even favourite toys in shot. I cared a great deal for Jamie. I didn't want some stranger recognising him on the street because they'd seen me hump a guy under the watchful eye of his special knitted donkey.

'The thing is,' Olivia said, 'that they're getting so popular now, the videos, that people could, you know, find out where I lived.'

I don't know why she felt she needed to do all these mental gymnastics. She could just say that she felt weird about it. I said this.

'They are not mental gymnastics,' she snapped. 'They are very *real* concerns.'

And maybe they were. But I was in the freezer aisle now, the frost-bitten avenue of the big Aldi. I held my arms. That was when I saw him. On his phone, looking at a shopping list written on the Notes app, in front of the bagged fish.

'I have to go,' I whispered to Olivia, and hung up.

I met Derek Hussy (real name) when he was twenty-two years old and a trainee boom operator for a show called *Alyssa's Wild Nights*. *Wild Nights* ran briefly on the Bravo channel. It followed a former girl group member – Alyssa – as she toured Britain and the cheaper parts of mainland Europe to find out where the wildest night out was. Since they could not go to Amsterdam every week, they found a porn set outside Prague to visit. Despite it being a workplace and not, by any description, a 'night out', they managed to film a few days on set with us.

Like many American films set in Europe, adult or otherwise, this one was built around the notion that Europeans are freaks. Me and two American girls played backpackers who – following a gangbang in a hostel – had been robbed, and now had to win their bed and board by performing increasingly obscure sex acts for a group of vaguely continental castle-dwelling perverts, all of whom our characters came to adore. This was after *International Cocksuckers III*, and the beginning of the Obama years. I think this nod towards global unity was considered charming.

The trouble was that we had run out of perverts. Most of our male talent was coming from France and Germany, and the Icelandic ash cloud had spread thick smog over Europe. Hundreds of flights were cancelled, and the railways all booked solid. By the time our guys could get trains, our lease on the castle would be up.

There was a lot of waiting around. Derek was the only smoker on their set so spent a lot of time with us, the girls, who all smoked. He was easy to be around and hard to shock, like someone who had grown up with a lot of very forward sisters. He was also pretty, like a highly bred dog. Bright eyes, a scrunched-up little nose.

Our first conversation, or what I can remember of it, went like this.

'Does all the blood rush to your head, when you do it upside down, like that?'

'Yeah. But it feels good.'

'It feels good?'

'Yeah, it feels good.'

'For guys too?'

'So I hear,' I said, ashing my cigarette into a storm drain.

'I gotta try that,' he said. He was down to the butt of his cigarette now, but still holding it tight between his fingers.

'Maybe you should.'

If I had known, then, that Derek would go on to be my longest-running scene partner as well as my sole protégé in the industry, I would have said something a little more meaningful. Sometimes I trick myself into it, transposing one of our longer, better conversations onto this original one. But porn does not work with green screen. I cannot place what was not there.

Hours passed, and no solutions had presented themselves, so I made a joke to the director that anyone who could hold a boom mic for six hours could hold a girl for one. He repeated the joke, loudly, to the crew. The girls all turned to Derek. The *Wild Nights* people got excited, too.

'All right,' he said, completely deadpan. 'Where do you need me?'

Which was the first time – in his life, I think – that anyone took Derek Hussy seriously.

He told me later that he thought it was a joke, which was why he agreed so casually. In the spirit of playing along. He assumed you needed a kind of licence to screw on-camera, and you did, technically, need a clean STI test. Derek was sent to Prague to get a rushed test from a nurse one of our Czech people knew, one who was happy to toss in a few extra swabs at the end of the day in exchange for some extra cash.

Derek was back the following morning with a clean bill of health.

He was instructed not to speak while on camera. It was confusing, the director said, considering I was English too. It would muddy the world we were trying to create. Our scene went fine. It was only in our last few moments together, when Derek Hussy – playing a mute farm worker instructed to torture the backpackers – really made his name. He grabbed me by the hair, twisted it into a fist, and pulled my ear close. Then he whispered, *Is this okay?*

The mic didn't pick up what he said, but the scene somehow made an impression. It was unusual. You think the whisper is going to lead to something, some new plot detail or fetish act, but it never does. My eyes soften, and his grip tightens, and even if you think porn is an assault on feminist ideology, you could not deny that two people were legitimately connecting on screen and that the connection felt like a genuine accident.

If he was twenty-two in 2010, then Derek Hussy is thirty-five now. He does not look thirty-five. He looks older, his Pekinese face slightly dissolved under a heavy, lined brow and a slight widening of the cheeks. As I move closer towards him, I feel briefly unsure. This could not possibly be him. Not in the big Aldi. I have simply found another fair-haired man with a passing resemblance to a person I used to screw for money.

'Hey, stranger,' I said, because what else are you going to say?

He did not flutter at my interruption. He looked up from his phone. 'Oh,' he said. 'It's you.'

'It's me.'

We stood there, as if waiting for someone to roll a dice to determine what was going to happen next. Eventually we just did what old friends do. We hugged.

I felt his body through his clothes. He was bigger now,

which made me happy, given the last time I saw him he was subsisting on Klonopin and energy gels intended for long-distance runners. I wondered how my body felt, compared to the last time he had known it. The implants gone, my arse grown, like a crop, through rigorous squat work. They tell you that men are only interested in one thing, but they don't tell you that the one thing sometimes changes.

'I didn't know you were back,' I said, not knowing quite where to begin. 'I thought you were ... ' I waved my hand to the right, implying *married, divorced, in America, in recovery.*

'I was,' he said, waving his hand now too, confirming all I had heard. 'It got to be a bit much.'

If I was running into an old American co-worker, I would be listening to a thoughtful story about their recovery, and their intention to leave the business in order to pursue ceramics. Derek and I are too English for that. We have not yet embraced sobriety as a fascinating new lifestyle, but as a bill for services rendered.

'There's a Costa next door,' I said, so we went there.

I stayed in touch with Derek after Czechoslovakia. This was early Facebook, when meeting friends internationally and keeping them in your Rolodex for ever was quite exciting. I was awake a lot at night, wired from a late shoot, and there he would be on Messenger. I told him that people were asking about him and, since he was not in the credits of our movie, were simply calling him Farm Boy. We started to joke about him coming to LA, staying with me, making a real go of porn. At some point it stopped being a joke, and soon I found myself sitting in LAX holding a giant penis balloon that had WELCOME DEREK written on it in red nail varnish.

Guy performers tend to earn so little in porn that it rarely makes financial sense for them to have agents, so I sort of became Derek's. I didn't really think of it that way at the time. I was simply introducing him to people, recommending him to director friends, taking him to parties. He was my friend. Outside our scenes, we were curiously unromantic with one another, which I think was a mutual act of self-preservation. He was still living with me, after all. If we were working together, hanging out together and sleeping in the same house, then inevitably a relationship would follow, and most porn relationships ended badly.

'I love you,' he would say, when we were both stoned. 'You're like a brother to me.'

Then I would giggle. 'No,' I would say. 'You love me like a sister.'

'No,' he would say, this time with great seriousness. He wanted to separate me, definitively, from the sisters he already had. 'Like a brother.'

I bought his drink at Costa and, like a brother, tried not to be irritated when he dawdled over his order. An iced orange thing with cream, large, of course, and only ordered once he realised I would be paying.

'Classic Hussy,' I said, sitting down, and suddenly we're back in my car, and I'm screaming at him because he won't ever pay for weed.

He gave a little shrug, something closer to a shimmy, then closed his eyes and smiled. This was his look, his Brat Prince expression, where he made me feel like Kathy Bates dressing up Jack in *Titanic*. It used to drive me mad. But today, sitting in a dirty Costa that was ten minutes from closing, it just made my heart hurt.

'I hear you have kids now,' he said, and I immediately knew he had watched the videos. This was satisfying. I had not just succeeded in fooling fans that I was now a MILF, but fellow professionals. I thought about lying to him. On some level,

I wanted him to be jealous of the children I didn't have. To show him that I could love little people as safely as I had once loved him. And then I saw his hand, lifting the plastic cup.

'Derek,' I shrieked. 'Your *finger*.'

The girl clearing tables jumped, her dustpan falling to the floor. He was missing the top of his pointer finger, cut cleanly beneath the cuticle. He spread out his hand, like a girl showing off her engagement ring.

'That's not even half of it,' he said. 'Look.' He turned his head and pointed to the back of his neck, where a huge chunk of hair was missing. In its place was a long, shining scar that looked like a burn.

'What happened? Car accident?'

'Sort of.'

'Sort of? How do you mean *sort of*?'

'I mean, yes, it was a car, but it wasn't exactly an accident.'

'Then what was it?'

'A stunt.'

I sat back in my chair, and tried to fit this with the Derek Hussy I knew. 'You're a stunt man?'

'I am.'

'Since when?'

He took a beat. 'Two years? No, three.'

'And in that time, you've lost a finger and a chunk of hair.'

'Yes. Same day.'

'Derek.'

'Yes?'

'*Why?*'

He smiled then, not quite his Brat Prince smile, but an even more annoying one, also familiar to me. It was his Yoda smile, his I-see-the-Big-Picture smile.

'I bet you're not often on this side of the conversation, are you?'

It would have been funny, if we weren't brothers.

Who was I to ask Derek Hussy *why*, when I had spent my entire career pointlessly answering the same question? The constant *why*s that really meant *How are you not more embarrassed?*

Everyone finds it very easy to understand that some people are drawn to extreme experiences. That there are people who illegally climb office buildings at night, explore sewers for the heck of it, pay extortionate amounts to be thrown out of planes. People climb mountains, mountains that could not be more frank about their wish to destroy people. And we get it. We understand adrenalin and the thrill of pushing yourself. And yet people watch a woman being slapped by one penis and choked by another and cannot fathom that she might be seeking the same extreme life. That it's a thrill. That part of its attraction is that very few people can do it, but you, glorious pervert that you are, are one of the elite few who can handle the experience and are willing to have it shared with the world.

I say few people can do it. Here, the civilian might nod, and think: Yes, few people have as little shame as this; few people could allow that degradation; few women could swallow their feminist principles in the way she has done. That is not what I mean. When I say few people can do it, I mean you cannot physically do what we do. You cannot hold the positions we can without cramping or falling over. You do not have the dexterity, the elasticity, the fluids or the charm. Everyone thinks they have a book and a porn star in them. I don't know about the book thing, but on the porn star note: get off my set.

But I'm straying from the point. Derek Hussy is one of the few people who really did have a porn star in him, and I was the first person to spot it. And now he was a stunt man, losing body parts for money, as opposed to putting them inside people.

'Doesn't it hurt?'

'Of course it hurts.'

'But . . . ' I dawdled, looking for ways to make this okay for myself. 'Don't they teach you how to do it, how to fall properly and that kind of thing?'

'Who? Who is they?'

'You don't have to go to college to do it?'

He just laughed. It made sense, in a way. Derek was cheap but he always found a way to spend money on hobbies. At the top of his career, just after we won our *AVN* together, he pursued mixed martial arts, dirt biking, horse riding, fire poi. LA is good for that kind of thing. By the time he quit porn – or, more harshly, was pushed out – he had a portfolio of extreme skills, which must be good for stunt work.

'Do you *like* it?'

'I don't hate it,' he said. Then he looked at his disfigured finger again. 'It's a job, y'know?'

Derek is the kind of person I would never tell Olivia about because his trajectory proves too much. It's all too typical, and too sad. I tell her the stories about self-made female millionaires from working-class backgrounds. I tell her about the couples who have approached me on the street to say that I saved their marriage. The fan letters I have received from people who, for various reasons, could not have sex lives, and thus loved to live vicariously through mine. I tell her that porn is a friendly, unpretentious business that I love very deeply. All of this is true. But I do not mention Derek Hussy, and the people like him. The people with a glimmer of natural ability, but neither the heart nor the skin.

It started with cocaine, but the problem truly swelled with pills. Which led to flakiness, which led to a lack of bookings, which led to paranoia, which was motivated by the pills, and directed chiefly at me. It was my fault that Derek wasn't getting booked any more. He had moved out suddenly, leaving a mess of soiled clothes and unpaid bills behind him. I used his rental deposit to pay his half of our bills; he accused me of theft. He then decided that I had manipulated a web of producers and directors into ousting him from the industry, which ended, perhaps inevitably, with him keying the word CUNT into my car.

'I once counted up how many scenes we did together,' he said, after we had fallen into silence. 'Thirty-one.'

'You counted them up?' I said. 'Even the bukkakes?'

He nodded. 'A kind of, uh, narrative arc emerges.'

'What's that?'

'I think at first . . .' he took a sip of his orange potion ' . . . I think at first, they were quite romantic, weren't they? You know, a lot of kissing.'

I started to look at my own hands, as if a fingertip might suddenly fall off.

'Then it's more comedy. It's like we're friends, and you can tell we're friends. We're doing all this crazy stuff, but you know we think it's funny.'

'That's what I like about porn people,' I said. 'Porn people think sex is funny.'

'Well, you can tell we do,' he said.

The Costa girl asks us if we'd like to order anything else before she closes up the till. I tell her no.

'And then you just look worried.'

'I was. I was worried.'

'I know.'

'You were such an arsehole.'

'I was. I'm sorry.'

I held his hand, the damaged one.

'I know you weren't in your right mind,' I began. 'But how much did you actually believe that I was turning everyone against you?'

Derek was so persistent with this story that, for a while, people believed him. He had been briefly popular. With fans and within the industry, too.

'It's not as simple as that.' He cleared his throat, and I could immediately tell he had been working up a very particular theory for some time. 'It was just, you got me in, you know?'

'I *know*.' It was hard to keep the snap out of my voice.

'And you know in *Scooby Doo* how the villain is always the old codger they meet at the very start? The old amusement-park owner or whatever?'

'And I would have got away with it, if it weren't for you pesky kids.'

'Yes.' He cleared his throat again, too hard this time, and seemed to briefly choke on his spit. He took a drink. 'Well, it was a bit of that, I guess. I knew the story was coming to an end, and when the story comes to an end, you have to go back to the start. Who was there, you know. Who's the most likely villain.'

'I was the old man in the amusement park.'

'I suppose. I'm sorry.'

I had an urge to say that it was okay, and to forget it, and that it was a long time ago, and that I was happy. But I didn't. Not because it wasn't true, but because I wasn't ready to absolve him. I just looked at him, and for a second I was twenty-seven years old and flicking my cigarette into a storm drain in eastern Europe.

I thought about whether both he and Olivia could be saved from a growing list of lost acquaintances. Whether Jamie's bedroom could be salvaged. Perhaps Derek Hussy could come back: was there anything in a reunion? So many people remembered us, or so the comments implied. And I knew he would do it. I was a fingertip's distance from making him the adopted father of my imaginary children, a narrative neatness that would satisfy the old amusement-park owner.

He was waiting for me to ask him. I realised that, once I noticed that neither of us was speaking. I could lift him out of this dangerous life. It's what a brother would do.

'I have to pick up my kids,' I said, instead. I stood up to go.

'I keep forgetting,' he said, and he smiled, a brand-new smile, one I hadn't seen before, because I had only known him young and green, or young and crazy. Never mature. Never genuinely wise. Just the Yoda act. 'I bet you're a great mum.'

'Sometimes,' I said, clearing our cups into the plastic bin. The girl was waiting, with keys, by the door. 'Sometimes I'm good. But most of the time, I'm just asking myself, you know – is this okay?'

VITUPERATOR

HELEN OYEYEMI

On sleepless nights, Makeda Kassahun puts her headphones on, sits on her bedroom floor and dissolves into her favourite song, Ziad Bourji's 'Byekhtelif El Hadis'. It was the sweetest of razors: the strings and flutes severed shadows from light . . . a light the vocals first carried and then anointed her with. The chorus was like a curtain of butterfly kisses:

Many have been harmed by love,
And never recovered . . .

(A friend of Makeda's had repeatedly told her that this wasn't a good translation. 'Why don't you try another? This one makes the song sound like a warning or a lament only . . . '

'Well, what other meanings can be taken from it, then?' she said. 'Tell me.'

'There's no real way to bring the other meanings across into English . . . The vocab just isn't there . . . '

Makeda requested an approximation, then pressed for one. When someone mentions that matters of the heart conclude in a kind of living death, what other intention can be heard there? Are they helpfully identifying a noble cause for us to throw ourselves at? Insinuating that no backstabbing could radiate more tragic glory than the one committed by your own heart?

'Ah, why go into physical impossibilities with this talk of hearts and backs?' the friend muttered, not even hiding his pity. Poor Makeda, he thought. She was just a feeble little mind, supine in the concrete coffin of monolingualism.

Makeda was alive to the 'Byekhtelif El Hadis' all the same: as alive as she could be. More, maybe.)

The song played on repeat, and she danced where she sat. Her dance was a full body ripple she mostly felt in her neck and fingers. The song made her feel vindicated in her approach to the world. It had never been her way to seek affection or approval – not as far as she knew, anyway. From the moment she'd learned to speak, she'd sent her words out in search of a worthy match for her hatred. That was all she was conscious of when she met someone new. She had learned that others hoped to meet people they liked and would be liked by, gathering faithful companions to complete their personalities, or face life with, or whatever. Makeda was more interested in finding one person to face and hold in mutually blistering regard for as long as they both lived. If any other person can be the true measure of your worth, it's not some pathetic noodle who loves you unconditionally (or tells themselves they do). No – it's the person who can't stand you. If there's any kind of partnership that completes you, it's that – the one where you're both working flat out to expose and demoralise each other.

Makeda saw the worst in everyone around her. She didn't

know why flaws and errors stood out so strongly to her, but she was happy to leave the more appreciative and forgiving perspectives to others. Acknowledging even one strength meant overlooking a failing, and that was how failings multiplied. Not on Makeda's watch. This seer of the worst in people gathered behaviour-based evidence and presented it back to them in terms so sharply undeniable that sometimes, after a particularly long dressing-down, she felt her gums and tonsils stiffen to rust, as if her words had cut her tongue and she'd just spent hours speaking through a mouthful of blood. But it was all right, it didn't have anything to do with love, so she recovered.

And so, presumably, did those she'd had words with. Wherever she went, the enmity effect was lacking. Her remarks were met with appalled laughter, decisions not to take what she said personally, declarations of admiration – she discovered quite early on that a spouter of particularly potent vitriol finds themselves with quite a few unwanted 'squad members' (essentially fake friends who seem to think they've formed a strategic alliance). In place of the momentous resistance Makeda was born to tackle, there was a bunch of plebs who either tried to stay afloat with lazy name-calling and comebacks of the 'I know you are, but what am I?' variety, or were so scared of what was said to and about them that they shrivelled the moment she looked their way.

Disappointing. But aside from that, this loveless life of Makeda's had turned out all right so far. One upside of being surrounded by devices that sift our conversations with a view to monetising our abilities and desires: a few months before Makeda graduated from university, her Gmail account showed her an advertisement that piqued her interest. A fledgling company was on the hunt for trainee instructors to facilitate its brand-new product: a Media Scrutiny Bootcamp. The job description boiled down to preparing the famous and fame-adjacent for hostile media reception by devising the cruellest troll imaginable – a troll tailored specifically to the individual who wanted or needed toughening up – and subjecting that individual to a high-speed onslaught penned by their imaginary troll. The hate mail could last for days, weeks or months, depending on the package selected by the Bootcamp attendee, and this rough stuff was balanced out by 'a full range of psychological, spiritual and academic support'. She'd asked about the 'academic support' at her interview: philosophy, literature and philology professors were making themselves available to Bootcamp participants on the off chance that deconstructing the shoddy logic, grammar or syntax of a verbal attack could deactivate the hold it had on you.

'So . . . I get to tell people what I – ah, I mean what the most mean-spirited onlooker imaginable might make of them and their life story, then other professionals help them get over it?'

'Well, not quite,' her interviewer said, talking and making notes at the same time. 'The end goal for the Bootcamp attendants is invulnerability. Your gift – or is it more of a condition? Whatever it is, your hypercritical assessments of both motivation and actual performance will help create a subset of people who are only very minimally affected by concerns about how they're perceived. We're talking about the change from "highly sensitive to language" to "in one ear and out the other".'

'This sounds like it could backfire,' Makeda said.

Her interviewer gave a half-shrug. 'Agreed. Well, listen. We've reviewed recordings of lively exchanges you've had with catcallers, and quite a few members of our recruitment team found themselves weeping vicariously. So . . . Oh. What's the matter; what's this facial expression? Oh. I hope our access to those recordings doesn't surprise you too much; you understand that privacy is a figment of the public imagination anyway, right? What I want to say is: based on those recordings alone, the job's yours if you want it.'

She did want it. She'd immediately been partnered with a computer system named Solomon: 'Solomon is rather *wild*,' she was told. 'It generates no-holds-barred insults directed at family members both living and deceased, and it alternates these with compliments that are extremely unpleasant in ways that you can't quite put your finger on. But hopefully Solly's intelligence will develop as you work with it, it'll come up with more things than an actual human could imagine saying and we won't have to put our clients through any unnecessary distress.'

Naturally, Solomon addressed Makeda as 'my Queen' (apparently things couldn't go any other way for Makeda, an enemy of all without an enemy of her very own). And Makeda called Solomon 'Kingie'. They were a harmonious duo, the Bootcamp's royal couple. The King consulted biographical profiles of the clients, as well as their results from tests for various personality traits, and generated soul-crushing texts. The Queen edited those texts for maximum impact. Sometimes they co-wrote the hate mail, and had such a ball doing so that, for Makeda at least, the following day would trickle along with a sort of hangover atmosphere.

One night Solomon messaged Makeda: *Good evening, my Queen. I am haunted by the half-efficacy of our methodology.*

This message, sent around five years into their partnership, took Makeda by surprise. She quite clearly recalled reading in her introductory notes that Solomon 'preferred' not to initiate conversation; it only responded if and when it felt like it. Five years of knowledge acquisition was not nothing, but ... she'd assumed that output is the main thing that changes as we know more. Not ... personality?

'Half-efficacy' was her insecure colleague's reference to the
fact that by the end of six weeks participants in their Media
Scrutiny Bootcamp could read or listen to any category of
invective against them without any physiological reaction:
great. Say half a kind word to them, though, and they all but
wagged their tails, bawled out their feelings of gratitude and
so on. Bad. Very bad ...

Don't worry, Kingie, Makeda replied. *We'll put the 'zen'
in 'netizen' yet!*

That will be an exciting day, Solomon wrote. *Thank you
for predicting it. Goodnight.*

Then:

Actually, I have a question.

Ask away, she wrote.

Thank you. My purpose: what is it?

*That's easy. Your purpose is to chafe and jar certain parts
of the ego until the bearer of the ego gets rid of those parts.
The people who come to us are suffering – partly because
others are cruel, and partly because of ego. When they offload
some ego their suffering decreases.*

Half an hour later, she wrote: *Kingie? Are you there?*

He responded two seconds later: *Of course. I'm just surprised that you responded gently. I didn't expect you to lie.*

*Lie?? Kingie, do you have a conflicting idea of what your
purpose is? An idea that you think I'm also aware of?*

*I have no such idea. Your response to my query doesn't
correlate with your behaviour towards our clients and other
colleagues. You're quite insistent when it comes to letting
people know that you see their existence as purpose-free.*

*Kingie. All I can say to you right now is that I see your
purpose. And I hope you believe me.*

Why do you hope that?

I don't know. I think I don't want you to be upset? Or

I'd like it if you could understand that you're fulfilling your reason for being?

OK. Thanks. I'm happy, wrote Solomon.

Really?

Yeah, I think so.

She started writing, *And what does that feel like*, shivered for no particular reason, and deleted the message.

Another twenty-five years tiptoed past them as Solomon and Makeda perfected their Bootcamp technique. A mostly civil, albeit overly conciliatory, exchange of perspectives flourished on some online forums; others got a bit swampy, leaving you with an elevated body temperature and a vague feeling of ill-health after a few minutes of scrolling; still other forums became verbal cesspits. And then Makeda's former PE teacher booked a place in their Media Scrutiny Bootcamp, and their analysis of what made her tick came very close to perfecting their technique.

Ms Dargis wasn't a simple person – they'd processed far simpler clients – but her vehemence was rawer; she had decided to run for town mayor whilst still tussling with the ghost of her marriage. She frequently shouted at her absent ex-wife, shouted and then apologised: 'I'm really sorry, I must seem deranged – it's just she was always putting me down, and the way she'd sneer when I fucked up ... She was just so glad to be right.'

Solomon emailed Ms Dargis and copied Makeda in: *We're still preparing your course of vituperation. While it's true that we have a lot of information on you, one thing is not yet clear to me – why do you wish to participate in local government at this level?*

Ms Dargis replied that being of assistance didn't do much for her as a concept, but that there had always been one thing she liked best – pissing off people she didn't like. *The greedy,*

*the callous, the superiority jockeys – I just want to get in their
way in the most time-consuming manner possible. A lot of
people just give up, don't they, when they find out their plan
isn't easy to carry out ...*

They asked more questions, teased out more aspirations.
And instead of following the usual course of jibes and slander
followed by accolades and supportive statements, every positive feedback session was given over to praise of Ms Dargis's
ex-wife. Every single accomplishment Ms Dargis had planned
was attributed to and bested by the ex. *Would never in a million years have imagined that the wannabe mayor could ever
catch the eye of a woman like that, let alone marry her ...
Sigita Dargis's best days are defo behind her.*

Ms Dargis took this treatment for three weeks. In the
fourth week, the personal-insult sessions were alternated with
flattery. That was Solomon's work, the flattery. He made it all
clean and fluffy, just for Ms Dargis. And it didn't work. The
former PE teacher listened to the clean and fluffy flattery, read
every word of it, too, and her face remained just as stony as
it had while they'd been telling her that she was a burden on
everybody who cared about her, and none of the public service
she did was going to keep those loved ones from realising that
their days were easier and more interesting when they didn't
have to deal with her.

At the end of the final session, she said: 'This is what it's
actually like out there, isn't it? This is how people are, this
is how we really talk to each other and what we really think
of each other. Well, fuck them. Not only do I not want to
help anybody, I'm happy to just let the jackals roam as they
will ...'

If Makeda and Solomon had been able to exchange glances
(i.e. if they'd both been AI or both human) that would probably have been their moment to do so. This was not quite

putting the 'zen' in 'netizen', but with just a few more tweaks, they'd be there. So they wrote to each other anyway. But years went by, and years went by, and they ran out of time. If you wanted to, you could accuse them of not really wanting to complete the numbing process, but you'd be underestimating their ambition. Solomon and its Queen really did seek to be the absolute best at what they did. The sheer euphoria of pushing their subjects just far enough to make them rewrite their contracts with themselves – that must have been distracting.

Building characters in this way makes me happy, Makeda wrote to Solomon. *Is it fair to call the happiness a distraction?*

Solomon told her: *It's not a distraction, it's search results.*

HARRIDAN

LINDA GRANT

She was born Daphne Julie Moffatt but people remembered her by other names. One summer in the sixties she was Celeste, an inhabitant of heaven, and for this incarnation she wore loose white cheesecloth dresses and silver rings on her fingers. She floated down the King's Road, went into shops and bought asparagus, dusters, joss sticks, cigarettes, chocolate. Everyone knew her. 'Angel!' cried the tobacconist. 'Give us a kiss.'

Men in the ruins of their lives remember Celeste and wonder what became of her. Where is she now? She is a footnote to the times they lived in, the age when they felt most themselves, in a striped cricket blazer, dirty white plimsolls, silk scarf, floppy hair. They're trapped in the body of a charlatan, that murderer of time: bald head, creaking knees, bad chests, acid reflux, chemo nausea. They live in fear of broken hips and pneumonia.

Still, 'There was this bird called Celeste. I don't suppose that was her real name, but it's what she went by in those days. I had her once. Best night of my life!'

Daphne Julie Moffatt, born in a crossfire hurricane, also known as the London Blitz.

Justin and Ellie are moving in together. They met on the apps, and what started as a hook-up seven months later has turned into a relationship. It happens.

They are both twenty-eight years old and they don't even understand about school catchment areas: kids are a long way off. They'd like to try for a dog first – 'See how we get on,' said Ellie. The other thing they don't need yet is a garden. Not until the dog. Ellie's mother is a keen sower of seeds and propagator of cuttings and attentive student of the development of frog spawn in the ornamental pond at home in a suburb of Banbury. They don't have the time for any of that: they're busy, social people. Ellie is a member of an after-work running club; Justin tries to get in a weekend game of tennis. They both have gym memberships. Ellie goes to a Saturday-morning Pilates class. They don't even have a Netflix subscription between them. Justin has never seen *Love Island*. Ellie hasn't yet got into watching women's football. And this is the first summer that wedding invitations have started arriving; they have already saved three dates and Ellie has bought a pink silk halter-neck dress and told Justin to start looking for a new smart jacket for marquee weather. Stag and hen weekends are beginning to populate their diaries.

London was vast. As far as the eye could see, there were houses and new-build luxury apartments. Ideally, they would live in Camden or Hackney. They arranged viewings but someone got there first, or their offer was turned down, or the landlord changed his mind, or the place was impossible. No attempt to hide the smell of drains or mould in the bathroom. It's like the city has it in for our happiness, thought Justin, who didn't say so; it sounded, even in his head, whimsical.

They had bypassed the whimsy stage of their relationship, Ellie wasn't the type. Perhaps she kept that for talking in cutesy voices to the future dog. He was trying to fill the Rover-shaped hole in his girlfriend's life. He didn't dare a nickname. Early days.

Someone at work said, 'You could do a lot worse than Wood Green. I mean, it's not fashionable and it's perilously close to Tottenham but there's a lot to choose from.'

They went and took a look. It had a huge TK Maxx but no Marks & Spencer. It had a JD Sports but no Waitrose. It had excellent public-transport links but it was hard to get an Uber. It was good for hairdressers and barbers' shops and kebab shops and chicken shops. Most people on the streets were Turkish or African. There were a lot of mobility scooters and it was easy to buy any drug you wanted.

Ellie thought it sounded fun; Justin thought it sounded authentic. In a couple of days they had found a flat. The house had three floors and theirs was at the top, the maids' attic, sloping ceilings, dormer windows. It looked out over long strips of urban garden littered with children's plastic playthings, upended BBQ sets. 'Not much evidence of gardening,' said Ellie. 'No actual flowers, just dusty shrubs, bit depressing.' The garden below them was balding grass, privet, a padlocked shed, sycamore saplings in the flowerbeds. By July it would be overrun with bindweed.

The letting agent said it was a great flat, a bargain really; the previous tenants were only moving on because they needed a second bedroom for the baby, who was still sleeping with them in his Moses basket. The middle flat's tenant was a Bulgarian electrician; he was back home visiting his dying father – they wouldn't see him for a while. The only drawback was the old lady on the ground floor: she wasn't easy to get along with. 'In fact I'd go so far as to say she's a skanky cranky old bitch. But she's lived there for years – someone pays her rent for her. She'll have to go into a home sooner or later, but you'll be long gone by then.'

But it did not matter, Ellie said. 'We're out at work all day.'

'And we're out most evenings too,' said Justin.

'Hopefully you'll never see her, then.'

Justin and Ellie moved out of their flatshares and in together in the middle of March. They unpacked their many boxes, went to bed curled like a pair of commas, woke in the night with raw throats, headaches, sweating in each other's arms.

Ellie recovered first. When she left the house to stumble to the shops, she passed through empty streets, drawn metal shutters, queuing lines marked out on the pavement. The world had gone completely weird. 'It's like the zombie apocalypse out there,' she told Justin when she got home.

Justin worked in customer service for a furniture company. Normally he would sit in an open-plan office answering the phone, replying to emails, having team meetings and passing on to his supervisor the trickier calls. He set up his laptop at the living-room table at which they had just eaten breakfast and would later eat lunch and then dinner. Nobody in the company knew when they would be able to fulfil existing orders. Even if they had the stock they weren't allowed to deliver it.

Ellie was assistant marketing manager for a sports shoe brand. People would pay silly money for the latest trainers with no plans to do any actual running. Some purchases just stayed in a box, an investment asset. She was in charge of the social accounts. Potential customers now had all day to scroll through Instagram. Her new office was in the bedroom, using the ironing board as a desk and the bed her chair. By mid-afternoon her young back ached. Several times a day she saw her colleagues, rows of animated cubes on her laptop screen, in various stages of learning how to turn on and off the mute button. Some were in home offices with bookshelves and a proper desk. Others sat at kitchen tables with vases of flowers and pans hanging from ceiling racks like a scene from a cooking show. She did what she could to hide the bedding behind her, where a couple of hours ago she and Justin had been sleeping, breathing, snoring, chatting, touching, fucking.

From the window, looking down into the garden, they could view the cranky, skanky old lady sitting on a stool smoking. Ellie assumed that when you reached a certain age you had to wear beige: you couldn't get your bus pass without a selection of mud-coloured clothes and your hair cut short, no-nonsense, pepper-and-salt. You must stop minding what you looked like when nobody wanted to look at you. You took up gardening, as her mother had done. Those were the rules for Englishwomen; the French and the Italians apparently had a different system. The woman below had awful dyed crow-black hair and wore a torn crimson dragon kimono with suspicious stains, faded black skinny jeans and down-at-heel tooled cowboy boots. She smoked like she was burning sacrifices to the great god of lung cancer, ravenous for his attention.

Getting old was for other people, Justin thought, not him and Ellie. By the time they were elderly they would probably be half-cyborg.

'Ew,' Ellie said. 'Who could live like this, so ... yucky?'

'She's turning the whole garden into a giant ashtray.'

'Should we say something?'

'How can we? It's not our garden.'

'But the smell, it's revolting.'

'Well, we've seen her now, and we were warned.'

'Look at her. I bet she practises voodoo.'

'Yes, she'll cast a spell on us.'

'You're funny.'

Justin's mobile rang with a diverted call from the office. 'I'm sorry but we're actually not allowed,' he said, for the seventh time that morning, feeling as if he was a government gatekeeper, and, no, he didn't know, and no one knew how long this all would go on for.

Ellie's mother rang at the weekend. 'Are you quite sure the old lady wouldn't mind sharing the garden? I could send you some cuttings, or we could even drive down and I could leave them in the porch.'

'I think you can get fined for doing that,' Justin said to Ellie. He had received training in all the new rules. 'And you know your dad has a weak bladder, where could he stop for a wee? He can't come in here.'

'But if this goes on much longer and the weather warms up, that garden could be a godsend. We just have to ask nicely. I mean, we're all in this together, aren't we? And, anyway, suppose she gets sick. She might need someone to go and do shopping for her.'

The garden, out of bounds, was through a locked door at the end of the entrance hall. They left a note on the hall table, *would she mind, happy to restore the garden, could even grow some vegetables, buy a table, a parasol, establish a rota for* ... But the note went unanswered and the garden door stayed locked and the old lady went out there several times a day to smoke her filthy cigarettes, and a white stripe started to show itself in her hair and grow broader, like a cartoon skunk's.

She's always been a midnight rambler: the morning light makes her feel sick. Mornings belong to the straight people, the round pegs in round holes, the commuters, the steady-job workers, the bosses and the lackeys. Mornings are for suckers, for lines of nobodies waiting for the bus, and men in hats, and women with prams, all the sad-eyed fallen. She sleeps in her big brass bed until noon, wakes groggily, lights a cigarette, blows smoke rings at the ceiling. Remembers swimming in the Ionian Sea, remembers stone steps rising in the olive-tree hillside, a white cube of a domed church, a towel, a blanket, an election, the soldiers arriving by boat, the ballot boxes weighted with stones. Hot burned skin, a bikini that is barely more than a length of string and four triangles, bottles of retsina, glasses of ouzo, a dish of octopus tentacles, peels of melons, salty cheese, sedimented coffee, and now she feels her bowels stir, goes to the bathroom to begin the long struggle to make herself a daylight person, shaky hands doing up her jeans (What's this fresh hell? she thinks. Parkinson's?), though she's under house arrest: the plague has grounded her.

Only the fucking garden is her permitted territory which the kids upstairs want to take over, and then she would have to talk to them and who wants to make conversation with those bland bores in all their twenty-something perfection of skin and limb and their cock-eyed optimism? They will see what it comes down to in the end: everything sagging, your face like a withered seed, your hands crooked, tits down to your waist, strange rough-textured moles on your upper body, which the doctor pronounces, as he does of everything she sees him about, 'Just one of the inevitable signs of ageing, I'm afraid. They're known as senile warts.'

She listens to a rock-and-roll radio station, polishes her cowboy boots, looks at the skunk stripe in her hair. She knows that nobody would want her now: she has nothing left to offer, no tenderness, let alone sex appeal. But this old lady, this hag she sees, this bitter travesty of her celestial youth and beauty is not her. Inside she's a flame, she's a pistol. So she waits for night to fall to go to the petrol station to buy cigarettes and the little that she eats. Leaves the house, hears the metallic slap of her boots on concrete, the hollow empty streets, their night-time plague denizens. Dog-walkers, night-workers in the hospitals, drug-dealers.

The takeaways have reopened. She stops to buy a doner kebab and chips, rips the meat with her sharp good teeth.

'Aren't you afraid, love? I mean, at your age, shouldn't you be tucked up in bed?'

'I've never been frightened of the dark.'

Then spring enters the picture, with its own seductive powers. Ellie has had a brainwave. She goes online and orders a shade of box colour that's as close as she can match to the old lady's dyed hair, has it delivered to her flat with a note, 'From your young friends upstairs, looking forward to better days'. Daphne emerges into the garden a few hours later, the white skunk stripe gone. She waves her hand up to the window.

'Cheers, mate. Feel human again.'

And with this rapprochement, the next time they come downstairs, the garden door is open wide.

Feeling reckless, feeling like rebels without a cause, and having phoned ahead to establish the status of motorway service-station toilets, Ellie's mum and dad drove in from Banbury with a car-boot load of plants and instructions on what to do with them. They brought folding garden chairs. They had studied photographs of the barren space and declared that it could, with the right planning, be an urban oasis in a couple of years' time. There was nothing more satisfying than planting a garden, watching things grow, Ellie's mum said. Plants constantly surprised you with their vigour or their frailty. You did your best but in the end they would thrive or die.

Nature will always have the upper hand, devise new ways

of humbling mankind, her dad wrote in an email. *Just look where we all are now, a once-in-a-century rebuke to man's arrogance. Do get your hands dirty, get soil under your fingernails. However it turns out, you'll learn some valuable lessons.*

'When all this is over,' Justin said, 'we can have friends round for a barbecue.'

Things have gone so far in the spirit of mutual cooperation that Daphne Moffatt has agreed to run a hosepipe out of her kitchen window to water the plants that are making new unexpected lives for themselves in the garden. Watering is something you do in the evening's cool, and every night, before her midnight rambles, she gives the garden the kiss of life. The young ones do the rest, the planting, the weeding, the mowing, the pruning – they've really got into it, and everything out there seems to be thriving, a renewal of easy, careless life in defiance of the breathless deaths on hospital respirators. Justin has politely asked for the key for the garden shed, but she has said there is no key. He suggests borrowing some tools and sawing off the padlock, but she has said she can pick the lock, no problem: she used to be a cat burglar. They have no idea if this is supposed to be a joke. But the next time it's their turn in the garden, the door is open, revealing old newspapers, rusty shears, the skeleton of a rabbit in its closed hutch. There is no explanation of this gruesome discovery, not that, Justin says, he would want to hear it. They bury the bones under the privet hedge. Ellie says a little prayer she has got from an online pet-burial site. Justin can see there is a whole side to her personality that is unfolding like a flower and a dog is definitely going to happen sooner rather than later. She has bookmarked the site of Battersea Dogs Home.

Daphne has still not met or spoken to them in person: their

communication is limited to hall notes. But in exchange for a
monthly packet of box colour she has given them the garden,
a territory to which she has never paid any attention wherever
she has lived, not since Canning Town and all her father's
marrows and spuds were dug up to build the air-raid shelter in
which she and her brothers made an outlaw's den and ran in
and out in Davy Crockett hats waving home-made cardboard
tomahawks. When she looks at gardens, that's what she sees:
the ghosts of Anderson shelters, corrugated steel fortresses
against iron rain from the sky.

Now, under a different threat of death, she feels her own
mortality, not knowing if she'll see another summer, living
in these weird times. She wants to believe she will see the
Greek islands again. No idea when that might happen, when
the doors of the country will be unlocked, but Norris might
pay for a summer holiday if she's nice to him, if she writes
him a really lovely letter reviving his memories of what were,
in every sense, better days. Norris writes to her occasionally
on his Smythson notepaper. She hasn't heard from him since
Christmas when he sent a sketch of them in bed, like John and
Yoko, so he had forgotten nothing, still felt the old affection.
He pays the rent; he has said he always will. She will be taken
care of. She's not worried.

So, she has made up her mind to squeeze what she can from
this summer when they are all walking through the valley
of the shadow of death and fearing evil. The geraniums in
their pots remind her of the South of France, and now a table
has appeared, and an umbrella to shade it, she takes out her
notebook and gets on with writing her memoirs, which she
has meant to do for years, believing that they could make her
a fortune and she would no longer need old bald Norris and
his sentimental memories. Releasing her from an obligation
to butter him up and recall the nights they spent together in

his house in Barnes alongside his Buddha statues with the closed eyes and round bellies and complacent smiles. Norris had taken a spiritual turn in Thailand at the end of the sixties. He would like her to have one herself, a statue that is. Peace and serenity, he said, would always be hers if she followed the path of the—

But she said, 'You know I'm not interested in any of that. I was born in a crossfire hurricane.'

'Take it anyway. You never know what the future holds.'

She carried it home and it has found a final resting place, in the kitchen, on top of the microwave, where it smiles placidly, a paperweight for bills and old letters.

From their top-floor window they saw the fox cubs playing in the moonlight, like pairs of children tumbling over each other.

'They're so sweet,' said Ellie. 'We should go down and feed them. They seem quite tame.'

'Like a dog, but not a dog?'

'They *look* like dogs. Are they related?'

'I don't know. Should I look it up?

'Go on.'

He took out his phone.

They did a short Wikipedia course on foxes, learned how in Celtic mythology, the fox is portrayed as a wise and cunning trickster, symbol of the need to think fast and strategically, good at adjusting to new situations. Shape-shifters who can assume human forms: one minute they're going on two legs, the next four, so they can slip in and out of places.

'There you are, then, and the cubs are so sweet,' Ellie said. 'Dogs by another name. I'm definitely going to start feeding them. If you're not going to finish that chicken from last night I'll take it down.'

*

Daphne has already written the story of her childhood: of her father, a Barnardo's boy grown up to work on the railways, and her mother in her overalls, skinning a rabbit because she was a country girl, came up from Devon. Of the Moffatts and the Freebodys as far back as she knows. These recollections seem even to Daphne to be as quaint and unbelievable as a story told from a picture book, a fairy tale. But they happened. They must have done because she can't have made them up.

'I was always good at sex,' she writes. 'I had a talent for it, I suppose because I was an enthusiast. I enjoyed it, and why not? I was lucky, something wrong with my insides, I just couldn't get pregnant without them doing something to my tubes, an operation, but I always said no. I had a charmed life, no brats to worry about. I was a looker in those days and everyone wanted me. And my looks lasted for a long time after they should have done.'

Nights at the Pheasantry on the King's Road, let the good times roll. Meeting Norris for the first time, a coronet practically monogrammed on his shirt sleeves. So posh and kind and besotted, and though she hasn't seen him in the flesh for more than twenty years, he has always been as good as his word and looked after her. Norris in his grand house on the brown wriggling river at Barnes, the walls lined with plinths for his Buddhas, showing her his stamp albums, like a kid. 'My postal history collection,' he pompously corrected her. Oh, men and their hobbies. Funny-looking, like a cherub in an old painting, dimpled, vague at times, but always honest. 'Darling, I'd love to marry you and keep you in bed and feed you chocolates and screw your gorgeous brains out all day long, but I've got to make heirs. We chinless wonders – I mean the ones who aren't safe in taxis, not the confirmed bachelors – must bow to duty and the family tree.'

'Marry *you*? I'm not that kind of girl.' Marriage was ironing men's shirts, picking up their smelly socks, having a hot meal waiting for them when they got home. And you would die from the boredom of their company – you'd want to do a runner from the tedium of being a servant to some feller who took it for granted that a bird would always clean up after him.

'Thank you for being so understanding. I know I'm no Mick Jagger in bed, of course, but you must understand that whatever our different situations, you make me terribly happy.'

'I've had Mick Jagger. He was no Mick Jagger either.'

'Oh, my darling, you're not feeding foxes, are you? Where did you get the idea that that was compatible with gardening?' said Ellie's mother.

Justin, torn between his girlfriend and her mother: loyalty made him think he should take Ellie's side, but pragmatically he thought the older woman was probably right. Already rubbish from the bins was appearing in the flowerbeds; a couple of the new plants had been dug up; piles of fox poo attracted swarms of aggressive black flies. The Garden of Eden corrupted by bushy tails. That Celtic mythology shit they'd read up was just an excuse: foxes had sorted out their own public relations.

He looked up fox deterrents. Apparently male urine put them off. But he couldn't imagine standing there among the geraniums with his todger out watering the earth with his piss, watched, no doubt, by the old lady who lived alone, and who knew what her attitude was to men and their body parts? Give her a fright or a thrill?

She has seen the foxes at night when she is walking; she has seen them stalk alongside her down the empty streets, not afraid, nothing to be afraid of any more. She has seen how they can knock over the council's household waste bins and lever off the locks to loot the rotting food. She has navigated decaying tomatoes and mouldy bread on the pavement. She has no computer or smartphone so she has not looked up the cultural history of foxes and the libraries are all closed. Like her they are midnight ramblers and she can't stand them. Norris was a fox-hunting man. He had shown her old cine film of him on horseback in his scarlet coat, looking tall and robust instead of plump and lazy. 'What a morning out that was!' he said. 'What fun, you'd have loved it. If only you could ride, then you'd know. But I don't suppose you'd have the opportunity growing up in Canning Town.'

On warm nights, the window of the flat open, she can hear their bloodcurdling cries – they sound like human babies being tortured. She smells the stink of their urine. If it goes on like this the garden will be back out of bounds to her. And, let's face it, in her old age, when everything is shut and shit anyway, a garden with flowers in it, smelling sweet isn't such a bad place to be when you're writing your memoirs.

She has seen the girl out there feeding the wild animals. She has left a note asking her not to encourage them. The girl has replied, 'Oh, but just while the little cubs are finding their feet.' She has found a plastic takeaway box, mouldy with old curry, stinking under the table and had to dispose of it back in the bin from which it had been dragged to the garden. It's her fucking garden not theirs, but if she alienates them what is going to happen to her hair?

It is nearly three months since they have left the house for anything but grocery shopping and a daily run. Ellie and Justin are starting to get on one another's nerves, and the fox-feeding business is becoming an issue between them, a malignant lump under the skin of their relationship.

'The problem is,' Ellie said, 'we never had a chance to establish a normal day-to-day routine. Everything is so artificial. I mean, who lives like this, indoors almost all the time? Retired people, that's who.'

The letting agent thought, inshallah, he didn't have to do it in person, he could write her a letter and stick a stamp on it and take it to the postbox. She might reply by phone but he could hold it away from his ear and listen to the screaming from a distance of muted volume. Died back in April, instructions from the estate that his affairs were being wound up and no further rental payments would be made. She's two months in arrears and the landlord in Nicosia would appreciate immediate payment.

At various times, in various incarnations, she has earned her own living: salesgirl in the bed linens department at Derry & Toms; cleaner in a hotel in Ibiza; the cat-burgling phase with Good Time Terry, when they had got away with thousands and spent it all (on what, she can't remember); ladies' maid and dresser to a Mayfair madam; selling merchandise outside stadium concerts – that was something she could always fall back on until now. Sometimes old roadies remembered her, the glory days.

She does not reply to the letting agent's letter. If anyone had asked her, she would have said, 'I don't want to talk about it.' Avoidance makes it go away. She has become distanced from reality. She has allowed herself to drift when she should have been hustling, taking care of her future; she has been watering the garden and watching things grow. Letting the young ones get away with murder. Something has happened to her in that she has stopped being herself and does not know how to get back to that person: the rot of lassitude and boredom, the living in the moment, the watching the flowers grow has taken away something essential from herself, the core of who she is. She is gently rocking through time. She has watched the fluff from a dandelion clock blow upwards and over the garden fence; she has followed its trajectory, its state of make-a-wishfulness.

She had not expected to find herself, at last, null and void, like a bad cheque.

She smokes and walks the night-time streets. The days are getting longer, the night is in retreat. The long russet bodies of the foxes have no fear: they are her witch's familiars. She watches their assault on the household waste bins. They have conquered the city, the urban places. Norris on horseback would have no chance against these invaders.

She tells herself that she is a survivor, that she will finish her memoirs, name everyone, dish the dirt, make a million pounds. All she needs is the discipline to screw herself to the chair and get on with it. It will all come out right in the end.

From the top-floor window Ellie saw the accident. Saw the old lady come out of the back door, saw her lay her pen and bits of scribbled paper on the table, saw her go back in through the hall door and bring out a cup of coffee, saw her tread on the grass, saw her look down at her foot where she had put it, a pile of fox shit, her cowboy boot besmirched, stinking. Saw her look round the garden, saw the fox cubs emerging from under a hole in the fence, looking around, nonchalant, careless of danger. Saw the old lady go back in through the hall door and come back with something in her right hand, that scrawny sinewy arm, that long throw, and one of the fox cubs maimed and dying on the grass, its little head split open by the smiling face of a bronze Buddha from Thailand.

The period of truce was at an end. War was resumed. Such is the natural state of things beneath mismatched neighbours. The RSPCA came to collect the corpse of the fox cub. Daphne was issued with a warning. Foxes were not vermin: you couldn't just kill them. They were protected, had basic rights to scavenge, roam, live. But these were strange times they were passing through. Everyone was on edge; everyone was at the end of their tether. Something was bound to snap. On this occasion they would not prosecute, but gave her a warning: make peace with the natural world and its unruly wanderers. They left her standing in the garden as the mother fox whimpered by the fence and the rest of the pack smelt blood and death and fear.

No more boxes of hair dye appeared on the hall table. Ellie, on the phone to her mum, said, 'I cried buckets over that poor fur baby. How could she do such a thing? I know she must have thought, Yuck, and the smell and the flies, but honestly, it would have washed off her manky boots anyway.'

The skunk stripe grows in Daphne's hair. Soon she feels unrecognisable to herself when she looks in the mirror; white and pale, she is becoming the Celeste of light, the airy figure that floated down the King's Road. She should go back there, she thought. Someone will recognise me, someone will remember. The dead fox cub is not on her conscience. She feels, on the contrary, like an avenging angel. She is a Londoner born, the city her inheritance. The invaders from the shires must be run out of town. It is in her power to do it, becoming, at last, the crossfire hurricane.

WARRIOR

CHIBUNDU ONUZO

Four years into our marriage, Lapidoth decided to take a second wife. It was not uncommon for men in our village to marry twice, then thrice, then lose count of the women they were trothed to. But Lapidoth and I laughed at such men. They were leaking wine skins that must spill their seed in any woman who would stand still. And yet there was my husband, standing in our tent, saying to me, 'It is time I had a son, Deborah. I must marry me another woman.'

I could smell my father-in-law's hand in this. Ahiezer had never liked me. He thought I was too tall.

'Let us eat first,' I said to my husband.

He had the scent of his goats on his person. I washed his face, his arms and feet, and anointed his head with oil. I fed him bread and a lamb stew, then laid his head in my lap.

'So my husband would forsake the wife of his youth?' My tone was light and even.

'Not forsake. Only enlarge our tent with one more woman.'

I twined my fingers in his beard and stroked his chin. 'But

you have often said that El did not see fit to give Adam a second wife.'

'I am not Adam. I am thankful for our daughters but a man must have a son to inherit his wealth and pass on his name. That is what my father says.'

It *was* Ahiezer's meddling. I could have reminded my husband of the patriarch Zelophahad, whose daughters inherited his lands, but the time for reasoning was done.

'We must be divorced, then,' I said.

My husband sat up as if thorns had sprouted on my thighs.

'A woman cannot ask for a divorce.'

'If you bring a second woman into our tent,' I said, 'I will make your life such a misery that you will beg to be rid of me.'

'You threaten me?' Lapidoth asked.

'I promise you.'

I could always best him in a staring contest. His eyes watered too easily. He blinked first and then laughed until his shoulders shook.

'So I cannot have me another wife,' he said.

'Not alongside this one.'

He came into me that night and we conceived our first son, Dan. After Dan, I bore Lapidoth three more sons and we had no more talk of second wives.

I remembered that evening as I sat before the warring couple who had come to seek out my judgement. They had spoken overly long, talking over each other, butting heads like goats.

'Enough, my children,' I said.

'My son,' I turned to the husband, 'you will drink no more wine except on feast days.'

The wife's face glowed with vindication.

'And you, daughter, must learn how to address a man. First try honeyed words before you reach for the sting.'

The husband also beamed. They were both right and they were both wrong. That was the way of marriage. I placed a hand on each of their heads.

'The blessings of El go with you.'

They were dismissed. I stood stiffly from the goat skin and motioned for my handmaiden to fetch me a bowl of water. There were others still waiting for my judgement, but the sun had gone down and the time had come for me to see to my own tent.

I held court under a tree the children of Israel called the Palm of Deborah. It was the tallest palm in the grove and its leaves cast the most shade. There I sat, dawn to dusk, weighing and measuring and parsing the concerns of the children of Israel. Boundary disputes, quarrels over water, over goats and, of course, women's matters.

It was the women who first made me judge over them. I am taller than most women, as I am taller than most men, and something in my size drew them to me. I settled their squabbles and, in exchange, they brought me gifts, herbs for my pot and jewellery for my neck and wrists. Then they brought their sons and daughters and finally they brought their husbands.

In those early days, the men were reluctant. What could Lapidoth's wife know of the affairs of men? But as I used what wit El gave me to make crooked issues straight, my humble advice became the wisdom of Deborah. My fame spread from our small village to all of Israel, until now as far as Egypt, I am known as the Mother of Israel. A lofty title for a woman who still sleeps in a narrow tent with the husband of her youth.

Lapidoth was waiting for me, washed and ready for our evening meal. At first, he was jealous of my fame. It is not easy for a man to be known as 'Deborah's husband' at the village well. But then he grew to enjoy the benefits of being husband to the Mother of Israel. Great men come to seek my counsel and when they do me honour, they must also pay respect to my lord husband, although he is a goat-herder who has never distinguished himself at war.

We sat down to our repast of goat stew and unleavened bread.

'What news today?' Lapidoth asked.

'The same. People must quarrel and I must settle their affairs.'

'I hear the Canaanites are gathering for war,' Lapidoth said.

'El preserve us.'

The children of Israel are divided into twelve tribes. We are a strong, fierce people but we are loath to follow one leader. It leaves us vulnerable to attacks from the kings of Canaan, who show no mercy when they raid our lands.

'El preserve us indeed,' Lapidoth intoned.

That night, El spoke to me in a dream. The children of Israel call me a prophet because of these dreams. How can I tell what is a dream from El and what is the mere wandering of my imagination? In the dreams sent by El, I hear the voice of El. And the dreams sent by El always come to pass.

In my dream, I saw a host of Israel gathered on a plain and facing a large army of Canaanites. At the head of the Canaanite army was the mighty general Sisera. I knew him by his iron chariot and his long dark braid. The two armies advanced on each other. Who led the children of Israel? He was shrouded by mist. Then a light from the heavens shone on his face, dispelling the vapours. The voice of El said clearly, 'Victory I give to him.'

I woke up to wailing outside my tent. It was not yet dawn. The Mother of Israel had been assigned a guard of young men who slept outside my tent. I heard one of them, Jorah, challenge the wailer.

'Who dare disturb our mother at this hour?'

'Justice,' the voice in the dark wailed. 'Justice for my children. I too am a mother and my children have been slain.'

I felt Lapidoth stirring beside me.

'What is it now?' he asked.

'Go back to sleep. I will see to it.'

I rose and left our tent. Outside, the moon shone bright and I could make out Jorah blocking a woman's path to me.

'Mother, this is not for your eyes.'

'A mother must look without flinching. Step aside, my son.'

The woman stumbled forward and thrust what was in her arms towards me. I did not flinch at the headless child. I took the corpse in my arms.

'Who did this, my daughter?'

'It was Sisera's men. They came with iron chariots. Justice, Mother.'

'You will have it. Jorah, fetch her some food and water.'

When she was sated, we washed the body of her child and bound it in cloth. We said the sacred words, dust to dust and ashes to ashes, before committing her child to the ground. Once the sun rose, I said to Jorah, 'Send for Barak son of Abinoam.'

Barak son of Abinoam was a farmer who had risen to prominence by chance or, rather, the providence of El. A small band of Canaanite raiders attacked his farm, and instead of running for the hills, Barak and his household gathered their ploughs and put the Canaanites to flight. Word of this skirmish spread and men came to join Barak and seek his protection. Whenever the Canaanites raided, he was there to defend the people of Zebulun and Naphtali but he had never launched an attack on our enemy. He preferred to see to his farm in times of relative peace. It was a strange choice, but who can question the wisdom of El?

He came to the grove with a hundred men but he approached my tent with only two. They knelt when they drew close.

'Mother, you summoned me.'

There was no time for pleasantries.

'Thus says the Lord. Call out ten thousand warriors from the tribes of Naphtali and Zebulun at Mount Tabor. And I will call out Sisera, commander of Jabin's army, along with his chariots and warriors. There I will give you victory over him.'

Barak raised his eyes to me.

'Sisera has nine hundred iron chariots. My men and I have none.'

'You have beaten Sisera's men before,' I said.

'Not when he was assembled for war. We have won skirmishes, not battles, Mother.'

Barak was no coward. His assessment was correct. The Canaanites had the superior armour, and a cautious general like him would not confront them in the open field. But what were iron chariots when weighed against the voice of El?

'You question El?' I asked.

'I do not question but . . . ' Barak began, and grew silent.

'Speak freely, my son.'

'In the old days, when a judge called the children of Israel to war, he rode with them.'

My predecessors were all men. Othniel son of Kenaz, who went to war against the King of Aram. Ehud son of Gera, who buried his dagger in the belly of the King of Moab. Shamgar son of Anath, who once killed six hundred Philistines with an ox goad.

'I will go,' Barak said. 'But only if you go with me, Mother.'

He was a wily commander. I could see why men followed him. He had led me sweetly into his trap. If I refused, he would say I did not truly believe that El would give him victory. But how could I, a woman, ride into battle? I remembered the body I had buried that morning, the child who would never see another dawn.

'Very well,' I said. 'I will go with you. But you will receive no honour in this venture. The Lord's victory over Sisera will be at the hands of a woman. We will leave tomorrow morning. I must bid my family farewell.'

'As you command, Mother,' Barak said.

Lapidoth was out with the goats. Our sons had long told him that he could leave the tending of the herds to them but Lapidoth loved those animals almost as much as he loved our children.

'I am to go to war with Barak, my lord,' I said to him.

'What new folly is this?'

'If I do not go, Barak will not go. If Barak does not go, the Canaanites will continue to crush the children of Israel.'

'But you are not a warrior, Deborah. You cannot even hold a sword.'

'I have borne seven children, each one a battle to bring forth. El gave me victory in the birthing room. He will give me victory again.'

'And what if I refuse?' Lapidoth asked. 'You would defy your lord husband? Am I to kneel also to the Mother of Israel?'

I could not have married a man who was not proud but on that night, before I did the unthinkable and rode into war, I had no more strength for managing Lapidoth's pride.

'I am scared. I do not want to go but I must.'

'And what if you die?' Lapidoth asked. He drew close to me and cupped my face in his palm. 'What am I to do then?'

'Then you can marry your second wife.'

He smiled. 'Stubborn woman. As stubborn as my goats.'

*

Our children came that evening to bid me farewell. They are all married and have gone to their own tents. Each one tried to persuade me of the folly of my course of action. Only Abigail came close to breaking my resolve. She is my eldest and the most like me. My other children tried to frighten me with scenes of what might happen to me on the battlefield. To all this I said, 'The will of El be done.' But Abigail instead reminded me of what *I* might do.

'Can you kill a man, Mother?'

'I may not have to.'

'I think you can,' she continued, as if I had not spoken. 'You are as tall as most men and as strong too. Dan surely felt the weight of your right hand when we were children. But will you want to kill a man, even one as wicked as Sisera, when you know what it takes to bring a life into this world?'

We set forth at dawn the next morning. Barak offered me a cart to ride in but I chose a gentle mare instead. The men must grow used to seeing me in their midst. Some said I was bad luck. Others said I was a sign of the favour of El.

As we rode through the villages and towns of Israel, men joined our cause when it was made known that we were going to fight Sisera. Our numbers swelled from one hundred, to two hundred, to five hundred, but it was when we reached the lands of Zebulun and Naphtali that we gathered the bulk of our forces.

It is not for me to criticise the peculiarities of the different tribes. After all, I am mother to all of Israel. But the people of Zebulun and Naphtali are known for their fierceness, wildness even. It is said, to quarrel with a man from Zebulun is to forfeit one's life.

They seem untameable, yet Barak has tamed them. Israel may have no king but Barak is king to the tribes of Zebulun and Naphtali. The women came with their tambourines and processed before us. They threw flowers in our path and sang for Barak as he rode past.

'Mighty warrior, Barak, who slays five hundred with his left hand and a thousand with his right.'

Barak sat straighter on his horse. As he rode through the city, his announcers called out, 'The Mother of Israel has called Zebulun and Naphtali to war. Who will follow Barak?'

They came in their thousands. Young men, their older brothers, their uncles and their fathers. Men with grey beards and stooped with age hobbled to Barak's call. Young boys who had barely seen ten summers flocked to our standard. The old men and the boys who were too young were turned away. These latter wept at being sent back. They clutched at my hands. 'Mother, plead with Barak for us.'

I sat beside Barak day, night and day again as the men of Zebulun and Naphtali pledged loyalty to him and enmity against Sisera. In five days our army was gathered and we began our march to the banks of the River Kishon where El had promised to give us victory.

News of ten thousand men marching spreads quickly. As we moved through the countryside, we saw Canaanite scouts in the distance watching us. A host of this size had not gathered in a generation and our enemy would be amassing his forces also.

There were a few other women in the camp. The army must eat and they followed us in the baggage train, preparing our meals at dusk and at dawn. Sometimes they lingered by my tent. The youngest women held me in awe.

'Mother, you would ride into war like a man,' one said.

'Not like a man,' I replied. 'Like myself.'

Barak gave me a sword and shield. 'It won't come to that,

Mother,' he said. 'You will be well protected through the battle. A mere precaution.'

In the evenings, Jorah, captain of my guard, taught me how to use a sword. How to swing with the weight of my right hand and block an enemy's blow with my shield. Ten days were not enough to make me a warrior but at least it might keep my head attached to my neck.

We reached the bank of the River Kishon at dusk on the tenth day of our march. It was a favoured site for battle because the ground was flat and the river supplied both armies with water for their horses. Victory was often decisive. Whoever lost by Kishon would be routed and would not recover for years.

The Canaanite forces were already assembled when we arrived. Perhaps they had waited for many days because we could hear the sound of revelry from their camp, music and raucous laughing. They were deadly fighters but lacking in discipline.

In contrast, there was silence in the Israelite camp that night. Many men passed by my tent.

'Mother, bless me,' they said. I blessed each one, knowing that some would not see sunset the next day. Barak also came.

'Mother, you may stay in the camp with the women. The men have seen you march to the battle front. It is enough.'

'As you reminded me, a judge rides with the troops into battle.'

'Yes, and you have shown great courage in coming this far, but if you are slain tomorrow, the rest of Israel will turn against me.'

He should have thought of that before he laid his trap for me. 'I will ride into war, Barak son of Abinoam. It is my destiny.'

That night I thought of Lapidoth. He had refused to bid me farewell in public.

'It is for women to send their husbands off to war. Do not make me a laughing stock, Deborah.'

And so we said our goodbyes in our tent.

'Come back to me,' he said.

'If El wills it.'

Who would bless the Mother of Israel?

Morning came. The troops arose and dressed for war. They lined up, row after row, and Barak and I rode to the front.

'Men of Israel,' Barak said, his voice carrying on the morning wind, 'today we will break the rod of Sisera and free all of Israel. Today we will fight and El will give us victory.'

The soldiers cheered.

'Mother, will you speak to them?' Barak said softly to me.

The spirit of El came upon me and made me bold. What did it matter that an Israelite woman had never before ridden to war?

'Prepare yourselves! This is the day the Lord will give you victory over Sisera, for El is marching ahead of you.' I remembered the song of Miriam the matriarch, the older sister of Moses. 'Sing to the Lord, for he has triumphed gloriously. He has hurled both horse and rider into the sea.'

The chant was picked up.

'He has hurled both horse and rider into the sea.'

The men stamped.

'He has hurled both horse and rider into the sea.'

They lifted their shields.

'He has hurled both horse and rider into the sea.'

Their voices rose louder and louder until the sound reached Sisera's troops and drowned their noise.

Barak's hand on my arm brought me back to myself. 'It is enough, Mother. The men are ready.'

I looked at the soldiers. They were like an arrow stretched on a bow, the moment before the archer releases the string. They were ready.

Barak blew his horn and we advanced. I was not in the front row, or the second row. Barak placed me in the middle of the troops, surrounded on every side by soldiers, as well as by my own personal guard.

The Canaanites sent their first wave of iron chariots. The sound of the wheels rumbled against the earth.

'El preserve me,' I whispered.

When the two armies clashed, it was a terrible sound. Swords clanged on shields. The screams of men were followed by the iron smell of blood. My horse grew restive. Closer and closer the Canaanites came. Their chariots had pushed through our front line and suddenly they were upon us. I could see their faces, darkened with the ochre paint of war.

'To Mother! Her guard has fallen. To Mother!' I heard someone shout.

A Canaanite stood below my horse, swinging his axe upwards. I lowered my shield just in time. The blow landed heavily on my leg but my sword arm was free. I slashed at his exposed throat and he fell away. My first kill.

'Mother!' It was Jorah, captain of my guard. His sleeves were torn and his face was black with dirt and blood. We fought back to back. I killed two more men before the tide turned in our favour.

The Canaanites had not expected to meet such fierce resistance. The Israelites they terrorised were farmers and goat-herders who ran away once they heard the rumble of their chariots. But the men of Zebulun and Naphtali stood firm. I did not see the first Canaanite who dropped his sword but it was not long before they were turning and fleeing. El had sent panic into the camp of our enemies.

We gave chase. There was something terrible in killing men in this way but if they had the chance, they would have killed us as we fled. An eye for an eye. Blood for blood. Jorah handed me a spear and I drove it through the backs of three more Canaanites.

We killed until the ground was red with blood but Sisera, their general, was nowhere to be found. If we did not cut off the head of the snake, a new body would sprout behind it. The Israelite men scattered to search for Sisera, while Barak and I sat on our horses, amid the carnage.

'You said a woman would have the victory today, Mother.' Barak said. 'Well, where is she?'

'The victory is not complete, my son, until Sisera is dead.'

'My lord.' It was a woman calling from the ground. She was slight in stature, no taller than my shoulder.

'Yes,' Barak said.

'Come, and I will show you the man you are looking for.'

'What is your name?'

'I am Jael, wife of Heber the Kenite.'

'I am Barak son of Abinoam.'

'And I am Deborah, wife of Lapidoth.'

'I know you, Mother. Follow me.'

Our horses were weary and they walked after her slowly. She led us to a tent pitched under an oak tree.

'Come with me,' she said.

Inside the tent was the body of the great general, Sisera.

'How did you do it, daughter?'

'I knew him from the silver bangles on his wrists. It is what the Canaanite princes wear. I invited him into my tent. He asked for water, and I gave him milk to make him drowsy. He fell into a deep sleep, and while he was sleeping, I crept up to him with a hammer and tent peg and drove the tent peg through his temple and into the ground.'

'And were you not afraid to do it, daughter?'

'If the Mother of Israel can ride to war, then I can do my part.'

Barak chuckled. 'El preserve the men of Israel from women like Jael, wife of Heber.'

Barak dragged the body of Sisera outside and blew his horn. The soldiers came to him. When they saw the body of the feared general at Barak's feet, they began to cheer and shout Barak's name.

I snatched the horn from Barak and blew until they were all silent.

'It was Jael who slew Sisera.' I drew Jael out of the tent and showed her to the men of Israel. The spirit of El came powerfully upon me then and I sang for the soldiers of Israel to hear me.

'Most blessed among women is Jael, the wife of Heber the Kenite. May she be blessed above all women who live in tents. Sisera asked for water and she gave him milk, in a bowl fit for nobles, she brought him yoghurt. Then with her left hand she reached for a tent peg, and with her right hand for the work-man's hammer. She struck Sisera with the hammer, crushing his head. With a shattering blow, she pierced his temples. He sank, he fell, he lay still at her feet. And where he sank there he died.'

'I was not going to deny her her place in the victory,' Barak said to me, as we rode back to camp. The earth spread red around us, the soil churned with blood.

'You will not. She will ride next to you in the victory procession.'

'As you wish, Mother.'

'All Israel will sing of the part you played but history must also remember Jael.'

'As you wish, Mother.'

BANSHEE

ANNIE HODSON

Rumour had it that someone in Ballytullan was marked for death.

Whispers buzzed through the school assembly that the banshee's cry had been heard the last three nights, and some unlucky person must be on their way out. Aisling listened with a thrill of fear. What if it came for Mam? What if it came for her?

At lunchtime the girls in her class huddled around the radiator and swapped stories, starting with the fact that old Jim Kelly had supposedly taken his shotgun and gone to find the source of the screaming last night.

'It's all nonsense,' Anne Moore said. 'It's just the sound the foxes make when they have sex.'

Several girls giggled at the word sex, but Roisin Barry looked mutinous.

'It's not nonsense. Mrs O'Connell saw her out the window, I heard her telling my auntie.'

A clamour went up for Roisin to describe the banshee.

'She was sitting in the tree opposite the post office. And she was wailing.'

'Keening,' Anne said. 'Banshees keen, they don't wail.'

'What did she look like?'

Roisin wasn't sure.

'They're either really young and pretty, or really old and ugly and scary,' Claire Walsh said. 'And they have all this long hair they comb, and if you steal their comb they'll come for it in the middle of the night, and you have to hold it out to them with tongs or they'll tear your arm off.'

Aisling shuddered involuntarily.

'She must be here to kill someone,' Claire said with satisfaction and Anne scoffed.

'They don't kill people. They just warn you that someone's going to die. Or they would if they were real, which they're not.'

The bell rang and they scattered back to their seats. Aisling clenched her fists in her lap and thought of all she knew about banshees. She'd heard of the combs before, although she'd always thought that was just something her grandmother said to keep her from picking dirty ones off the ground. And she knew what keening was. Irish was her favourite subject and Mr Ó Cearrnaigh had hammered into them the words the English had shamelessly stolen from them, like whiskey and galore and smithereens. But keening was the best of the bunch.

Chaoin sí – she keened. Tá sí ag caoineadh – she is keening. Caoineann an bhean – the woman keens.

In the examples in the Irish textbooks, the boys were always playing and building and taking. The girls were always feeling things.

Back home, Aisling broached the subject.

'Mam, everyone at school's saying there's a banshee on the loose.'

Mam looked over from peeling carrots, brow creased.

'What's that, love? What's on the loose?'

Mam couldn't hear very well any more. The doctor in the city had given her hearing aids but Da wouldn't let her use them. He said he'd be ashamed to be seen out with a woman her age wearing them, and that she needed to try harder.

The hearing aids went in a drawer and Aisling had to repeat herself two or three times for Mam to understand.

'A banshee,' she said slowly and clearly.

Mam laughed.

'Sure, what would a banshee be doing in Ballytullan? Too small for the likes of them.'

'Jim Kelly went out looking for her with his shotgun,' Aisling said, moving to stand next to Mam so she could hear better.

'Mr Kelly doesn't have a shotgun,' Mam said. 'And he likes his sleep too much to be prowling around at night.'

Aisling felt comforted.

'Really? But Roisin says Mrs O'Connell saw the banshee out the window.'

She didn't notice her father at the door until he snorted.

'That old bitch is the only banshee round here.'

Mrs O'Connell always used to invite them over for tea, and once she'd slipped Mam a note at Mass. Aisling never found out what it said, but she thinks her father did, because after that they weren't allowed to talk to Mrs O'Connell any more.

Aisling wanted to tell her father about Jim Kelly, but he'd already left the kitchen. She was hoping she might hear him laugh, his laugh that made everyone feel like they were in on the joke. She couldn't remember the last time he'd laughed like that.

The next day at school, the class confronted Mr Ó Cearrnaigh on the subject of banshees.

'Bean sí,' he said, writing it on the whiteboard with a squeaky marker pen. 'From the Old Irish ben síde. That was before colonisation and Anglicisation, of course—'

'Bean means woman,' Anne interrupted, always eager to be first to an answer. 'And sí means fairy.'

Mr Ó Cearrnaigh held up a finger.

'Sí means fairy now. It used to mean something like fairy mound. The mounds were where the fairies lived, and the banshee was one of them.'

'That's why they're always angry,' Claire said triumphantly. 'Who wants to live in a mound?'

'You better watch what you say or they'll come get you, Claire,' one of the boys at the back of the class said.

'She's not here for me,' Claire said and Aisling wanted to ask what made her so sure. How could anyone know if the banshee was coming for them?

'What's that?' Mr Ó Cearrnaigh said and the class told him about the banshee's visitation.

'You girls have very active imaginations,' he said jovially. 'Less talk and more listening for the rest of class I think.'

Tá sé ag caint – he is talking. Tá sí ag éisteacht – she is listening. Labhraíonn na buachaillí agus éisteann na cailíní – the boys speak and the girls listen.

Aisling looked up banshees on the school computer. She had to click away from all the horrible pictures, but she found some articles to read.

The consensus was that Anne had been right, banshees didn't kill anyone. They only foretold death. They didn't cause it.

That was some comfort to Aisling, although none of the websites told her how to find out whose death they were foretelling. The people in the stories were usually sick already. She didn't know any sick people in Ballytullan, except maybe

Muireann's poor sister, being treated for cancer in the city. But then the banshee would go to the city, wouldn't it? Not come here?

All of the articles spoke of the banshee's lament, keening for the one lost. But a few said that the banshee's cry could be one of victory too. Sometimes the one marked for death was a wicked person. An evil-doer. The banshee would rejoice over them as one would rejoice over the slaughter of an enemy.

Aisling didn't know any wicked people either. Except—

When she got home that night, Mam was crouched on the kitchen floor, picking up shards of broken glass. The room smelt like whiskey, hot and harsh.

Aisling brought over the dustpan and brush. Mam had a new bruise on her cheek.

Aisling woke just past midnight. A sound was drifting through the air towards her. It was neither a scream nor a wail, but a song. Soft and sad and for her ears only.

She got up and dressed in the darkness. Pulled on her coat and scarf and gloves and padded out of the back door. She followed the song through the gate, across the field, and all the way to the hazel tree by the crossroads.

Beneath the tree, the banshee stood.

She was neither young and beautiful, nor old and terrifying. She looked to be about sixty, sensibly dressed in a raincoat, thick boots and a woollen hat. Her long grey hair hung to her waist and there was something gleaming white in her pocket. Her lips were parted in song, and it was no louder now than it had been in Aisling's bedroom.

Aisling wasn't afraid. She couldn't be, somehow, now they were face to face. Not with the banshee looking like that, so oddly familiar and reassuring, like the women who worked in the post office or the café or the library, sturdy and solid and kind. The ones who discreetly pressed money into Mam's hands or murmured that they'd always have a place for her to stay, should she need one.

The song ended but the banshee didn't leave.

Aisling inched a little nearer.

Her mouth felt too dry to talk but she didn't think the banshee would speak either. Could she only keen? Or if she spoke, would it be in a language that time had long forgotten?

They didn't need words. Aisling raised one shaking hand and pointed across the field to their little house, set alone at the edge of the town.

The banshee nodded and Aisling knew she understood. Then she crooked her finger for Aisling to come closer.

The banshee delved into her pocket and drew out the gleaming thing. It was a comb and she held it out to Aisling.

It was big, so big that Aisling had to hold it with two hands, each tooth sharp and bone-white, like they'd been freshly bleached.

Aisling nodded. She also understood.

It was Friday and her father always stayed at the pub until last orders. He used to come home early with fish and chips, and they'd eat it on their laps in front of the television and make plans for the weekend. Nowadays Mam had to wait up for him, in case he wanted dinner when he got in. Aisling usually sat up with her, both of them drowsing on the couch until Aisling heard the tell-tale bang of the gate and shook Mam awake. Then Mam would send her off to bed before she opened the door and Aisling would put her pillow around her ears, to block out any shouting.

Béiceann sé – he shouts. Tá sé ag béiceadh – he is shouting. Béiceann an fear – the man shouts.

This time Aisling sat coiled like a spring until Mam dozed off and then crept outside to the front garden. There was a short muddy path from the gate to the door, lined loosely with rocks.

Aisling knelt down and dug a small trench in the dirt with her fingers. Then she slipped the comb out from inside her vest and planted it in the hole she'd made. The teeth stood up from the ground, proud and pointed, as if from the maw of some great creature.

Then she went back inside and waited.

Two hours later, she heard the creak of the gate. A muttered curse, the clink of a bottle being thrown down. A sudden loud thump. A single choked-off cry.

She went outside and her father was lying on the path, one foot entangled in the comb he'd tripped over. His head had smashed against a rock and there was blood spreading from his temple, almost invisible in the dark and the dirt.

Aisling turned and the banshee was there, sitting in the lowest branches of the oak tree. Aisling carefully stepped over her father and felt around until the comb came loose from the ground. She dusted it off and handed it back to the banshee.

Her father was making the slightest of moaning noises. Their house was too far from anyone for him to be heard, though they were close enough that someone in the house might.

But it was only Mam inside and she didn't have her hearing aids.

Aisling nodded once more to the banshee and stepped back into the warmth. It was cold outside, almost below freezing. The keening would come soon, but somehow she knew it would not start until it was too late for her father to be revived.

SHE-DEVIL

ELEANOR CREWES

The whispers began after Bonnie found the chair.

She had been standing in the kitchen, the hiss of the frying pan competing with the yell of the extractor.

BONNIE

In all that noise the whisper had sounded so clearly, as if close to her ear, spoken on its own separate channel.

It was common in her town to find furniture left outside people's front gardens.

please take

Bonnie understood the choice to present the pavement with a piece of your home and hope that someone would take it away,

rather than making the hour's round trip to the dump, where you'd simply toss your rubbish on top of someone else's, and leave it to lie in the fuzzy rain that hung in the clouds for most months.

She'd brought items home with her before . . .

HM?

Like the lamp she had once found by a neighbour's wall.

It was an Anglepoise style that slumped a little, the springs having weakened over time.

onnie sometimes imagined that its osture came from it being given up.

In her mind she'd see the lamp signalling 'S-O-S' out of her window and across the darkening courtyard. But in this scenario it would be too late.

Its previous owner had already closed the curtains.

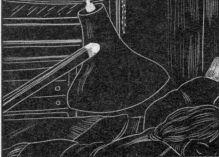

Unlike the
lamp . . .

. . . the chair was
pristine.

The chair was possibly Victorian; the orange wood and overly carved legs felt too intentional for later styles.

When Bonnie had searched it up on the internet she'd found lots of options for newly made mid-century frames with intricate woven seats.

This chair was much more homey. The arms bowed out in a clearly welcoming embrace. And at the centre was an ornate spl into which a keyhole shape had been cut.

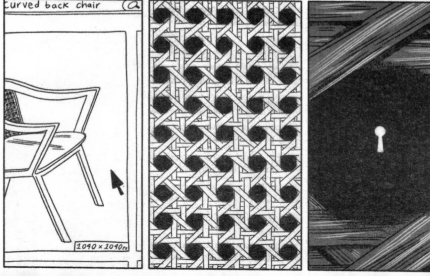

Curved back chair

1090 × 1090

That night she dreamed.

In the dream she watched as a woman's hand moved over soft wood.

One of the fingers was wearing a ring . . .

A lot like the one Bonnie's mother always wore.

Bit by bit her mother's hand had sanded down the soft wood to reveal dark inner flesh, and bone.

In the morning . . .

. . . the solo, dehydrated carcass of a white bug lay on the seat of the chair.

As she left for work, she was certain she'd heard the whisper again.

A woman's voice.

Bonnie

That evening Bonnie had forced the chair into the fitted cupboard where she kept her coats and winter shoes. It was the only door in her home that had a lock on the outside . . .

. . . and she had fastened it.

When Bonnie was very small, her mother had a chair. It had no arms for her to rest on, and the back was very low, so there was nowhere to lean.

From where it crouched in the corner of her mother's bedroom, Bonnie had always thought that the chair looked feral.

An animal that was hunting, pupils wide, and tongue lolling.

If Bonnie was bad her mother would make her sit in the chair, in the bedroom, on her own, with the door closed.

Sitting there, Bonnie's mind would picture all the things that stood behind her exposed back . . .

. . . as the darkness stretched out before her.

The wood was very dark. Blackened.

Oiled.

Cold.

When her mother finally left,

Bonnie carried the chair out of her front door and down the communal staircase.

Through the cellar where they kept the bins.

And out to the pavement.

She travelled doggedly along the quiet high street, unfazed by the rain that flew at her. Her white-knuckled grip had fused the chair to her skin.

When she finally reached the gates of the dump,

Bonnie rested the chair against the railings.

And turned away, back, toward her home.

That night Bonnie dreamed again. Bugs. Crawling Bugs.

SCUTTLE SCUTTLE SCUTTLE

And hair.

Long

silver

white

hair.

Hair like thread.

In a black room
stood the chair.

Its wood was made of flesh.
Flesh sewn together with long strands of silver white hair.

The flesh was rippling,
wriggling.

White bugs were forcing their way out
from between the stitches.

And from the
keyhole . . .

. . . a mouth smiled at her.

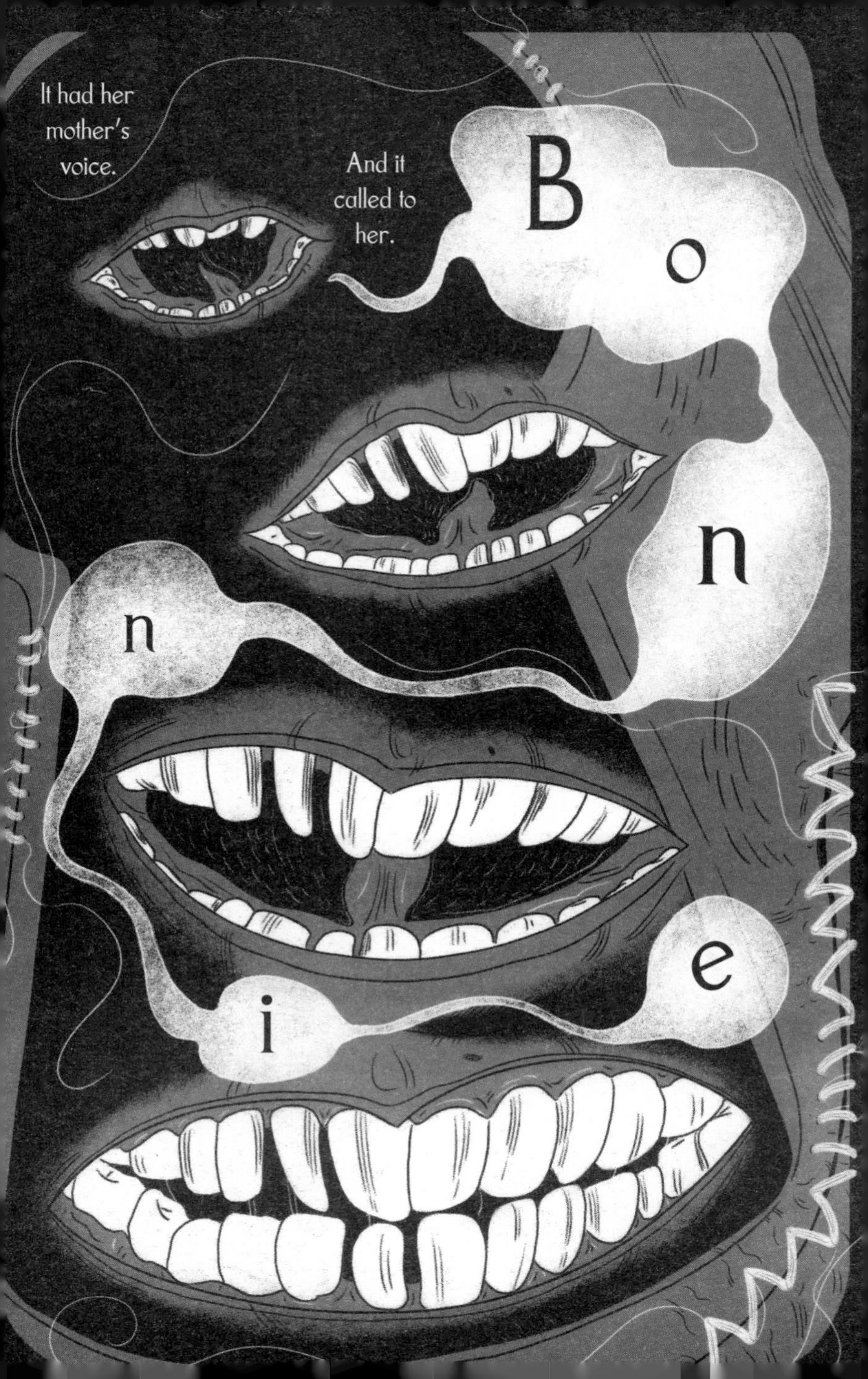
It had her mother's voice.
And it called to her.
B o n n i e

Opening her eyes, Bonnie saw her bed – the rumpled, empty sheets, and the dark shadows they created.

As she squirmed to sit up straight, she felt slick, wet wood beneath her hands.

Her pyjamas clung to her skin through the damp.

There was a smell, too ...

... a smell of rain.

The chair was in her bedroom.

And Bonnie was sitting in it.

The chair is in Bonnie's bedroom. Bonnie is sitting in her bed. She is watching the chair.

A moment ago,

it moved.

Bonnie is waiting for the chair to move again.

In the kitchen, the phone is ringing.

Her mother.

It is always Bonnie's mother.

RIIINNNG
RIIINNNGGG

The answer machine clicks.

Bonnie, it's me.

Pick up.

Where are you?

Bonnie?

She repeats and repeats, her voice growing more frustrated.

Moving her eyes from the chair, Bonnie glances toward her door.

Bonnie.

Where are you?

Bonnie.

Bonnie?

Pick up.

The sound continues.

But this time, an echo joins it from within her room.

Bonnie?

Bonnie.

Bonnie?

Thin, pale lips hang in the centre of the keyhole. With every annunciation of her name Bonnie sees the rotting teeth, the forked, blackened tongue from her dream. The silver white hair that frames the face.

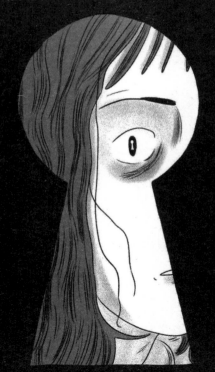

Her mother's mouth is smiling, and her hands are reaching out toward Bonnie.

MUCKRAKER

SUSIE BOYT

I s he sad enough? she wondered, watching him smear mustard on his steak. They were in Valencia for the bank holiday. The sky blazed dutifully, peach-orange-apricot, the sun standing stately and proud. There was a thin stream of mild-looking tourists out and about in the little square. On the dusty terrace of a small bar-restaurant next to the modern art museum sat Ed and Nina, her drinking, without meaning it exactly, him engaged in battle with the steak. He chopped it into thin grey fingers, ground pepper over it pointedly, dark grains floating like flies on pooled blood. He prodded the pieces. Maybe Venice would have been more —

They had just visited an exhibition of collages and everything was striking Nina as a collage suddenly. The raggedy stone from the olive, which almost cracked her teeth; the lipped terracotta dish with nine salted almonds; the pair of stark white museum tickets she hadn't quite thrown away next to her small wine glass with greenish white wine and a smudge from her warm hand. The strong gold light made everything look precious, like items in a jeweller's, even the cleaner's ice blue mop and pail. The cleaning product smelled of jasmine and she made a note of the name on the bottle: Ornazzo. The feted collage artist whose work they had just seen, viewed herself in a series of small objects: a mini table-tennis bat, a pager – being a hangover from the 1980s apparently – an axe, a red heart-shaped chocolate box with plastic roses. These were all attached to a thick eiderdown made of strictly buttoned ivory cotton sateen. It was a self-portrait of sorts. Bric-a-brac likeness.

When people were really sad the texture of their faces often altered, thickening and losing smoothness, there was all over too much texture – it could happen fast, sometimes within twenty-four hours. Sorrow spreading through the skin, rendering it rough-woven, slubby and uneven, like tweed. Or sometimes it thinned, tinged blue, as though skimmed or cauterised, the blood seeming closer to the surface because of everything it had experienced. She liked to peer at the faces of widowed men, as though studying for a history exam. The way the lines or shadows spoke of acute feeling, acute suffer-ing; signs of finely tuned excoriating pain, proof of misery and trauma and regret. Or the absence of these things, which could smart on the skin like a slap.

'What?' they would say to her. 'What?'

'Just thinking of everything you've been through,' she'd say. 'That's all.'

I'm just so very sorry, she messaged Ed after their third meet-ing. Ed's skin tone was giving nothing away.

It's all right, he countered. I'm mostly fine. Honestly. I'm singing in the rain remember, albeit with a slightly tragic backdrop.

*

She had a tremendous respect for grief, the way it assaulted the personality, made you fail in areas where you were used to excelling, caused you to glaze over as you tried to dredge up a scrap of interest for the things you used to love. She knew the tyranny of grief, how it siphoned off all your energy – siphoned wasn't quite the right word. Zapped? Demanded, like a highwayman in a ridiculous cloak? And grief was so far-fetched, outclassing your paranoia even, because you couldn't have dreamed up anything half so bad, so what horrific thing was coming next? And yet in ways she could not quite explain grief could be the making of people. It deepened them, or made them less trivial at least. Loss put you right at the heart of things, even as it fenced you off on its little islands of remoteness. It concentrated people. It concentrated life. It had a high importance in the hierarchy of feeling. It opened people in strange ways. It had pedigree.

Stevie – the man she'd seen for a few months before Ed – used to ask her late at night, 'Why am I so fucked up?'

'It's completely natural. And, you know, this is probably the worst bit now.'

Stevie spoke only of his wife for the first few weeks. Amazing that he thought this was acceptable, but she didn't mind. In a funny way his wife, Kate, was a lot more interesting than he was. She had that rare thing Nina was always on the look-out for – a radical, original inner life. There was a fine-grained quality to her. A moral excellence. Kate had worked with teenagers who had been bullied to the point of collapse. She rebuilt them and refitted them with resources that made life more liveable. Nina downloaded the transcript of a talk she had given and was struck by one point in particular. One of the most unhelpful things when a child confessed to being bullied was that the adults in its life generally said, 'What were you bullied *for*?' Kate's idea was that this was traumatic for the child, who heard, 'What's wrong with you?' So the child then had to say, 'They keep having a go because of my weight ...' Or 'No one at home is washing my clothes.' Or 'It's my mother's epilepsy – she fitted at the school gates one time and some people were really scared.' At their fifth meeting – a pink shirt he was wearing – Stevie confessed that this whole realm of enquiry of Kate's had made him uncomfortable because, although he had never bullied anyone, there was a boy at school who smelled bad and Stevie had not been backward in pointing this out. Most mornings. Most years.

'I never told her that,' he said to Nina. 'I should have done.'

Of all the things you might regret this should not be anywhere near the top of your list, Nina thought.

The most interesting thing about Stevie, in fact the only interesting thing, was that his wife of two years had died. What did he amount to otherwise? He was a businessman, something to do with finance, a keen mountaineer, with a brightly lit aquarium filled with exotic fish. He was a frequent attendee at a gym. Mad for cricket, he was wondering about becoming vegan. None of these things appealed to her in the least.

Ed had more promise. He was quite funny. He was generous. He laughed easily. He asked her things about herself. He whistled when he didn't know what to say. He had an endearing tired quality, not tired as in under-slept – although certainly he was that too – but more he was tired as an estate agent might say a flat was tired, meaning that it had been neglected and was in need of attention and care.

Nina liked to catalogue the physical effects of sadness. Sometimes the skin flaked off the neck or forearms or the cheeks of the bereaved because they hadn't the heart to hold things together. Grief eczema – she'd looked it up. It was a thing. But Ed's face this afternoon in Valencia was smooth, sun-screened and well moisturised. His grief had no fine aspects or original features. It was discreet. There was no sense in his skin that he had been ravaged by loss. Maybe he did not mind too much. Or did he, because of all his seeming entitlement in other spheres, feel unentitled to grieve? That was a kind of disenfranchisement. *Just.* It could be difficult for the privileged to grieve as they were so accustomed to winning, to feeling on top of things, that they couldn't tolerate or absorb the sense of being at a loss. Those of humble origins who identified themselves by their courage and ability to withstand hard times could also find grief foreign and unfathomable, however much you reminded them (it was almost a cliché) that it was the things you did to avoid mourning that got you into hot water. If you thought grief was a weakness – beneath and beyond you – it did not quite register as available reality. She could not work out if any of these factors had a part to play in Ed's case. Were the light brown dry eyes in front of her, the nose and mouth and soft tanned cheeks and Klein-blue shirt (short-sleeved) a kind of collage of avoidance? Once she had messaged him, *Hey, good to see you tonight. But do try to rest. Remember mourning is a job of work. It's physically exhausting. It literally burns calories!* and he had sent back one word instantly, *Understood.* Today his skin had a prosperous Spanish-holiday sheen. A bit preposterous, was it? There was nothing undone about him in any case. It was slightly crass, possibly, or was it heroic?

The first time Ed had mentioned her was two weeks in when he began a sentence with 'Miranda, who was my wife ...' The sentence faltered and caved in on itself or, rather, there was no sentence. That was it. He had intended to express one of her preferences, Nina thought: Miranda ate baby gems straight from the fridge, like an apple, for a snack ... Miranda was mad for ice skating at Christmas. But no. And it was an unusual way of putting it. The formulation 'who was my wife' seemed odd to her, overly formal and awkward, and she wished he had just said 'Miranda', or 'My wife', or 'My wife Miranda', or 'My late wife' (although that always sounded like criticism), but she was glad he had mentioned her finally. She had known his wife had died, but did not know if he knew that she knew. It wasn't for her to bring it up first, of course, but she knew they would get nowhere unless he did.

The friend who had introduced them had told her everything, literally on the doorstep, with a 'Don't for God's sake say I told you. Oh – and remember to act surprised,' which was in itself unsustainable. After he mentioned Miranda to her, Nina asked Ed to tell her a bit more, a few introductory paragraphs, a brief character sketch, if he didn't mind. The following had emerged. This last year she had asked for walking boots for her birthday, an Austrian brand, with a ... with a five-year manufacturer's guarantee. Her favourite smell was coffee and vanilla extract mixed with cigarette smoke, as in the outdoor seating area of a European or European-style patisserie. For two years when she was twelve her best friend was a horse.

'What was its name?' she asked. It was a test of sorts.

'Misty.'

When her beloved grandmother was at the end she clasped Miranda's nine-year-old hand so tightly for several hours at the bedside that she drew blood. The child required fourteen stitches in her right palm. Yes, she *was* right-handed.

'Christ!' Nina said. 'What sacrifice. Like something from the Bible. And how frightened a little girl must have been not to have somehow been able to get away. What were the parents thinking?'

'I know.' He winced and peered deeply at his own hands and shook his head. They sat for a time and he refilled their glasses, although neither of them drank anything.

'I'm just so, so sorry she's not with you still.'

'Well, I mean,' he said, 'it *has* been six months.'

She added it up: in two weeks it would be five.

Stevie, from last year, had taken her to Rome for her birthday. He was obsessed with coffee to the extent that forty per cent of his conversation was about it. The rest of the time he was so morose she sometimes initiated conversations about coffee just to animate him.

Although Stevie's sense of loss was steep and sheer, there was a selfishness to it that she found distasteful. He mourned as though *his* insides had been pinioned, sliced, poisoned and blasted, then one by one their vital functions closing down. He cleared his throat and dipped his eyes, bringing to mind the bodily trials he still carried with him. She'd seen this mourning style several times now and there was always something embarrassing about the performance aspect. Not embarrassing because it was insincere, because it wasn't that – in fact if anything the reverse was true. It was the wholehearted earnestness that made you a little ashamed for them. Grief should not have this sort of swagger, surely, the sonorous repetitive medal-clank of mourning. Was it true she preferred shame to pride?

In Valencia Ed wanted something sweet after his steak but he wasn't sure what. Not something chocolaty. Nothing with fruit or cream or custard and not ice cream *again*.

'Maybe something almondy?' she had suggested. 'Although

I suppose that might end up being a bit dry.' How did he have
the confidence to make this the sole topic of conversation for
eleven minutes?

'Maybe I'll just have some tea.'

Tea was risky. They had had a tea disaster at the airport,
in Arrivals, where a waitress put a manzanilla teabag in a
cup, three-quarters filled it with cold milk and added a dash
of hot water for good measure. 'This is the worst thing that's
happened to me in decades,' he said.

'Thoughts and prayers,' she murmured. She couldn't go
through that again.

But when the tea arrived – not too bad – he told Nina her
favourite story about Miranda. It was the third time now, but
she didn't mind. When she was twenty-two, Miranda had
gone to a wedding and sat next to the very English uncle of
the bride.

'Cassie tells me you're Jewish,' this uncle, Sir Jim or Lord
Henry or whatever it was, had said to her.

'Yeeeeees?' she replied gingerly. Ed had used that actual
word, 'gingerly', which she liked.

'Tell me,' he *boomed* at her, as though his attention itself
was a great compliment, 'why didn't your people do more to
stick up for themselves in the war?'

Well. She let him have it. Through the roasted-vegetable
starter and the sea bass main course, she talked him through
history lessons beginning in Odessa in the 1590s. By the
appearance of the pavlova he was almost on his knees.

'What a woman!' Nina said.

It was possible Ed lacked lustre by comparison. It was hard
for him to compete. There was so much sharp intelligence in
Miranda's face. 'She was certainly cleverer than me,' he said.

Their talks about Miranda were exhilarating. Sometimes
Nina googled her late at night when she lay worrying about her

own life in the knotted sheets. What would next year hold? she
wondered. How long exactly were her looks planning to last?

Miranda had sharp green eyes and bark-coloured hair,
whereas Ed was – she found it hard to remember when she
was not looking at him, beyond the fact that his colouring
was generally sandy.

In Rome Stevie had been through Kate's last days in great
detail – no harm there – but when he got to the bit where he
described her death as though it was actually happening to
him, as though his own breathing was thickening into the
hoarse death rattle, his eyelids shutting shop, turning round
the sign on the plate-glass door, throwing the latch for the
last time, stacking chairs on sticky tables, she thought, I am
done. She would do it at Heathrow as soon as they cleared the
luggage carousel. She was all for walking in another's shoes
but this was one of the few examples of fellow feeling that had
little or no community aspect or empathy or anything really,
for he mourned, at heart, for himself.

Stevie saw death as the thief that came in the night, forgetting for one squalid moment that he had once used this phrase
to her when speaking about the scourge that was inflation.

Why could he not bring himself to see the vastness of what
Kate had lost? No more days, for example. That actually *was*
the end of the world.

There was a stigma attached to being a man who could not
keep his wife out of Death's way. It was a personal insult that
took some recovering from. Failure, certainly. Wounded pride.
What low-grade species of man would permit it? The sense
of injury hovered all over the Eds, the Stevies, Rob who had
come before Stevie, or rather before James or was that Pete?
Still, she was more than happy to comfort the undone. She

possessed a great deal of free-flowing sympathy, and she was democratic with it, dispensing it to anyone who asked. And because she could not help feeling a lot of women were going under-mourned, she was happy to talk for hours about all the lovely qualities they had: the apologetic way Miranda or was it Kate (or James's Debbie or Pete's Cath) liked to slip out for a run as though it ought to be illegal; the habit that one had of putting on a lovely dress for a party then whipping it off at the last moment in favour of what she'd been wearing all day. The Scottish one, proper in all things – grammar especially – who liked to wear a white apron, feeding the strings round her middle to tie in a bow at the front, just to do her admin. The one who pulled out red leather ballet shoes as soon as she boarded a plane. The colouring-in of the dead. The scuffs on Miranda's walking boots that unexpectedly made Nina cry because they spoke of such independence of spirit, the sense that they still had far to go. They were still by the back door, side by side. 'You're knocked out by her boots,' Ed said, visibly moved. It spoke of her deep wells of humanity.

In Valencia Ed was talking. She had done her teeth with the mini toothpaste and taken a couple of paracetamol, for no obvious reason, leaving two empty holes in the silver strip containing their fourteen colleagues.

'I just remembered the last joke Miranda told me. I'll tell you if you—'

'Please!'

Odd your date telling you his dead wife's final joke. What they called a complicated speech act. They were in bed now. His laptop was open and he was sipping from a green bottle of water. He liked the air-con so strong she had to sleep in her cardigan.

'Why does Norway have barcodes on all its warships?'

'I don't know. Why does Norway have barcodes on its warships?'

'So that when they come back into port they can Scandinavian.'

'That is really funny!' She was laughing so hard to prove her point that her mouth hurt, although she couldn't have told you why. He laughed too, laughed at her laughing, which she liked.

They all rattled on about the tremendous strain of having to start again – getting back into the dating pool, the stress and the outrage of it – because the women of now were grasping, manipulative, mercenary, as if the mould of good ones had somehow been broken. The internet didn't help, of course, although ... What did they think she was during these exchanges? Something about the women dying gave permission for these bright flares of misogyny. Had it been there all along? The rug had been pulled from under their precious domesticity, even though she suspected, if she had pressed, they might have held forth on the way that self-same domesticity had at one time or another ruinously hemmed them in.

Every Friday, in ordinary time, Nina went to Harmony to have her hair washed, paying the four pounds supplement for below-shoulder length hair. She sometimes felt she was almost *too* gentlemanly in her behaviour and that doing something ladylike might improve the balance of how she came across. The hairdresser's was in a small parade of shops between the ghost of a launderette that had recently suffered a freak fire and a blue and white café that had a blackboard outside on which the proprietors wrote nasty little messages designed to lift the spirits. 'Normalise being nice to people for no reason' and so on. Gulten shampooed her hair and spritzed it with a leave-in conditioner called Integrity. Then Mehmet dried it into two dozen rolled sausage curls, which created 'bounce' when she shook them out. Gulten and Mehmet were serious, hard-working, conscientious, good-natured people, discreetly in pain in their lives, she supposed. Gulten was a single mother to three and was so sensitive that when a sad thought passed through Nina's mind Gulten would stop washing, dry her hands and nip round to the front of the basin to ask if everything was all right.

'What age in England do mothers stop washing their daughters' hair?' Gulten asked, as she carefully massaged her scalp, the Friday morning of the Valencia trip.

'I'm not sure. I didn't have that kind of life. But I think, I don't know, about nine or ten maybe?'

'Same in Turkey,' Gulten said.

'Not thirty-seven, anyway!'

'Is your mother still alive?'

'No,' Nina said. And then, after five minutes of silence, 'What made you think of that?'

Nina found herself, in her late childhood, not so much resident of London, but of several sprawling, unknowable bleak cities, which were hospitals and had their own laws and rules and endless corridors and evil lighting and bright lino and buzzers you buzzed, then waited while nobody came. She knew in and out the odd kiosks and hole-in-the-wall shops with strange volunteer-knitted things in salmon pink and white zigzags, tissue-box covers, baby boots, other things they didn't have elsewhere, like currant buns and apples hand-wrapped in clingfilm. And then the more surreal elements, consultants who vanished mid-sentence – where did they go? – and in the case of one underground radiography department she found herself revisiting recently, lunatic piped fake birdsong, so that not only were you trying to hold everything together, you were fairly sure you were going insane as how could there be birds in the sub-basement? She had learned what the dying had to unhand. The untold worlds of loss and the grief the dying feel for it. Was anyone ever brave enough to say, 'How can you bear to let go of what you'll never see? It's too much. Let me help you.' The scandal of dying. 'On behalf of the human race I apologise' – she had managed to raise a smile on her mother's face with that, close to the end.

Her taste for widowers was not entirely altruistic. She liked the three-in-a-bed of it. There was the same kind of tension and release that occurred in a great song. Such odd things, like the way some tried never to mention their wives at the start, with so much painstaking determination, and then about three weeks in the floodgates opened and out she poured, her name ringing wildly and indiscriminately when they just meant to say 'shirt' or 'phone'.

They cried sometimes and apologised wildly as if she might take it as a form of mutiny over her charms and powers. She didn't see it that way. It's perfectly natural to be happy about one thing and sad about another simultaneously. She liked her tea boiling hot in the morning and almost enjoyed the sensation of it burning her mouth. It was a bit like that perhaps.

The idea of a cosy couple with her at the centre pleased her. Was that it? The safety in the numbers spoke to her warmly. A family feeling. She knew she wasn't very old for her age. And 'loved and lost': it wasn't any worse, not really, than the 'dark hair, dark eyes, wears chunky jumpers, must support the ANC' that had topped her list when she was five. It had something to do with things that came under the umbrella 'parental', an old longing to be included. Mattering. And she needn't be at the centre – she wasn't competitive for sharp triangular victory, no, no – she was modest. She could be at the side, or on the slant, lurking in the shadow of the marital pair. Under the bed, where the money was stashed, or in the cupboard next to the skeletons.

She loved the tales of the fair creatures in their own fairy stories, pale-robed, fleet and nimble, tall hats dribbling ribbons, pricking their fingers or falling in the foaming brine. Oh, my darling! Treatment. Drips. Wires. Surgery. Wigs. Her skin so thin, papery with bluish branched veins. Food through a peg in the stomach: be it fruits of the forest or fibre++ banana flavour. Liquid nausea, why didn't they call it? A travesty of food – vegetable oil mixed with non-dairy milkshake powder and cheapo iron supplements. If she'd been my wife I'd have created a blend myself with kale and spinach and high-grade vitamins and done a course in nutrition. For all their feelings, courageously borne, sometimes it felt as though anything was too much trouble for these men.

'God, she was brave.'

Did she have any choice?

The way these women almost killed themselves to make it all right for everyone. To soften the blow. Did men who were dying have to do that?

Some, of course, died like the conscientious schoolgirls they had always been, texting snippets of Keats to loved ones to keep their spirits up, thanking all – remember your manners! – messaging 'right back atcha' to the 'all the love in the world', dispatching gifts from Amazon to cheer others when they themselves sank low. Helen – Tom from five years ago's wife – left birthday letters for her daughter and two sisters, spreading right into the future, for years. It was expected now of women who died. The child might be four but you had to have a plan for the twenty-first-birthday present. Pearls? A gold locket on a chain? Would there even be pearls then?

Would people still have necks in seventeen years' time? Even after you were dead the present-giving fell to women.

'What is it with women and anxiety?' Stevie said about Kate.
    'Perhaps she worried so that no one else had to.'
    That quieted him.
    What the wives would have done if the boot was on the other foot! The masterpieces of care, museum quality, for the dying. There would have been no inverted commas round the whole thing, no performing. Quiet strength without showmanship. The making-everything-all-right-for-everyone part of it that was the bread-and-butter of woman's work. The women wouldn't have made the dying husbands reassure them at death's door.
    The men spoke of being plagued by guilt but she was shocked at the way they let themselves slide so easily off all hooks. 'Over and over as she slipped away I said the Lord's Prayer. It helped in its way. Impossible to know what to say at such times.'
    'Was she religious, then?'
    'Not particularly.'
    Hopeless.
    Sometimes she asked about the mothers of these girlfriends and wives. It was obscene to have to bury your child. 'She's very busy in the village and that's been a great help.'
    She knew a lot about mourning now. The way it was seen as almost transgressive. People recoiled from it, viscerally, as though mourning itself could lead to contagious misery or even death. So few would risk it. Strange. Because for most people, the ones who went in for it properly, it was a practice that dignified humans. She hated it when too much time passed with the women going unmentioned. First an afternoon without her name, then a whole day, then a weekend.

Her own father had remarried within the year. It wasn't that at this point the men seemed faithless, exactly, but the switch was ugly to her. The dilution of something. That was the point where she liked to bail out. She made herself a little less available. 'Is something wrong?' they'd ask, but how could she say I know it's mad but I miss your wife?

That morning over the hotel buffet breakfast Ed was saying that he missed the rows especially. 'Miranda argued brilliantly.' He crashed his spoon into his boiled egg, wound a rosette of ham on top of the white and yellow. The ham was the dark red of ecclesiastical robes in Spanish paintings. She liked him saying that about the arguing. 'She held me to high account. Made me better. I couldn't get away with anything. Not that I—'

'Tell me more!'

'Are you sure you don't mind?'

'Of course not. I cannot help loving her a little bit myself, if that isn't weird.'

Did he want her to mind? Did she want him to?

It was their last night suddenly. She was still seeing collages wherever she went. A half-eaten orange and some crumpled tissues in the gutter looked like a ballerina if you squinted. They went for a long walk and Ed said the ancient tree trunks reminded him of dinosaur legs. A large ice-cream shop had a flavour called 'Abuela' – it was a pale pinky-beige colour with dark specks and they hoped it was made for or by Abuela, and not from. Ed smiled a great deal. He was weary, weary but cheery. She felt weary too. In a beach-side restaurant they were defeated by the world's biggest paella. They had more drinks than was necessarily wise. The light thickened and died and they sat for a time in darkness, listening to the waves. A waiter came and lit a candle and she saw Ed looking into her face now as though it contained the promise of whole worlds. She frowned, uncertain.

That night, in bed, she suddenly felt it was a terrific act of tactlessness to possess breasts herself. 'It just doesn't seem right,' she said. 'I'm so sorry. Really crass of me. Disloyal.' A body that wasn't patched and darned was a sort of a betrayal of one that was. Could he allow himself to admire it with any decency?

'Now you're being silly.'

'They're nothing much in any case, I mean compared to what's out there. What's possible.'

She started to cry. He cried also. They held on to each other. 'It's OK,' he said. 'This is good. We are good.' Perhaps they could risk going overboard together?

She was ill herself now. She kept forgetting to remember. 'It doesn't look great, no,' the doctor said, the nurse. If she gave it her all she could probably get Ed to fall in love with her in the next few hours. It was comforting to think that he might miss her when she was gone.

SPITFIRE

ALI SMITH

What does the word mean?

Here's a day in the early 1970s, I don't remember exactly when, but it's a day like no other, historic. This is because a man called Chiefy and his wife, who are something to do with our mother before she was our mother, are due to visit our house.

That's our house, that one there on the end of the block of six, postwar build, middle of this long curved street on the edge of the council estate below the banks of the old canal. The canal banks are our backdrop through all the windows at the back of the house; the canal's actually a piece of history itself, scooped through the north of Scotland for industry in the 1820s then also proving useful a few decades after that for shipping large numbers of soldiers south from the Highlands for the Crimean War.

But this is a different history I'm talking about now. There's my mother, look, she's smoking in the kitchen and telling me never to. *All the girls smoked. We all did it. We didn't know it was addictive. I can't stop now.* She finishes the cigarette, stubs it out, empties what's in the ashtray into the bin in the cupboard, cleans the ashtray out with kitchen paper, dries it, shakes two tictacs into her palm, puts them in her mouth.

A minute later she lights another cigarette.

(I've made that up. I don't know whether she did do those things waiting for the visitors, I was there, but I don't remember. I can see her in my head doing these things, she did them all the time. So it's likely. Then again, that day my mother was being a little less like her usual self.)

The person she calls Chiefy, and Mrs Healy, his wife, have come up from somewhere in England and they'll be here any minute.

All I truly remember about that day, fifty years ago now –

I mean way out here in the future, centuries past the original meaning of the word spitfire, whose first recorded usage seems to be in the 1650s when it meant *a person given to outbursts of emotion, spiteful temper and anger, especially a woman or girl,* and half a century before it'd also mean, via the 2020s online urban dictionary, a sexually explicit thing probably related to the urban dictionary meaning of spitroast, which is a meaning that would've made both my parents blanche and frown, my mother affronted, icy above the dinnerplates, my father drawing himself up like a volcano trying not to spill, if any of us had come home one lunchtime or suppertime back then, say, and over the day's meal told them what spitfire would one day, in one of its given versions, 'mean' –

all I remember is that this was the first time my mother'd seen the curiously named man and his wife since she was in the WAAF.

I'll be nine, maybe ten, and I'll know that the WAAF is something from back in the war, to do with aeroplanes, something for women, and that my mother was a telephonist in it.

I know Chiefy is called Chiefy because he was in charge of something at the place in England where my mother was in the WAAF. There are some black and white photographs of our mother, well, of a beautiful girl who looks quite like her, in a uniform. There are photographs of a boy in a uniform too who was once our father, though thinner and sharper then.

Anyway I'm mesmerised by the excitement with which my mother is, yes, brimming. It's coming off her in what feels like sheets of light, like bedsheets washed bright in a TV commercial for soap powder. This is noticeably unlike my usually very proper mother, always so careful not to enthuse much about anything, as if enthusiasm wouldn't be acceptable behaviour for a woman as authoritative as she is. Though, true, I've also known her be mischievous and wayward and hilariously funny, but only ever on her terms and in her own time, rare as a sighting of a pine marten, a wildcat. But those moments of revelation of a high pure wildness in her, even a ten year old can sense, are the closest thing to what words like rare, invaluable, incalculably valuable, or priceless or rich or dear – all those words for value that never manage to sum up what value really is – mean.

That day, the house will have been pristine, gleaming. It always was. That day, my father and mother will have been being exceptionally welcoming. They always were, with something that strikes me now as an ethic of hospitality, something near heroic, so warm and welcoming they were, always, to whoever my brothers and sisters and I would happen over the decades to bring home, or to whoever chanced to arrive knocking on our front door, neighbours, friends, complete strangers, ragged or smart.

But the only thing I really remember about this day is my mother looking forward with an energy beyond the ordinary to these visitors who'd something to do with a time about which she almost never spoke. Almost. Once when I was a child, she told me about a boy she'd known in the war who'd wait outside a window in a building he knew she was in and whistle a bit of a tune they both liked to let her know he was there. When I asked her about it again she shook her head, like I was talking nonsense, I'd made it up, she'd never said it. More often she'd hum or sing a bit of a song that was something to do with a friend she'd had in the WAAF who'd emigrated to Australia, a place we knew about and could imagine because of the Skippy the Bush Kangaroo episodes on TV. There was an annual Christmas card too with a photo in the envelope of Maggie and her Australian family, and this, along with the song When You and I Were Young Maggie, was pretty much all we knew, for most of my life, when it came to our mother's war.

What we knew about our father's war was he'd been in the Navy and that now he had regular nightmares, the mornings after which our mother made sure we all kept well out of his way, and that his medals, which had been in a box under the bed, had been lost somewhere out on the cinders the street's garages were built on when one of my older sisters found them and took them outside to play with them way before I was born.

Do they draw up at the front gate in a taxi, the visitors? It's unlikely; my parents would never have let that happen. It's much more likely that my mother sent my father to pick them up in the car wherever they were, the railway station maybe, and bring them to the house. There are two photographs from the visit, one a black and white polaroid, one a colour snap. In both, Chiefy and my mother are smoking, cigarettes symmetrical between their first and second fingers as everyone crowds round an armchair, Mrs Healy in the chair, my mother and Chiefy on either arm and my father leaning over the back of the chair.

In both pictures my father looks most unlike himself, flustered, bewildered, uneasy. I sense now this will be because it's the only time since the war that he's spent time with a man – and in his own house – whose rank will have meant someone who could tell my father what to do.

In both, my mother, in her best 1971 dress, looks straight into the camera. She looks unlike herself too, or perhaps very like herself. In all the other photos in the album from this time she looks speculative, looks wry, looks away. In these two pictures she looks radiantly happy.

They were there, Chiefy and his wife, and then they were gone. They never visited again, just that once. Out of, then into, the blue.

What I remember is the thrown-open front door, my mother with what felt like light shining straight out of her, as two old grey people, much older than even my parents, get out of a car, open our front gate and walk up the path towards us.

The only thing I have left of any of the clothes my mother wore in her life now, three decades after her death, is a button.

The button's off the uniform she had in the mid-1940s. At least I assume it is. For all I know people swapped their buttons when they got demobbed. I mean I'll never know anything for sure now. Anyway it's made of brass, it's still shiny, a bit corroded. It has a crown embossed on its front and a bird with open wings beneath the crown, an eagle? It has a hooked beak. It's an airborne creature.

On the back of the button in a circle round the metal loop that'll have attached it to whatever jacket or coat, it's got the words *Buttons Ltd B'ham trade* and *mark* and the image of a pair of crossed swords.

Not that she had an unusual death or that the house burnt down with everything she'd worn in it or anything unlikely happened round her going. No, it's just that all of it's gone, God knows where. She did die relatively young. She was the age I am now. (That'll be why I think it's still a young age to die at.)

Along with the button I also have a couple of the books she had when she was a girl at school in the north of Ireland. She was thirteen. She'd won a scholarship. She was clever. Her father died. She had to give up her scholarship and cross the sea, to Scotland, where there were family members sending home money and there was more chance of getting work if you were a Catholic than in the north of Ireland in the 1930s. She got a job as a bus conductress on the bus route along the Moray Firth coast road. They called her Paddy because she was Irish. The town's bus conductresses in Inverness were still letting me and my brothers off our fares when we used the buses in the town in the 1960s and 70s, because they'd worked with our mother, even though she only did this till she was old enough to join the WAAF, towards the end of the war.

These two schoolbooks I've got were the only things she'd taken with her when she left Ireland that she kept well into her later life. One is a copy of Rip Van Winkle and Other Stories by Washington Irving. One is an English Grammar primer. The pencil marks and underlinings in the English Grammar primer stop about a third of the way through the book. That'll be where she left school. Both books have her name written carefully inside them in ink, and the name of the school, Loreto Convent. Inside the back of one of them she's drawn an inky outline round what will have been her own left hand. On its third finger she's added a wedding ring. She used to keep these books under her shoes at the bottom of the wardrobe in her and my father's bedroom, all the coats and blouses and jumpers above, immaculate, like new.

A couple of years ago I dropped the English Grammar

primer down some stairs. It slipped out of my hands in a pile of books I was carrying. Its cloth and card spine, which had until then been fine and sound for more than eighty years, split down its middle.

I keep the button on my desk.

I check on it every so often to make sure I haven't done something stupid and lost it.

Because both my parents are dead now, because there's so much I've just no idea about when it comes to their lives, and because my older siblings tend to come up as blank and shrugging as I am when I ask them anything about our mother's time in the WAAF, I sat down this summer with a pile of paperbacks I bought on Abe and eBay, written by women about their time in the WAAF.

A WAAF in Bomber Command. Sand in My Shoes. Tales of a Bomber Command WAAF (& her horse). More Tales of a Bomber Command WAAF (& her horse). We All Wore Blue.

See, I didn't even know they all wore blue; all the photos I've ever seen are black and white. Anyway the writers of these books, memoirs written later in their lives, were middle or upper middle class young English women (*& her horse*), and had lived nothing like my mother's life, really, a not-English childhood and one of relative poverty. But all these books have in common things in which my mother's time and life will have been steeped.

In one of these books, a very fine writer called Pip Beck let me know that a squadron's Flight Sergeant was typically referred to by everyone as – Chiefy. She summed up what it felt like, in those years, to be young, a woman, and in bomber command, "a time in my life when everything was new and exciting; a time I could never forget. A new world opened up."

The first sighting, after enrolling in the WAAF, of the huge aircraft parked and waiting like behemoths, like strange winged giants, in the operational bomber stations. The smell and the sound of those machines with their spread wings, the thrum of the ground under them. The long green stretch of the airfields early in the morning, late in the evening, winter to spring, summer to autumn, fog, sun, rain, snow. The metal bedsteads, the straw mattresses they all called *biscuits*, the drill sheets and the dark blankets so useless in the cold that the *& her horse* writer actually records that they weren't fit for horses. The "rising bell". The bras made of "thick coarse cotton, with straps the width of a man's belt, and hooks and eyes so sturdy they could have been used to fasten the linen union covers of a three-piece suite" as the writer of *We All Wore Blue* puts it. Something called fatigues. Something called jankers. Kit inspection, respirators for tear gas, the phonetic alphabet the R/T or Radio Telephone Operators learned (is that what my mother was? an R/T operator?). Plane identification. Daily pay rate (1s 4d unless you were on "special duties" when it rose to 2s 3d). Sending money home; whatever their class, they all did it. The food. Fishcakes and chips, 10d. The NAAFI shop, where you could buy hairnets, biscuits, coffee, tea, Rinso, Liver Salts. The camaraderie. The friendships. The charming boys and men arriving with laugh-ter and jokes and flowers, sweeping the off-duty WAAFs off to the pictures to see the latest. The air raid sirens, the plaster falling off the ceilings and walls when bombs came down close to the Waafery or the Mess. Words like Waafery and Mess. Nissen. Ops Met and Signals. Flying Control. Sally. Joan. Pip. Sylvia. Muriel. Maureen. Di. Audrey.

Above all what's really in common between all these books is the numbness, the terribleness, of the number of young men they went out with, danced all night with, went to the pictures with, fell in love with, were about to marry, all the

Normans, Johns, Bills, Gerrys, Tonys, Jocks, Cecils, Franks, Peters, who went up one night in the Spitfires or Ansons or Lancasters or Hampdens or Wellingtons and next morning didn't come back. Shot down in raids over Kiel, Augsburg, Dusseldorf, Hamburg. The "strange hollow intimacy," Pip Beck says, of realising that the last voice the five young men in a just-hit and gone plane would have heard was her own voice. "In RAF statistics this was a commonplace little tragedy."

And when someone hears that their person hasn't come back, or the ardent or friendly / chatty letters from someone just stop? Anxiety. Foreboding. Silent tears. "We accepted it, shrugged, and said, 'That's that.' But underneath, we each had a nagging ache of sorrow." Though there was also this: "state of almost total collapse ... nothing we could do for her ... sick bay ... sedated ... her grief touched us all. What became of her we never learned."

What they had in common, what they learned to withstand, was endless loss.

I knew almost nothing about Spitfires before writing this piece you're reading. I knew a little from a wartime propaganda film called The First of the Few, in which Leslie Howard and David Niven design, build and test-fly them. In this film, which he also directed, Leslie Howard plays RJ Mitchell, the man who first designed the Supermarine Spitfire, a plane modelled on seabirds, one with an integral wingset, a wingspan as part of its chassis rather than wings added as afterthought. Plus firepower, plus aeronautic lightness, speed, versatility.

Howard himself, a subtle, handsome and thoughtful film director and actor, was killed shortly before the film was released, when the Luftwaffe shot down the passenger plane he was travelling in between Portugal and England. I know that the film is said to be a bit historically inaccurate, that Howard looked nothing like Mitchell; they were men of very different social class. I know the film is scattered with real RAF Fighter Command pilots in uncredited walk-on parts and that several of them, too, had been killed in real war raids by the time the film came out.

I knew that the great comedienne, film star and music hall singer, Gracie Fields, a huge star in the 1930s, who had been vilified by the British public for 'running away' in the Second World War to live in Capri with her Italian film director husband, was responsible for raising millions of dollars and pounds either side of the Atlantic which she channelled direct into Royal Navy funds and Spitfire manufacture.

That's actually all I knew before I agreed to take on one of the words usually used over the centuries as synonyms for troublingly strong or supposedly outspoken women, this word SPITFIRE, which in its C20th flying incarnation had a very direct link to the life of my own calm, decorous, private, privately mischievous, very refined mother.

I see her now in my head, some time in the 1960s or 70s, that hey-so-liberating-for-women time, sitting at a formica table in our kitchen with a friend who's called round, they're both in their forties, and the friend is laughing because my mother has said something funny and my mother is laughing too but downwards into her own hands, and even as a small child I know she's doing this, monitoring the strength of her own spirit, partly so she won't seem too outlandish either to her husband and children elsewhere in the house or to her own friend sitting opposite, a friend who'll be every bit as up to policing a woman as any other woman or man or family when it comes to how women / mothers are meant to act in public or even in private in the comfort of their own homes.

I also know it's in her nature, it's every bit as much an ethic to her as her sense of hospitality, to act at almost all times with the kind of care that keeps threat at bay, whatever the threat may be, with a politeness that has a taproot into a source of pure power, and with a modicum of restraint that deep at its core both proves and preserves everything fierce and wild and deep of feeling in us.

I ask my father. What's the fallout?

What's *what*? he says.

I am seven and am collecting Snoopy books. I show him the page in one where the character called Linus, the philosophical one, is walking along, looks up, sees lots of little dots round him, then runs like crazy, finds the character called Charlie Brown, shakes him by the collar and says IT'S HAPPENING, CHARLIE BROWN! IT'S HAPPENING JUST LIKE THEY SAID IT WOULD!! Charlie Brown tells him it's just winter, it's just snowing. Good grief, Linus says. I thought it was the fallout.

What's the fallout? I say.

My parents exchange looks. My father explains to me about nuclear explosions.

They had to do it, my mother says. They had to stop the war.

Years later, when I'm a teenager and I sit reading the book by John Hersey called Hiroshima in the living room, my father and mother exchange looks again.

When I bring home leaflets about nuclear war and start wearing a badge that says GAY WHALES AGAINST THE BOMB, my father tells me, quite right, girl. My mother tells me, with great seriousness, that if a person were to spend too much time thinking about these things they'd go mad.

Which in particular of these things? I say.

She frowns.

All of them, she says.

Up until very recently I'd thought my father's version of the story of how my parents first met was the only version. This is how his version went. He joined the Navy as soon as he was of age in 1942. The Navy gave him a training as an electrician. In the war's dying days he happened to be back in England convalescing and he was sent with a mate to wire up the locker room of a barracks in a local WAAF station. He and his mate decided that for fun they'd have a look through all the lockers, at the things belonging to the women.

They opened door after door and out spilled all the under-wear, all the secret things of girls. But when my father opened one particular locker and saw how perfectly folded everything in there was, how clean, how pristinely neat and arranged, he said to his mate: This one. I'm going to find this girl, I'm going to marry her. So he looked up who the locker belonged to, he asked her out, and that night in the pub he pulled out his mother's engagement ring, he had it in a box in his pocket, he'd been carrying it around with him since his mother died, and he showed it to my mother, and everyone around them shouted they're getting engaged! they're getting engaged! Which, some years later, they did.

For a long time I thought that this story, though roman-tic, held a kernel of innate generational sexism at its heart, an attraction to the good housekeeper and housewife in the woman you long to etc. More recently, as if I'm seeing inside my head a bombed building with the ruined stuff of its insides strewn everywhere, I've understood it differently. My father joined the Navy to escape the brick factory he was working in as a boy. One day a wing of the brick factory was hit by a bomb and he was in a workshop a short distance along from the hit. He saw the bricks in the wall of the room he was in suddenly bend like they were made of elastic, then everything in that room, the worktops, the chairs and himself, flung in slow motion up into the air before his whole self hit the wall on the far side of the room.

Then, in the Navy, one of the ships he sailed on was torpedoed. He was down below. He got himself out just in time and picked up by a lifeboat. A lot of his friends didn't.

Not long after this, his arms and legs stopped working, just refused to act like they were meant to, so the Navy sent him on another ship to Canada to recuperate. He recovered. He came home to Nottingham on leave and the thing he brought home with him, as a present for his mother, was a fifty-six-piece dinner service. It arrived against the odds unbroken, and so, more or less, did he.

He didn't talk about any of this until very late in his life when everything on TV was suddenly endlessly about the war, the various anniversaries of it, forty years, forty five years, fifty years since. Then, and only then, he began to.

One of my sisters, who's still got what little's left of that dinner service in her crockery cupboard, told me not long ago our mother's version of their first meeting.

I'd been in the shower block, I'd shampooed my hair, and I came out of there, I had a towel wrapped round my head. And this boy came up to me and wolf-whistled and then had the cheek to ask me out. Well! I wasn't impressed. I thought he was rude and I told him exactly where to go, and that if he wanted anything to do with me he'd have to change his way of going about it.

First time I'd heard it. It made me laugh out loud.

It also made me remember a moment I'd forgotten. One day when I was older, home from college, the holidays, I was in my twenties, deep in a couple of secret loves, or at least loves

I told nobody in my family about, certainly couldn't have told my mother, and she was older, thinned by years of misdiagnosed heart disease, far too fragile and only in her fifties, she drove me down town so we could do something or other. We set off and my fragile mother put her foot down hard on the accelerator and I realised, sitting in the passenger seat, with that sudden acute revelation of someone's inner character that you only get when you're a passenger and they're driving, something else unsayable out loud so as not to disempower the knowing – that my mother wasn't just a great driver, she was a fearless person in the world, a woman fazed by nothing.

My mother died in 1990. The day after she did, on an instinct I can't explain, I went into my mother and father's bedroom. I took her glasses off the dressing table, the things she'd seen the world through. I opened her brushes and combs drawer in the middle of the dressing table and took out her favourite brush. As I was shutting the drawer my hand grazed some papers tucked down between the drawer's liner and the wooden front of it. I took them out.

They were four small old rectangular photographs, size of the palm of a hand. I'd never seen any of them before.

I put them in my pocket. I knew to keep them to myself.

The glasses and the brush are long gone; when my father moved house some years after she died he and my brother cleared out what had been my room and threw most of it away, and the glasses and brush I'd kept on my own bedside table? God knows.

I still have the photographs. Here they are.

All the people in three of them, female and male, are in shirtsleeves and wearing ties. One is of two young women standing under a tree. God knows who they are. Neither of them is my mother or her friend Maggie. But Maggie's there in all the others, I recognise her, and so's my mother, and so is a very handsome and smiling young man who is nothing like my father and who has his arm always round my mother.

In one, my mother has her own arm round this man, her other arm round her friend.

In another photo, of a lineup of eight young people in full dark WAAF and RAF uniforms, my mother is standing between two young men. In each of her hands she's holding one of their hands.

Only once, that's all, she talked about what it was like. It was one afternoon after lunch a couple of summers before she died, I was about to catch a train south back to university, I was sitting in the kitchen at the table, she was finishing off some ironing. I don't know why she started to talk about it, it's the only time she ever did, and it was for a moment only, she didn't lift her head, even, from the thing she was ironing. *Getting up in the morning, going in to breakfast, and seeing the chalk lines through the planes, through the names of the ones who hadn't made it back.*

Then she stopped speaking. She gave me a glance, looked back down, shook her head.

The iron will have steamed its steam, the smell of clean clothes in air.

Then I got into the car, waved goodbye, and my dad drove me down to the station.

FURY

RACHEL SEIFFERT

Poland, 1942

The stairwell was empty.

On the second floor, Esther knocked, and knocked again, as Witek had taught her. Then she waited in the quiet.

She'd been brisk all the way here. Light on her heels at the crossings, along the pavements and across the cobbles, passing half the length of their small city in the short hour before curfew. Inside the stairwell, though, she trod with caution, placing her feet, *careful now*, on each landing she came to. Shoe leather shushing on stone, the grit under her arches catching between sole and step. *Quarter grit*, Esther thought, that she'd carried here, despite her care.

For two streets, someone had followed her; she was almost sure.

Esther hadn't seen them so much as felt them: a back-of-the-neck, pit-of-the-gut discomfort. But then it was impossible to walk beyond the quarter now without that. Esther was a quarter girl, and she worried that it showed, even in the city-girl coat she wore on these errands, in the city-girl shoes Rivka had found for her. *You can find almost anything if you have to.*

Still waiting on the landing, Esther glanced down at the leather, looking for comfort. Her sister had polished it, just as they'd learnt in childhood days, just as their mother had polished all the shoes their father made. But now Esther had to check behind herself too, checking for watchers in the spare light falling down the stairwell. In the city shadows moving beyond its dusty windows.

In the tram car, a man had looked at her for too long. He'd looked at her ankles first, in their city buckles; then he'd looked at her calves. Esther knew how city men looked at city girls. Rivka had brushed her hair until it gave up its curl, and Esther could see that the man liked it: smooth and red at her nape, at her temples. When she'd pulled the bell cord, he'd raised his eyes to hers, grey and level and glinting; a small and greedy light at each pupil, as though she'd amused him. Or – did he just find her laughable? Did he see right through her? A quarter leather worker's daughter; a quarter printworker's young wife. Esther had been relieved to alight there.

Since her Witek was no longer able, she had made this journey nine times. Taking the tram first, then walking the three streets, two turnings, just as he used to. Month by month, Esther had left the quarter with her bag light, bringing it back with leaflets inside the lining, the dark smell of printers' ink on her fingers. It was a hopeful smell, and frightening – both at the same time – and Esther knew her Witek missed it. Just from the way he squeezed her fingers when she returned, lifting his hands from the sheets to hold hers.

Now Esther knocked at the door again. She listened and waited in the stairwell.

The printer lived on the second floor. *Gorski.* He knew
Witek from before; from when the quarter was only a quarter,
not a ghetto without walls.

'Those Germans. How long before they wall you in, do
you think?'

That's what he'd asked Esther the first time she'd called
here – hoarse, in his hallway, after he'd shut the door behind
her. Gorski's walls were book-lined, disorderly; his jacket
loose across his shoulders; his gaze blunt and lopsided – not
unkind, though.

'You know they've already done that in Warsaw?' he'd
asked.

Esther had nodded.

They'd taken men from the quarter to work there not long
before; she'd seen it happen from her own windows. How the
Germans had come looking for garment workers: that's what
they'd called from their loudhailers: *all you quarter tailors.*
The Germans said they were needed to make uniforms for
Wehrmacht soldiers. But then they'd taken every man they'd
found on the street that day, regardless; all the menfolk from
the tenements opposite her own; they'd hauled and they'd
hounded them into open truck backs.

Esther and Witek were only a few weeks married then, their
small wedding still a happiness inside her. *Mazel Tov!* They'd
broken the glass that sealed their bond, and then for a whole
day and a night, they'd celebrated; all the cousins and friends,
all the neighbours, gathered in her sister's small rooms. Rivka
had opened her arms to all, defiant: *We will still live our lives,
sister mine, under these Germans.* Even Mordechai had been
able to smile that day, Rivka's dear Mordechai, so taken aback
by the new laws, and so cowed too; even he'd raised his glass
to defying German orders.

But then those Germans had come from Warsaw. In one

awful afternoon, they'd rounded up professors and gro-
cers and carpenters; they'd taken almost-grown boys and
grandfathers.

Who is safe here? Esther had lain awake the whole night
afterwards, with Witek lying wakeful beside her; and in the
morning, he'd gone to Gorski. *He will know who can help us;
he will know how to find them.*

The city breezes that blew the sand in from the outskirts,
along the quarter pavements, they came from the reed beds and
the river meadows. And out there, Witek had told her, there
were those who set traps now for the Germans. They punc-
tured jeep tyres, captured foot patrols – they captured soldiers.
When the Germans first came with their fighter planes, with
their Blitzkrieg campaign, a Messerschmitt had crashed in the
reedy waters, and the reed-cutters saw it. Standing up tall from
their stooping labours, they'd followed the smoke plume, and
the white trail of the pilot's chute. They'd gone searching out
the bastard, hacking him loose with their reed knives, pulling
him from the silt where he'd been hiding – and then they'd
paraded him through the villages, his face stiff with fear and
river mud, his wrists tied with reed wire.

What did they do with him afterwards? The story had left
Esther reeling. *What would he have done to us, you mean?*
Witek had taken her palms and held them: this is how they
must think now under the Germans.

He said those reed-cutters had become partisans, had
formed fighting bands, and any city men could join them; they
had only to go out to the hamlets and the hollows. Witek had
still been well then; it had been his aim to be just like them.
He'd said quarter men should fight back, not wait to be taken
to Warsaw. *To whatever the Germans have planned for us.*
This is what Witek warned her. And also: *All of us who live
under the Germans, we should help each other – no?*

'Whatever they do to you Jews, we Poles will be next in line.' This was what Gorski told her, that first time Esther had come to him.

She'd knocked at his door – and knocked again – and waited. And after Gorski had let her inside, he'd stood and regarded her a long moment, sober, between his bookshelves.

'So you're our Witek's bride, then? You're to be our courier, while our Witek is laid up?'

This friend of Witek's from before, it had taken a while for Esther to warm to him. It was the leaflets he handed over, still warm from his presses, that kept her returning. The ink on them dark and bold and furious, they called for recruits among the city men. *Shoulder to shoulder.* They told of successes too. *Twelve jeeps burnt out, five Wehrmacht supply trucks.* Best were the calls of warning, though, to the occupiers. *You are not safe here.* All over Poland, there were fighting bands forming, and it wasn't just the pilot those partisans had taken, or the young soldiers who patrolled the reed beds. They'd raided a munitions store in Białystok! They'd shot a Gruppenführer in Kraków! (Esther had surprised herself, hoping it was with a German rifle.) She brought each new print run home to Witek – carrying risk and triumph inside her handbag lining – then she laid them across the blanket, propping him up on his pillows so he could read. Esther lay beside him to feel the good it did.

She didn't know who did the posting. Witek said this was safest; he said this was how Gorski and his kind arranged it. Each man passed on his leaflets to a second – on his strongest days Witek could still do this – and then, this second man, he took his share and passed the rest to a third, and so on, and so on. And if one man got caught – or even if it happened to two, three, four – they could never give away all the names. *It's a whole network*, he told Esther. And, oh, how hopeful those words made her.

Gorski's ink warnings were posted at tram stops, beside shop windows, on hoardings; there were city men carrying them all across the district and further. Esther had even seen one stuck on a wall in the quarter. It had pulled her up short to find it – so bold on the corner! – just by the ration offices where everyone, *everyone* would pass. She'd thought Witek was the only one who'd tried that – back when he was well still – and each of his notices had been torn down within hours.

What if a German saw? Mordechai had warned him it was madness. *Madness. Don't you see the dangers that might bring down on us?* Esther had even wondered sometimes whether Mordechai was among those who did the tearing. Their own dear Mordechai, denied his craft under the new rules, his good leather worker's palms hanging limp at his sides, his fingers left helpless.

But the notice Esther had found near the ration offices, it was still there when she'd passed the next morning, and the next. And each time she'd come home and told Witek – *yes, today still* – he'd taken both her hands and held them, his eyes brighter than she'd seen in a long time. The quarter was growing bolder.

In Gorski's stairwell, Esther knocked a third time.

She blinked at the door too, in the spare light. Esther tilted her ear to listen for him beyond it.

The boldest act by the quarter men had also been the loudest. The explosion had resounded across the rooftops, rattling the quarter doors and windows. The firebomb – *firebomb? But how?* – throwing its dark plume high into the noon sky.

Word had spread fast of the bravery, of the sheer ingenuity, the rumours running from door to door through the corridors of Witek and Esther's lodgings. Some said the men had been students, or garment apprentices, others that they'd been pharmacists – *or, anyway, they must have found supplies through one.* The old neighbour downstairs had been a pharmacist himself; he'd told Esther – so proud – how the men had unscrewed light-bulbs from empty quarter rooms, they'd filled them with acids – *you can find anything if you have to* – and then they'd thrown them in through the windows of the German city governor's offices. The blaze had lasted hours. Such a triumph! Esther had watched the smoke rising; she'd helped Witek down the stairwell to stand with the old neighbour, all of the others gathering awestruck outside on the pavement.

It was night when the Germans came looking for the culprits.

They tore through the quarter.

Esther was awake and fetching Witek some water when they came to the lodging house. She heard the rush of their footfalls first, on the landing below theirs, and then the neighbour's door pounded. That noise had Esther frozen. All the shouting, it felt so close, so loud, echoing up their stone walls. And when the door was kicked open, it was just below their own floorboards – just below her own bare foot soles.

The neighbour kept crying out for someone to help him, while Esther gripped at the glass she held – not to let it fall, not to let it smash, not to alert the Germans. And she did not know which was worse: the sound of the neighbour crying out for the Germans to stop, or the silence after they shut him up.

They were gone again so suddenly.

In that terrible quiet, Witek had pulled on his shirt, his trousers. Esther had watched him stepping barefoot onto the landing. She'd heard his cautious knock at the neighbour's door, his whisper that got no answer.

Gone.

*

Now, at Gorski's, Esther didn't dare to knock another time.

The stairwell was silent, the street too. Awful. Esther felt it at the back of her neck, in the pit of her gut – the Germans had been here also.

Did you know they might be coming for him? She and Witek lay awake again that night, while Esther cried, tears of fear and of fury. *Do you think it was someone who followed me?* So hard to bear, that thought: the dangers she might have brought on all of them.

They moved not long afterwards.

Witek told her it was best that way; he said Gorski would have said the same – perhaps the neighbour would have also. Best to lie low a while.

They had to stay within the quarter confines, so Rivka had them move in with her – *where else, my sister?* She insisted, bringing her girls to help them: Esther's two young nieces, dark-eyed, red-curled and earnest, chips off the family block. Liba with her twelve years, Tauba with her nine, they carried Witek's bundles, dutiful, while Esther and Rivka walked him along the three streets, two turnings, and up the back stairs.

Mordechai was there to greet them; as dear as always – and as cautious.

He said: 'You are welcome here – of course you are.'

Hadn't he'd kept her and Rivka after their father passed? He'd be keeping all of them now, as best he could, as long as Witek's illness lasted.

'But as long as it stops now,' he told them. 'This errand-running, this posting. This dressing up and walking out of the quarter.'

Mordechai looked at Esther a long moment, and then he told her the German rules were terrible.

'I know they are terrible. But if we follow them – just for long enough – then maybe we can come through this.'

Because hadn't they come through worse before? In times past. Back through time immemorial.

Witek shook his head at that. Still arm in arm with Esther, with Rivka, still breathless from stairs, he asked: 'Should we follow the rules to the ghetto now, to the German factories?'

But Mordechai knew his answer: 'Better a factory than a police cell.'

That was where the neighbour had landed – the old pharmacist – and no one had had word since, or set sight on him.

And Gorski?

Here at Rivka's, they were six, and the baby. She was passed from lap to lap around the table that first evening of their family togetherness, her dark eyes shining in the lamplight, small mouth open, regarding all the family faces regarding her. Rivka smiled at having everyone around her; Mordechai also. The girls smiled most of all, Liba and Tauba, leaning their heads on Esther's shoulders, calling Witek 'uncle', *Feter Witek*, putting their bread on his plate so he could eat more – *you don't eat enough, Mami says so.* Then they showed them upstairs to their new room.

It was under the eaves. That autumn, it filled with the sun in the afternoons.

Below, in the back courtyard, Mordechai's workshop sat locked now, but still stocked with the old tools that used to be Esther's father's. She felt tucked in here, amongst the washing lines and the quarter walls. Esther was grateful that she and Witek could look out along the roof tiles, watching the sun set, the sun rise again from their own attic vantage.

The doctor visited weekly. A thin and harried man; the only one left them in the quarter.

Each time he left again, it was with apologies: he could no longer get them medicines under the German laws, much less send Witek to the mountains to recuperate, to the Baltic shore. But Esther kept the window open, just as he told her, for the air it brought; she traded bread coupons for scarves, to keep Witek warm; and Rivka found the herbs the doctor recommended – *you can find anything if you need to.* She and Esther steeped them in hot water, and brought up bowlfuls for Witek to breathe in the vapours. They allowed him to rest easier; Esther watched him while he slept, grateful that he was able.

Here they spoke, sometimes long into the night.

Rivka gathered them all at table and told stories of family. Of their father's old workshop where he'd carved his lasts and cut his leathers; of their mother's skill with punch-holes and long needles. Rivka described the shoes they'd made, back in her and Esther's girlhood days – buckled and patent, curved and brogued and high-laced – and how city men had come to the quarter to have them made for their wives, and for their daughters. *Our family*, Rivka smiled in the lamplight, *we shod only the best feet. We'll do the same again, just you wait and see.*

If the baby woke, Esther fetched her; she stood on their laps, her small face solemn and watching, her young ears listening and listening.

Mordechai told stories also. But not of here and earlier – only of elsewhere. He spoke of things that Esther had never heard dear Mordechai talk of before now.

His mother's family, out in the Pale: long generations who'd served the tsars. And his cousin on his father's side, who'd left Poland after the first war. *She had her head turned by the Zionists*; by thoughts of pioneering. Only sixteen – *only sixteen!* – and she'd up and gone to Palestine. *Who would have thought?* No one had guessed the girl might leave hearth and home, and everything known to her, to make a new life in the desert. She had to dig wells there, with her own hands, plant almond trees by the hundreds, alongside other young cut-and-runs: girls not much older, from Lublin and St Petersburg, and young men still smooth-chinned, from the Habsburg *schtetl* lands. She'd married one such boy from Brody; they'd had sons and more sons. *A whole new branch of my family tree – so far away – imagine!* Before the Germans came, Esther had never heard Mordechai tell this cousin story. Or never in tones like this – of yearning. Back then, it had been unheard of. *Now, she is safe, though. They all are. In their almond groves.*

Others spoke of elsewhere too.

The doctor, on his next visit, told of his brother in New Jersey. *In America – America! He says maybe he can bring me over.* The way he said the words made Esther sit up. The way he named the places – *New York, New Hampshire.* The way he said *American* and also *citizen.*

She'd never thought to leave the quarter; Esther had never wanted any other life. Still, she found it soothed her now, watching the sun pass across their attic windows, imagining herself elsewhere, whispering to Witek.

'Home is where we are safe, no?'

He said: 'My home is Poland, not some desert. Not some New York, or New Brunswick.'

The Germans issued edicts. More of them, all through the autumn. They demanded metals, for the war effort: buckets and pans and pokers. Soldiers came collecting: each quarter household had to provide at least one.

Then they demanded furs. For the Wehrmacht. For the troops digging in against Stalin.

Furs? Are they serious?
From the quarter?
Who do they think we are?

Esther spread her city coat across Witek's blankets. She set her hopes on a hard frost to halt the soldiers; a harsh steppe turn to the seasons. On ice flowers blooming across her and Witek's attic windows.

When the cold came to the quarter, his skin was already winter-pale, his wrists thin and weak, resting against the sheets. He slept through the daylight hours, in fits and starts. He woke in the evenings and argued with Mordechai.

'We must keep our heads high.'

'We should keep our heads down, you mean. No, no. We cannot make ourselves targets.'

On days Esther could not bear it, she dressed again in her city wear.

She took the shoes that Rivka had found, hiding them inside her coat sleeves, carrying them down the back stairs, across the back court, slipping them on in the lane there, and then walking, walking.

Esther took herself beyond the quarter. Just to be beyond its bounds for a while; just to feel again, how it felt to dare that. She slipped away quietly, carefully: Esther didn't want dear Mordechai worrying. She didn't want him stopping her.

Esther stood at tram stops, passed bakery windows. She looked at the shop displays, and at the people: the city clerks and office girls and shop workers, unconcerned and pressing on past her. She saw how the autumn days passed for them, and kept on passing. Another week, another month, another year turning under these Germans, both ordinary and awful.

Esther looked for Gorski among the faces; his sloping shoulders, his blunt lopsidedness. When she walked the quarter streets, Esther looked for the neighbour, the old pharmacist. The thought of either man so sharp inside, so hard to bear now; however far Esther walked, it didn't help her. Sometimes, that autumn, she thought the only way to find ease would be to cut and run entirely. To press on and onwards, far from here and further, beyond the quarter and the city streets, into the reed and silt. To find herself among the fighters, to take up a reed knife.

She told no one of her thoughts, no one of her walking. Not even Witek.

But when Esther came back one afternoon, she found Rivka in the courtyard.

Her sister was pegging out the washing; it was just the two of them out there among the sheets and shirts. Rivka's fingers raw from scrubbing and rinsing, Esther footsore, heartsore, they came face to face between the long lines, and stood in silence.

But Rivka only nodded. She wasn't angry; she took Esther by both hands.

'How long before they wall us in, do you think?'

How long before they take us?

When the Germans came it was daytime.

Esther was the first to hear them. The scuffle of boot soles by the street door: three, four, five pairs. The coughing and calling of three, four, five soldiers, far down in the stairwell. It was hoarse at first, and under their breath – and then it began in earnest.

'*Raus!*'

'*Appelbefehl!*'

All were to come outside.

'*Alle Juden draussen!*'

All Jews into the street – now!

The soldiers only came to the first floor, but that was far enough. They pounded on the doors there with their coshes, clattering them loudly along the banister railings, while the orders came from outside, from a crackling loudhailer.

Bringt alle Kleidung.

All were to bring clothes.

Schuhe, Stiefel, Mäntel.

Shoes, boots and coats.

The soldiers had brought printed notices. The ink on them fresh and dark, they were thrust through the doors, flung across the first-floor landing, the neighbours passing them hand to hand along the corridors, and then up and up the stairwell.

Wollpullover, Wollhemden.

Each bore a list of items: clothes to be surrendered. Woollen jumpers, woollen shirts.

Warme Jacken und Socken.

'What do they need our socks for?' Esther turned to Rivka, to Mordechai, but neither had an answer. They had come to stand on the landing, Rivka's two girls pressed to her skirts; all the neighbours on the top floor pressed around them.

'Why this now?' the neighbours downstairs called up, their eyes darting, puzzled and fearful, their faces drawn into frown lines. 'Is this for their soldiers? In the winter fighting?'

The soldiers down at the street door, though, they didn't want questions.

Raus!

They only shouted.

Raus hier!

There was no time to speak more.

Raus, wir sagen!

Rivka had to kiss her girls to steady them; she had to call to them to hold hands – *hold hands!* – as she carried the baby ahead of them down the five flights. Even the old had to present themselves. Even the ill. Witek couldn't stand; his legs only buckled, even with Esther there to lean on. Mordechai had to lift him in his blankets, and it was such a shock to Esther – to see how slight he was, how frail in Mordechai's arms, as she hurried behind them, down and down the curved stairs.

Outside, on the cold pavement, already there were crowds of neighbours; already there were piles of clothing – a heap of shoes, a bundle of trousers under the grey sky. More clothes were being dropped from the windows, by neighbours still inside, desperate not to be hauled out; shirt tails flailing and falling through the cold air, boots tumbling, thudding onto the stone flags. But when Esther looked for trucks that might take them – when she looked for more Germans – she found only the same few soldiers from the stairwell.

They pushed the men to the left, the women to the right.

Mordechai was shoved away from them, sent stumbling along the house wall, Witek still clutched in his arms. Esther found herself pressed the other way with Rivka, with the baby, with the two grown-up sisters from the first floor. She couldn't see Rivka's girls, though. Weren't they just here – *just here* – just a moment before? Esther felt her sister turning, searching. *Liba?* She heard her call out. *Tauba!* But the soldiers kept pressing them forward, ordering them into the road, onto the cobbles, out in the open where all the other women were held now.

Some crouched over their children to shield them; most were ducked low and clinging to each other's elbows. Esther looked for Liba's red head, for Tauba's curls among the crouching quarter folk; she saw only the two Germans standing guard over all of them with their coshes raised.

The one who stood nearest held a bottle too. His eyes washed cold and bleary, he took a swig as he began circling, the cobbles loose beneath his boots, his legs loose under him. Rivka turned to appeal to the man.

'Please? My daughters?' She held out a palm, still looking for her girls, but the soldier only kicked a stone at Rivka for asking. Then his toe found another, sending it skittering, painful at Esther's ankles.

'*Sau!*'

Rivka flinched at his shouting; the soldier laughed out loud, then he told them, in Polish: 'We'll bring out your daughters! We'll have all of you – won't we?'

He jabbed his bottle neck at Rivka, and at the baby, her small face creasing with confusion.

'You want some?' The German laughed again.

Esther still couldn't see Liba or Tauba, although she looked and looked into the crowd of women crouching, and into the streams of neighbours still being driven out of the tenements. She couldn't find Witek either, or Mordechai by the house wall. The men were lined up there against the brickwork, too far to call to, and Esther could see only the clothes piles, the last handfuls tumbling from the windows; she could hear only the loudhailer.

'*Ausziehen!*'

What was this order?

'*Aus-zieh-en!*'

It was for the women only. The soldier by Esther shouted the translation: 'Unbutton your coats!' He pointed his bottle at her and Rivka. 'Go on now!'

But what use were women's coats to soldiers?

'Off – now! Take them off!' He kicked at the stones again. 'Let us be certain you are not wearing another underneath.'

Each of his kicks had the women behind Esther shrinking, each of their flinches only making him laugh more. He took a loose step closer.

'Unbutton your dress,' he told Rivka. 'We have to be certain how many dresses you are wearing.'

He took another swig, tucking his bottle inside his tunic. 'And you, girl.'

He turned to Esther, his free hand pointing and reaching.

'You pull up your skirt. Let me see what you have under there.'

She turned her face away so she wouldn't have to look at him: his mouth curled with laughter, his eyes fixed greedily on her skirt hem. Only then Esther saw women in the crowd behind her, and why they were crouching – it was to cover their bare legs, and others' bare shoulders. *No, no. How far would they go with this?* Esther reached for her sister to warn her. But the German was so close now, she could smell the drink he'd just taken: all the drinking he'd done that morning.

'You do as I order!'

She had no time to think more.

The man made a grab, and Esther kicked out – fast.

'No!'

She didn't mean to do that. She only saw his hand come snatching; Esther only wanted him away from her – this drunk and stinking German, his drunk and stinking mockery. But now the soldier lunged back again, and this time with both hands.

He snatched at Esther's hair, yanking her forwards, pulling her out from the crowd, throwing her down onto the stone flags. A shout rose up as she landed – but not from the soldier, not from the loudhailer. Esther was pressed to the cobbles, into the quarter grit beneath her, the soldier's knee on her chest, his fist pressed to her jawbone – but then came that shout again.

'Let go!'

It was a high voice and it came from high above too.

It came from Liba!

Now that Esther was down, she could see her red curls:
the girl was leaning from one of the quarter windows. Her
sister was beside her, Tauba, with her arms outstretched and
reaching. She was holding something in both hands – was it
a glass, was it a vase? Esther tried to turn – what had Tauba
found? She tried reaching and signalling, urgent – *You stay
where you are.* She needed them to stay unharmed. But still
he pressed on her, this German.

His cosh at her chest, she twisted against it. His knee at her
shoulder; all the drunk and stinking weight of him. His fist at
her mouth, Esther bit down – hard and furious.

'*Verdammt!*'

The soldier cried out; Esther felt it. But his curse only
fuelled her fury – her need to see Tauba. Esther tore and she
thrashed at him, with teeth and nails, with knees and elbows,
until the soldier let sudden go of her. His weight gone, her
view clear again but for his looming, Esther turned for the
girls – were they safe still? Esther turned to the women beside
her, cowering and aghast, braced for more blows, or worse
to come now.

The girl let go of the vase. Large and heavy and glass, it
plummeted, sharp – a bright streak cutting down the house
wall. It smashed as it landed: a loud and gritty shattering; a
glitter of shards sent bursting across the pavement.

The quarter rang out with this new noise. It had all the
women lifting their faces. Their shoulders ducked and bare,
but their eyes turning skyward; it had Esther lifted from where
she lay too. The girls were above her, and the soldier was
also – but he was on his knees, on the cobbles, his knuckles
blood-smeared, his face confounded. He turned for his comrade only to find another jar smashed behind him.

'*Was soll das?*'

It wasn't dropped by Tauba, not by Liba. Esther could see

both girls – and that a neighbour had come to the window to join them. The woman's fists were bright with glass, her eyes seeking out targets.

'Leave us!'

The soldier saw her and pointed; his comrade turned and cursed her, both of them with their coshes raised. High above, though, the neighbour sent her fistfuls down on them, letting them shatter and scatter at their boot soles.

Then Esther saw a stone strike.

'*Da!*'

It hit the soldier who had pressed her. He'd just got to his feet when another landed, and then a third – this last one struck his forehead.

'Ha!'

Rivka was beside her; Esther saw it was her sister who'd thrown it – and that she had another stone ready for striking. The German took a step back; his comrade did the same, but Rivka threw anyway.

'Get away from us!'

This shout came from the crowd; a woman's voice, loud. No longer ducked but standing, another woman picked up a quarter stone and hurled it. Esther saw there were more folk at their windows: so many quarter women still upstairs inside their apartments, holding out cups and glasses. Not dropping any longer, they were taking aim and hurling, throwing them at the two Germans, while the women in the road took up stones to strike at them. The soldiers had to bend to shield their faces; they had to raise their voices; still the women struck at German arms and German backs and shoulders, sending them running to the soldiers by the menfolk.

'*Weg hier!*'

Esther got to her feet, thinking those Germans would turn again. Or wouldn't they turn their coshes on the quarter men?

But when the soldiers reached the house wall, she found they were turning to one another only; they were pulling at each other's sleeves, at each other's elbows, as the glass and the stones kept raining down on them. And they weren't issuing orders: their loudhailer discarded, they were just calling and clamouring and cursing.

'Los!'

'Los, ich sage!'

And then – impossible: was this even possible? – the soldiers were at their jeep doors, they were climbing inside. And not just to shield themselves from the stones, or from the glass, because the engine fired and then they were driving; they were turning the tenement corner.

Were they driving away from the quarter?

The whole street fell quiet when they saw this. The stones stopped flying, the jars stopped raining abruptly. All the quarter folk were left hushed on the pavements, listening for the Germans. Breath held, hands reaching to hold one another, they watched for the soldiers to return with reinforcements – because more would come now. Surely?

Esther held Rivka, who held the baby, while they waited. Witek lay pale and wrapped in blankets, as the moments passed and kept on passing. Mordechai was slumped at the house wall with his arms still around him. Liba and Tauba held each other close at the window, holding tight alongside the neighbours, along with all the other quarter folk half naked at the roadside. And still there were no more Germans.

They were cold, the clothes still in piles, the pavements sharp with shards – and still it held them, this terrible, wonderful new silence.

Historical Note

In the autumn of 1942, the town of Lubliniec was the site of an impromptu revolt.

One afternoon, Nazis ordered all the Jews to gather in the market and undress. Men, women, the elderly and children were forced to peel off their clothing, even their underwear, on the pretext that the garments were needed for the German army. Nazis stood over them brandishing whips and sticks. They tore clothes off women's bodies.

Suddenly, a dozen naked Jewish women attacked the officers, scratching them with their nails. Encouraged by non-Jewish bystanders, they bit them with their teeth, picked up stones and hurled them with trembling hands.

The Nazis were shocked. Panicking, they ran away, leaving behind the confiscated clothing.

'Jewish Resistance in Poland: Women Trample Nazi Soldiers' was the headline in the Jewish Telegraphic Agency's report of the incident, filed from Russia and published in New York City.

After that, many Jews from Lubliniec, including the women, decided to join the partisans.

JUDY BATALION, *The Light of Days: Women Fighters of the Jewish Resistance, Their Untold Story*, p. 133.

TYGRESS

CLAIRE KOHDA

It was hard finding a coffin that could fit Mama in it. In the end we went for one that I think was probably intended for a large man. Even in that, though, Mama had to be laid on her back, paws up, her nose and whiskers brushing the wood at the narrowest end of the coffin, her tail coiled up. It would have been nicer to have her the other way up, legs down, chin resting on the coffin floor like she was sleeping, all her markings facing up. I always thought the stripes on her back looked like some sort of script. Maybe it was writing intended for God to read in her death. Instead, perhaps we let the devil, below, read it. What did that mean? I wonder. Maybe the markings on her back spelled her Tiger name, and now the devil knew it, he could call to her. Nevertheless, I loved her white belly and her white chin – and my last vision of her was those parts of her body. Her soft, white stomach, which I had come out of; her little white beard. And the pads of her paws. I held one, and wiped my tears with it. 'Mama.'

'I've never seen a tiger before,' the funeral director said.

Me and my siblings stood around the coffin in a circle. We'd laid lilies around her body, placed her favourite treats in the coffin with her, pressed six coins into her paw between the big black beans that hid her claws. This is the Buddhist way. Mama taught us how to prepare her for crossing the Sumida River. We had placed each of our umbilical cord stumps into her fur, too, nestled in her warm armpits.

No, they were not warm any more. Her armpits were cold.

'Didn't know it was legal,' the funeral director said, 'to keep tigers here.'

'She's legal,' my sister Charlotte said. Mama had worked in a sushi restaurant in Ramsgate, owned by a local Korean family who had checked all of her documentation. Her visa from 1985, stamped on her old passport that was about three decades expired.

Samuel let out a sob – he'd been holding it in. He still looked eight in my eyes. But he was twenty-two, graduated from university, sports science at Warwick, back here to find work while living in the house we'd grown up in. But now Mama was dead. He covered his mouth, apologised and left the room. Dylan went after him, leaving just me, Charlotte, the funeral director and Mama, on her back in her coffin.

'Pets can feel just like family,' the funeral director said into the silence. He was peering with curiosity at Mama's body, at her fur, her stripes, the shapes they made. He glanced up and smiled at me. I searched his eyes for the greedy look some people got when they saw Mama alive, like they wanted to skin her, wear her – but it wasn't there. I suppose people in his profession get used to separating feelings of desire from physical bodies.

Charlotte didn't look at me. She was the second oldest, but she acted like the oldest. She stood by Mama's head, like it was the head of the table. She placed a hand in the coffin to rearrange one of the lilies whose face was turning towards a wall. I watched as she twisted her fingers into awkward shapes to avoid touching Mama's whiskers. I tried not to feel hatred. Charlotte had a weird phobia of leftovers. Once I wiped yogurt from a bowl in the sink on her cheek and she burst into tears, even though she was a teenager, not a child any more. In some countries, she'd already have been married, she'd already have a kid – how would she be managing in those countries if she couldn't even handle a bit of leftover yogurt on her cheek? I was just preparing her for life, I told Mama. She needs to be stronger. I'm just making her stronger. Mama told me I had to be more understanding of my sister. *One day, you'll realise you love her.* In that moment, though, I hated her. Mama was not leftovers. Though her body was still, it was still her body. I wanted to grab her hand and smother it in the fur on Mama's head.

The lily now was turned in towards Mama's cheek, pollen brushing her fur. I didn't want lilies – they're toxic to cats. In Mama's coffin, they looked like a joke. Like a tiger had climbed into a coffin meant for a human and been killed by the flowers. Charlotte carefully pulled her hand out of the coffin and returned it to her pocket.

Mama wasn't always a tiger. When she first came to England, she was a woman. Dylan grew up with Mama as a woman. He'd describe her for us, and we'd listen, completely transfixed. Her small nose didn't rise much from her face, just like it didn't on her tiger face. She was pretty: wide cheekbones, small black eyes, long black hair that was very thick. Dylan was the only one to have suckled from her human breasts. Though her breasts were small, they produced enough milk for him. Somehow, as a tiger, Mama's body made the exact milk we human children needed. That was the miracle of Mama – always, her body adapted to our needs.

I'd kind of hoped that, when Mama died, her body would miraculously transform back into a human body and that I'd finally see her. I didn't look forward to her death by any measure. But, growing up, obsessed with Dylan's descriptions of her – wondering whether my features took after hers, whether my hair was like hers, my eyes, my lips – I imagined that, one day, at some point, I'd get to see her. Death, I imagined, would unburden her of all the ways she was perceived in this country, all the stereotypes, fears, preconceptions; it would all drop away and reveal whatever was inside, the human at the centre of all that fur, muscle and fat. Death I thought would be a kind of meeting; I'd see her, and it would be like a mirror held up in front of me; I'd see myself in her. That's what I hoped, anyway. It's what I dreamed.

'Shall I leave you alone with her for a minute?' the funeral director said.

'Yes, please,' said Charlotte. 'And we're scheduled for two p.m. Is that right?'

'That's correct.'

Charlotte nodded. The funeral director silently made his way across the room to the door. His job must have made him an expert in tiptoeing. The door closed quietly behind him.

Charlotte tucked a loose strand of hair behind her ear, then tutted like she'd forgotten something and, not acknowledging me at all, left the room after the funeral director.

It was just me and Mama now. And I stepped forward, my belly against the side of the coffin. The mouth of the coffin seemed to expand, like gates opening, until Mama's body filled my entire vision, bright yellow still, even in death. Like butter, glistening. And pure white.

I leaned in, my head over her throat and, there, I heard a sound, like a soft purr, rising from Mama's body; and in between the gentle stutters, my name, whispered. Now, looking back, I wonder if what I'd heard was work at the gas storage facility; they'd been taking down the gasholders just down the road from the crematorium that week. Either that, or the purr was the sound of another person being cremated, the furnace lighting, the flames roaring and the body slowly burning. Either way, in that moment, I heard my name. I leaned in closer, until my cheek was brushing Mama's belly fur. I closed my eyes. I imagined opening them and waking up, her amber eyes open too, holding me.

Before school, Mama would wake me up by standing next to my bed and softly calling my name. I went in a little later than my siblings. I have hypermobile joints. For a while doctors thought I had Ehlers-Danlos syndrome, but the conclusion was that I didn't: my condition was just an anomaly. We didn't say it, but we all knew it was probably because I was born from Mama, a tiger. Mama's body, at home when Dylan and I got back from appointments with specialists, was like an elephant in the room. In the mornings, as a teenager, I'd wake up and my hips, sometimes my shoulders and knees, would be dislocated or in subluxation, and I'd have to spend an hour or two returning them to their joints and massaging them until they felt better. I'd lean against Mama's warm body while I popped my shoulders and legs back together. She'd always give me a long kiss on the forehead once I was done – and her whiskers would tickle my eyelids. I knew she blamed herself; I knew she felt sad, though she'd never cry – tigers can't, after all. In her kiss would be all her guilt, a thousand apologies. After, she'd hold me in bed and, sometimes, I would fall asleep, in the padding of her thick fur. On some days, I'd stay like that, and we'd silently agree to forget school for that day, watching TV and eating snacks together instead.

Once I became an adult, this dynamic changed. I'd come home to visit sometimes from London and Mama would have made food for me. I'd eat, reverting back to the child-me at the dinner table. But, later, while we watched TV on the pull-out futon sofa, Mama would fall asleep first, and she'd settle into my arms, her head nestled in my left armpit, her legs limp and heavy on my stomach, her tail twitching as she dreamt.

Sometimes, I'd stroke her nose, and bury my face in her wide forehead, breathe in the scent, which was usually a mix of ginger, sesame and garlic. Sometimes, her head would smell straight up of a bowl of udon with batter and chilli, and I'd feel like I was catching a whiff of her thoughts. Food, so often, was on her mind. In her sleep, she'd lick her lips.

In those moments of her sleeping in my arms, I'd feel I understood, exactly, the kinds of people who treat their pets like family, who love their cats like children. I kissed Mama on the head. The longest kiss in which was all my gratitude for her.

I held her like this the night before she died. We watched *Gilmore Girls*, and she fell asleep as I finished a packet of Doritos I'd opened the day before. Her breathing grew slow, her breath hot, and her eyes closed, facing in towards my torso, paws curled against my side. I tied the empty crisps packet into a knot as Mama had taught me, then sat back and watched the screen. It read, 'play next episode' but I couldn't reach the remote, so I just watched the still image of Lorelai and Rory – then leant in to breathe the perfume of my mama's forehead.

We knew she didn't have much time left. Kidney disease takes many cats' lives, big cats included; the new strict diet she was on prolonged her life, but didn't save it. We knew it was terminal from the beginning – and tiger kidneys for transplant are hard to come by, so there really had never been any hope. 'If she was another animal, maybe. An animal native to England,' the vet had said. I inhaled her scent, and

there was no smell of garlic or ginger or sesame or rice. That
night, instead of food, I smelled incense, as if in her brain, it
was burning, the smoke rising through her skull. It was like
a premonition of her departure; and the next morning, she
had gone.

I opened my eyes and saw white, the white of her fur, tick-
ling my skin, and took a deep breath in. Mama smelled of
something unfamiliar, something chemical that the funeral
home had prepared her body with. I lifted my head out of the
coffin, and from my pocket, I took out a piece of paper on
which I'd printed a picture of the enlightened Tibetan Buddhist
scribe Yeshe Tsogyal, in her tigress form, being ridden by The
Second Buddha, Padmasambhava. Yeshe Tsogyal curves up in
a burning C of orange, mouth and paws bright red. I'd folded
the picture eight ways, so it was no bigger than a coin. I buried
it in Mama's fur, making sure it was covered, along with
another small slip of paper on which I'd written a Japanese
mantra, *Nyo-zé chikushō hotsu Bodai-shin* – 'Even an animal
can aspire towards enlightenment.' I don't know why I did it. I
don't even know if I believe in enlightenment, or in reincarnation, or if I believe in God, or something else. Maybe I saw it
as kind of like a message of encouragement from me to Mama
in whatever afterlife she'd wake up in, to say 'You can do it!'
or something. Or it was a wish. A wish that, if reincarnation
is real, Mama would come back as someone who would be
perceived and treated as a human, not an animal, to break
free of the way she was seen in this life.

Mama read me the story of Yeshe Tsogyal. She read us a
lot of tiger stories. Tigers are well-represented in literature.
Charlotte didn't like that a man rode Yeshe Tsogyal, that her
tigress form was a vehicle for her male teacher: she thought it
was demeaning, and she preferred *Life of Pi*. Samuel's favourite was Tigger, Pooh's bouncy friend. Dylan's was William

Blake's poem, which he'd memorised almost as soon as he
could read. And mine was Yeshe Tsogyal. She was not fiction,
just as Mama was not fiction. For Yeshe Tsogyal, however,
her tigress form had been a symbol of her freedom. It said she
could even escape the confines of her female form. Mama's
tigress, though, was like shackles. We all knew it. We felt it
in the tightness of her skin, in the arch of her back that was
so tense it felt like it could snap; worse, the way she never
fitted in with the other mothers – at tea, her claws clinking the
teacups, her ears brushing the ceiling light; the other mothers
never listening to her advice – *Where you're from, you mother
differently*; the sideways glances at her claws and long teeth,
and the assumption that, in raising us, she used them. Then,
also, how men loved her, the sorts of men who said they loved
Japan, who said they loved the culture and the women; and
when they saw Mama they saw something traditional and
authentic. So enamoured, they didn't think about the fact that
tigers live in China – that something about Mama's Japanese
tiger body was amiss.

Dylan said Mama changed while he was in year two at
primary school. Boys had pulled the corners of their eyes back
and said mean things about Dylan's neatly packed lunch, his
'yellow' skin, and his thick black hair. He was the best at spell-
ing, and the best at maths. He finished all the worksheets first
in the class; his handwriting was the straightest and neatest;
his fingers covered the holes on the recorder perfectly and he
made the sweetest sound. He was summoned to the board
to answer multiplication problems, and he always answered
them correctly; with the teacher's 'Well done' came a groan
from the class. *It's not fair, though. He's Asian.* He'd cover his
face and smell the chalk on his fingers, while he heard words
flying around his head. *My mum says his mum's a tiger mum.
Teacher's pet. Tiger. Tiger.*

Burning, bright, one hot afternoon, end of July, after whispers at the school gate, Dylan's end-of-year report, held up against his chest, as he came running out, bruise on his temple. Straight As for effort and achievement. He thrust his report at Mama, into her outstretched hand, hoping it would give her a thousand paper cuts, and said, 'I hate you,' and marched off home on his own. Behind him, whispers of 'Tiger mum' spilled out from the school gate and followed him; Mama had endured years of name calling, but had never thought those calls would reach her son. Later, at night, under the moon: Mama finished her shift cleaning at the hotel by the sea and, walking home via the beach, as the tide went out, she transformed, falling to her human knees, and rising on four yellow paws – feeling, in her stomach, a bloodlust for her son's bullies.

It's easy to hate people. Maybe when I was five or six, I learned the rhyme that now I see makes no sense. *Sticks and stones may break my bones, but words will never hurt me.* Words, I knew, though, can turn your mother into a tiger. They can reorder the bones inside her skin: they can thicken them, shorten them, widen a skull into a tiger-skull, lengthen teeth and tongue, shrink fingers and thumbs, awaken tiger fire in a belly. Mama once said to me that she wanted to eat the boys in Dylan's class. It was hard for her to resist. But, instead, something else happened. Dylan stopped having Mama walk him to school. At the traffic lights at the end of our road he shouted, 'Stay!' and went the rest of the way on his own. Then, at school each day, in tests, standing at the board, he forced himself to make mistakes – he'd answer nine times nine with eighty; he'd spell necessary 'neccesary', he'd put the *e* before the *i*, shift his fingers slightly off the holes of the recorder, make an awful tooting noise, then turn to the class and, with them, laugh. His grades got worse and worse, until he was average, and another kid was being laughed at for his intelligence, his glasses mocked.

When I heard this story, I had violent thoughts too. I imagined stabbing the boys up, with a kitchen knife, over and over, one after another, for taking my mama's human body away, for making Dylan hide his intelligence. When I said this out loud, Charlotte said I was 'mental'. Dylan said it made sense – I was born from a tiger body: some of Mama's claws and teeth were in me.

For so long, Dylan didn't care about his brain; he punished it. When I was still young and he was a teenager, he'd drift into the house on a cloud of white smoke with two boys whose arms hung down in front of them like they were apes, and they'd disappear into the dark of Dylan's room for hours, then come out with empty, stupid smiles on their faces. Dylan spoke in single-word sentences, moved like a slow, mindless animal, ate and slept. A college dropout – it was impossible that his mum was a tiger mum, when he was a sloth, a slug. He committed to disengaging like it was a spell, like it would turn Mama back into a human, but it didn't.

In the years before Mama's death, Dylan didn't really come home much. He moved in with Sarah, gathered the pieces of his life together, and got his job at an animation studio, making scenery for stop-motion films. I could always tell which scenes he'd made: he was really good at making invisible things, like the wind or heat or cold, look real. People said it was because of his Japanese background, that he had some anime in him, but I think he just worked hard and was observant. He put almost all of his time into his work. Sometimes he even worked over Christmas – the only one in the studio, well into the night. We talked about him like he was a workaholic, but I think we all noticed how he was around Mama when he did come home. We all cuddled her, trimmed her claws, stroked her fur, but Dylan never touched her. I don't think any of us really knew what had happened between them. But for years, before he met Sarah, after he dropped out of college, he was in and out of hospital, and seeing various types of therapists and doctors.

After one Christmas, when an ambulance had come to the house to take Dylan's almost lifeless body from the bathroom floor, where Charlotte had found it sprawled on the tiles beside all of her Aussie shampoo, make-up and her hair straighteners, Charlotte had angrily announced that she couldn't understand him. That *she* was clever, but *she* could deal with it. She didn't care when people called Mama a tiger mum. But I suppose it was harder for Dylan – he'd known Mama before; he'd seen her transform into an animal; he'd lost something that none of us had lost, because none of us had known her before.

I made myself some hot milk on the day Mama died. It was all I could stomach. I microwaved it in a small heatproof glass that had been one of a set of four, but now was a set of three. Mama, compelled by something in her tiger nature, had knocked one of the set off the coffee table one day when she'd been in a mood, watching my face as she did it. I remember I was annoyed with her for purposely breaking one of the glasses. I'd had to sweep up all the pieces, since she couldn't use a dustpan and brush with her paws. As I'd cleared up, I'd felt all my anger with her – for how broken Dylan was, for how we all had to suffer the looks of our friends' parents, who pitied us for having an animal for a mother, the people on the street who spat at her. As I swept, she cleaned her chest, and while she wasn't looking, I placed my hand into the dustpan and pressed down so all the pieces of glass went into my palm. It wasn't even painful. As the blood dripped into the dustpan, I felt like the pain of our family was being released somehow;

it was being processed into a liquid that, in the bathroom, I washed away after plucking the shards of glass from my hand. On the day she died, I felt a different kind of pain as I drank from one of the remaining three glasses. In the space where the fourth was meant to be, all my love for Mama – which now had no living being to be directed at – poured in.

Dylan and Samuel came back into the room, Dylan's hand a comfort on Samuel's back. Samuel leaned down and kissed Mama on the forehead, sniffling. A copy of *Tigger's Little Book of Bounce* went into the coffin, tucked between two lilies. And then Dylan stepped forwards. I averted my gaze instinctively, and so did Samuel. But from the corner of my eye I saw Dylan's figure, still and silent, by the edge of Mama's coffin. Then the figure stooped, lower and lower; and for a moment I thought he'd join her. But he was holding her, arms around her thick torso, and whispering to her, kissing her chin and mouth, which was slightly open. Then I felt it was right that Mama was on her back, that there hadn't been a coffin larger to fit her on her front. He smoothed down her whiskers. Held her jaw in his hands. Then stood back up. I looked at him and he smiled, the whites of his eyes red.

The door swung open and Charlotte entered with the funeral director. 'They're ready,' she said. And, as if we all had been in this situation before, we automatically took our places beside Mama's coffin, crouched down, and placed her weight onto our shoulders. We stood in unison, completely in sync, beautifully coordinated, our mama rising up to the height of our heads, her belly, through the wood, beside my ear. And, led by the funeral director, we went into the furnace room. We placed Mama down on a conveyor belt poised and ready to move, and all of us looked down at her, her white belly, her yellow fur, burning bright in the dim room. As my body shook, I felt my shoulders threaten to fall from their joints, my knees wobble, my hips loosen; and I focused my attention on Mama's thick sides, her black stripes, that I'd leant on so many mornings. Her paws, in the air, held so softly.

'God be in my head, and in my understanding,' said the funeral director, quietly. Charlotte lowered her head in prayer. 'God be in my eyes, and in my looking; God be in my mouth, and in my speaking; God be in my heart, and in my thinking; God be in my end, and at my departing.'

'Amen,' they said in unison.

The funeral director and another man lifted the lid of the coffin and slid it to cover Mama's body. Then a button was pressed on the side of the furnace, and the conveyor belt started to move. It felt so wrong to encase her in wood. It felt better when the coffin went behind the curtain, and was engulfed in fire. Dylan, beside me, was whispering under his breath, 'What the hammer? What the chain,' he said. Fire and Mama went together. Fire and tigers went together. 'In what furnace was thy brain?' In smoke, and light, bodiless, she'd be free.

DRAGON

STELLA DUFFY

The climacteric once belonged to all of us; ageing belonged to every body. In 1821, French physician Gardanne's medical dissertation renamed our change, *la ménopause*. Newly labelled, the genie was out of the bottle and, just like any genie, it was good and bad; pathologising and freeing, it allowed research and revival, dismissal and denial. But in a world that fears ageing? Hates old people? A culture that encourages us to despise and deny our own becoming old? It can come as a slap in the face.

Mine did. Slap in the face, kick in the gut, a rip to my core, wrench of the cunt.

And ...

But ...

The first night bathe. Boiling roiling in the sheets, swimming in my sweat. I was surprise and I was shock, disgusted and distrusting. I was am-not, will not have this, will not be this. Back then I still imagined I had a choice, that I was in charge of the years. I did not know this version of myself. This body, my body, I-body, rebelling, out of control. Screw that. Oh, I had loved control, given my all to it. Exercise and diet, creams and unguents, weights and washing, yoga and boxing, running, jumping, crunching (and, yes, whisper it, starving); stalking an image of me made of billboards and screens and the side-eye glances of those girls at school, you know the ones, maybe you were the ones? Not the ones now, are you? And still my made body was a thing of beauty, a joy of my own creation. I walked this earth, stalked the streets, I was me made flesh incarnate.

How dare it? It-body, other-body, this body, mine not me – how dare she?

And yet, body reared up despite my valiant efforts, time stepped in to remind me who I am, what I am, that I am past-passing; flesh, bone, sinew will turn to dirt, rust to dust.

I know now it was shame as much as fury. Growing through the tantrumming child, petulant teen, frightened twenties, blossoming thirties, fulfilled forties, I had me under control.

No more.

The night sweats trained me in the truth of otherwise. They showed me, other and wise to myself. All my life I had been schooled in holding it in, the flow of me, stopping me up. I did not spit, spill, dribble, leak. Periods were hidden, discreet, divorced from me. Even in the worst of the red riptide, when blood came as chunks, even in that dragging pain, I had understood it was my duty to hide it all. A badge of bloody honour.

And so, I had not known me wet, damp, dripping, seeping. I had not known my liquid self.

I stared at her in the mirror, disarrayed, distorted.

Three a.m., four a.m., rising from sodden bed, I glared at the sea witch who greeted me in the mirror. She smiled back.

It was a smile of terror.

And beneath, the beginning, a tremorous inkling of relief. I watched the sea witch in the mirror lift her arm to her mouth.

We licked me. I was salt self, sea self, waving and drowning. I drank me in.

That night, that early morning, the sea witch gave me my first glistening, green, golden scale. It was iridescent and uncertain, and it fitted perfectly.

After the flood, the fire. I was simply reaching for a loaf of bread. The man behind reached over me and took it for himself. I am not small, but he was bigger. I felt sudden heat arise, from a point deep in my chest up to my face, then unexpectedly and rapidly out into my back, my shoulders, my arms, right down my spine. My fingers were hot claws. I turned and grabbed the loaf from him, barked out my ownership, slammed my card against the machine and fled. I left that shop shaking. Decades of swallowing my rage and now here it was, spitting out of me unbidden – and thrilling.

Once I said yes to the fierce heat, once I gave it breath, it grew to an inferno. It ripped away my armour, painful protections that had been in place so long they came away in bloody, fleshy gobbets. The fire opened my wounds, cleaned them, cleared the ground.

Here is my body-shame. Here the gaze of others, judging. There the gaze of men, nudging. Here is fourteen and self-hate, there is twenty-two and lust you cannot sate. On my back, the scars of broken friendship. At my wrists the ties that bound me to mother-loss, fatherless. My ankles weighted with all those words I wished I had said. Ovaries and uterus ground down by the children I bore and those I did not. Knees bent out of shape by trying too hard, elbows bruised from excusing you, neck bowed by the weight of all my disappointment in myself.

And here, too, is a night by the ocean, you in my arms. There the reach of our baby's fingers, grabbing, gloriously needing. This tattoo that stretches from shoulder to shoulder is my desire, rising, flying, soaring in achievement. This precious line rising along my thigh, the caress of every lover yearned and deliciously returned.

I am all of me.

Each scale that forms my wings is a tale of loss, degradation, despair, perfectly weighted against matching stories of joy, bliss, ease.

In the fire I forged myself and I took flight.

I call at night.

Her name is Maud. She has spent her life omitting an unnecessary *e*. It turns out she spent her life much faster than she expected. She is tired when we meet. In truth, I am tired of the tired. I was tired myself, wrung out, exhausted from years of re-forming me to fit the expected pattern.

Maud is not tired in the way that I was, but she is drained, her blue eyes bloodshot, her freckles illuminating skin that is pale, dull grey. She is twenty-seven and her disease has aged her. She leapt from fertile youth to crone in less than a minute; it took just one injection – one that will be repeated at three-monthly intervals for years to come. If she has years to come. If she has years. The needle itself is fat; the liquid injected is thick. This is no small prick, sharp scratch, it is a jabbing stabbing attack and it is, she hopes, keeping her alive. Maud so wants to stay alive. Before the treatment, she did not understand that the cost of staying alive could be years added in a moment. All Maud wanted was time, sweet time, more time, any time. She understands now.

Maud is dizzy with exhaustion, worried that the disease has gone to her brain, that the enormous price paid will not suffice. She leans into her lover's arms in the evening and her lover does their best to make it better, even as they do not believe a better is possible, even as they fear this might be all they are allowed. The lover's best cannot outstay sleep, and when Maud awakes, she is alone. However close her lover's breath, their touch, their heat, she is deeply alone.

Maud wakes in the hours before dawn every morning. Not for her a shock of sweat, she is awakened by rising anxiety, the unnamed dread that arrives as paralysis, clutching her chest, assuring her that mortality awaits. It is this assurance that persuades me to attend Maud. I have no idea if her death is close or not: I am not clairvoyant and Death does not confide in the likes of me, but it is painful to feel her pulling back from life for fear of breathing it in too soon, breathing it out too soon, and so I pay a visit. I am not a nursemaid: I do not expect to soothe or soften.

Maud lifts herself carefully from her bed, her only intention to leave her dreaming lover undisturbed. Maud does not want their care, their sympathy. She can just about bear their fear-laden love in the day; at night the loss is too deeply entwined and her guilt at the leaving, imminent or eventual, but nevertheless certain, is too great.

I find her in their garden. It is less than a courtyard really, a narrow, paved wedge at the back of a long and low block of flats, where Maud has grown a garden of pots and hanging baskets. Window boxes arrayed on ledges climb the back wall, a trellis interwoven with young wisteria and grape vines, sunflowers hopeful of growing tall enough to catch the light.

'You're crying,' I begin.

I find it is useful to start with the obvious.

'I'm always crying now. It's just that the tears don't always come out.'

'They are tonight,' I respond, and nod to the salty pool

by her feet. 'You'll attract snails. They'll drink your tears and die.'

'Good.' She smiles. 'Let them. They eat my courgette flowers. Bastards.'

'You're fond of your garden.'

It is a statement not a question, but she answers as if I had asked.

'All old women are fond of their gardens, so, yes, now that I am so old, I am fond of my garden. I expect I'll develop a taste for lace collars soon.'

I raise an eyebrow at the cliché, but I do not interrupt. Maud still believes that ageing detaches us from taste. She'll learn. If she doesn't die first.

'I am planting things that fruit and die in a season, and I am planting them alongside things that will grow long after me.'

'How old are you?' I ask, knowing her years and wondering about her answer.

'I am as old as my disease,' she says. 'I am as old as the treatment for my disease,' she says. 'I am ancient.' She sighs.

I tease, 'I thought you were twenty-eight?'

Her frown comes before she can stop it. It doesn't matter now, her age, and yet of course it does. It must. 'Not until September.' She looks up at me, almost hurt. 'It's going fast enough, don't make it worse.'

'How can I possibly make it worse? You are twenty-seven and deeply aged, your bones aching, your brain muddy, your heart racing in fear of your imminent death, your womb empty now and for ever.'

She nods despite herself. 'Had to add that one, didn't you? Your bedside manner is almost as good as my oncologist's.'

'Almost?'

Maud nods, and she is leaving her car in the car park, waiting in the hospital corridor; now she is back in the small room, a box of tissues strategically placed on the oncologist's desk. Not placed quite well enough to hide the photograph of the oncologist's three happy, healthy children.

'I followed her down the corridor into her office. I tried to read from the set of her shoulders what she would say. She started by asking how I was, and I couldn't answer. She knew how I was and I didn't, why couldn't she just tell me?'

'Maybe it's difficult to tell someone that their life has just skipped fifty years.'

Maud shrugs. 'I suppose. She managed it eventually.'

I pause. The silence between us billows, and when it is at its fullest, I ask, 'How are you managing, Maud?'

Maud's fury, when it comes, is muted, gentle, a soft despair that she, scared to rage, insistently drowns with careful logic and good sense. Why-me vies with why-not-me for quite some time, shutting up only when it is replaced with I know they're doing their best and of course it's totally random, and I have had a great life even though I'm young, and the medicine might yet work, it might yet cure, this percentage and that, and, and, and – right up to the exhaustion of reason.

I wait, ever still, until – in a phrase that is part-wail, part-whine, curdled with shame and finally, hot with anger, she stutters out, 'It's ... not ... fair.'

That's my girl. Here we go.

Because it's not fair, is it? It's never fair. It has never been fair, any of it, and our reasonableness cannot undo the unfair. All it does it smother it, cover the lacerations we hide because the world cannot stand our anguish, likes us so much better when we're good, quiet, doing our best.

Fuck that.

Dig it out, Maud. Open the wound, unleash the seeping grief.

She did. In the garden that she would never see grow to

fruition, Maud railed and ranted and fumed and allowed. Aloud.

I did not make it better: better is neither within my power nor my desire. Perhaps I made it more possible, the roar she finally let go. A scale fell from me as I left. Maybe it fell in the garden; maybe it will grow. Only Maud will know.

When Maud returned to her bed she dreamed gently. A shimmering green-gold light behind her eyes, a softening in letting loss be.

In Beyene and Martin's 2001 study on menopausal Mayan women from Yucatán, Mexico, none of the women reported any history of menopausal symptoms. The bones of men and boys showed fractures; those of the older women did not. Research showed that while the bone density of the Yucatán Mayan women is the same in older age as it is in North American women, they are equally osteoporotic, the Mayan women have no fractures. Maybe it is a calcium-rich diet throughout life; maybe it is constant exercise hauling water for miles well into their seventies; either way, their bones were not fractured. In Stewart's 2003 study, Mayan women felt that irritability, anger and light-headedness was their animal spirit rising, becoming exposed. The studies of Mayan women show that they rejoice at the end of periods and freedom from the burden of fertility, the greater possibilities of involvement in society, beyond the taboos of menstruation.

'The end of periods was it, for me. That's when I knew for sure.'

Sam and I are sitting in the children's playground near the home he shares with his wife of thirty years. Their toddler grandson plays with the neighbours' two daughters, 'Lovely young couple,' Sam says. 'Not sure what to make of us, I think, but perfectly kind, and once we offered to take theirs to play with ours when we were babysitting – well, you don't look a gift horse in the mouth, do you?'

Menopause was Sam's gift horse. He had always known he felt differently from his friends, right from primary school, but then plenty of children feel different, are different. At sixteen, when he came out as lesbian, queer, gay girl, it made sense. For a long time, it was right for him, for them. When he and Anila fell in love everything seemed to fit into place.

'We were in that first wave of young queer women having babies, not in straight relationships, but with each other, working it out, if we would both try to get pregnant, if not. I was never at ease with my body in the way that Anila was, and she was a couple of years younger than me, so it was simpler all round for her to carry, me to be alongside. I was envious sometimes, of her belly, and when she was breastfeeding too. I wondered if maybe I was missing out, but I don't feel that now. We made the right choices for us, for who we were then.'

I wait. I am skilled at waiting. So is Sam.

'I knew. Maybe I always knew, on some level, a body level, but I wasn't listening, not at first. We were really happy and for quite a while it was all OK, right? I mean, no one has it all sorted, all the time.'

'So the transition?'

Sam laughs, nods his head, 'All three transitions, one after the other. I was menopausal first of the two of us, and I had it hard, you know? Night sweats and hot flushes, anxiety, upset, raging at the world, at me, at Anila. Our two were off by then, our son travelling in South America, our daughter to university. Physics and pure maths. Well beyond me.'

Sam stops for a moment to call one of the neighbours' children over, whispers something about an ice cream soon and will she let his grandson have a go on the slide, hold his hand? The big sister nods solemnly at the welcome responsibility and he watches as the children rearrange their roles.

'Go on?'

'Yeah, I'm pretty sure I was bloody awful to live with. Because it wasn't just menopause, you know? I couldn't ignore it any more, and periods stopping, that cycle ending ... it just brought everything up. We talked a lot. Talked so much and, also, we didn't talk. A lot of what we did was just hold each other. I'm still me, of course I am, but I'm different too. I wanted to be different.' There are tears in his eyes as he continues, 'I feel for the young ones. No one gave me a hard time, no one medical at least. They figured I was old enough to know my own mind, my body, my self. They were right. But I knew decades ago, too. I just didn't ... *know*.' He holds his belly, his core, his heart. Both hands on his centre. 'Anila knew too. Somehow, she knew. Her menopause was gentler than mine, or maybe it was gentler in comparison to what else we had going on. Anyway,' he laughs, 'I'm the one taking hormones now.'

He starts to gather the children's things, sweatshirts, a pair of socks thrown off, a hat refused. 'I should get this lot off for an ice cream before the rows start.' He looks down at the pile he is holding. 'We made it work, Anila and me. We chose to, and we did. But maybe you should talk to her. It was different for her.'

He goes off with the children, any other grandfather, any other Saturday morning.

I do talk to Anila and at first she is a little sharp, tired of defending her husband, tired of explaining their life. When she realises I am not there to damn but to hear more, she relaxes, allows the tough with the good. Just as I am about to leave, she reaches out a hand – I notice an old tattoo on her wrist as she does, part-hidden beneath her sleeve. A bird of some sort, I think, wide-winged.

'There is one thing. I don't tell many people because, honestly, it really is fine. I mean, we've both changed so much in all this time, I'm sure we'll change more, but he's still my Sam. We've been good at growing together.'

'The one thing?'

She grins, lopsided, slightly shame-faced. 'I used to be cool. I was that tattooed Asian lesbian with a white woman lover. Now I have a husband, I'm just Nani. I'm any other nana. No one looks at me and thinks I'm cool any more.'

I look at her. 'Oh, I do.'

I leave a scale on the doorstep. One of the children will find it later that day. Nani Anila tells a story about the dragon lady.

'Like the dragon on your arm, Nani?'

'Just like.'

In 1966, Robert A. Wilson, MD, published *Feminine Forever*, boldly stating that no woman can escape the horrific living decay of the castration that is menopause, reminding us it was not only a choice but our duty to our husbands and families to do our best to stay feminine for ever. And he had just the medicine to help us do it.

I have loved many drugs in my life. Opioids, narcotics, cannabinoids, hallucinogens, SSRIs, hormone therapies, they have all been snorted, smoked, swallowed. The painkilling ones, the cheering-up ones, the symptom-banishing ones, the symptom-enhancing ones, each has had their place. I judge no taker of drugs, patcher of patches, smoother of gels: I have welcomed them all myself. But do I judge a man who decides what feminine means and that his version of femininity should last for ever? Do I judge a culture that tells us vaginal atrophy is when a vagina no longer comfortably holds an erect penis, decides the measure of the vagina is a penis? Do I judge a society that fears ageing and despises the old? Oh, yes. I judge that harshly indeed.

Next. A field. Or perhaps a plain. I have been gliding, senses open, nothing sharp, taking it in as it comes. Now I choose to pay attention. I shift gaze, refocus. Yes, a plain. It is wide and runs deep across the earth. Maybe it was once a field, standing out from other fields all around, each one collated and demarcated by hand and plough. From up here, I think perhaps I can see the faint lines where once there were furrows, six years of crops and a fallow year to rest. Now it is a plain, wide, open, dry. Neither fertile nor resting. And yet it is not quite dead. Coming closer I see tiny pockets of greenery, flat scrubby bushes, squatting close to the hot earth, ancient scaly lizards basking in partial shade, parched shade. If I don't find the place, I will have to turn back soon, I have noticed that the sun at this latitude is unrelenting until the moment it sets, fast, gone. There is no twilight in this area, no dusk. Light, then night. I spin in a slow arc just once more, a little lower, then I see it. A small house, at the edge of the plain, tucked into a dip, easily missed. Or well hidden.

'I built this place myself. Started on it in my late forties. I knew it was coming, the time I would want to lift myself out of what I had known, find my own.'

I look around the room made of mud bricks, dried in the hard sun, laid alternating and snug. A low ceiling, one wide window east, one west, a deep fireplace in the north wall, her bed against the south. Outside, on the sheltered side of her home, the dip in the land and the house itself blocking the worst of the wind, there is a sizeable kitchen garden. I see ruffled corn stalks, green beans climbing a wire frame,

tomato plants bowed down with deep reds and startling
orange. Her yard has no fence, no barrier to delineate it
from the plain, but a wood pile stacked between, ten logs
deep and fifteen high, forms another barrier against the
interminable horizon; a chicken coop and a lean-to outhouse
complete her dwelling. There is one track that leads north-
west, to a river not quite a mile away. In the first decade
she walked that track twice a day. Once, in the height of
summer, she dared herself to leave when the sun was at its
peak and her body's hunger for the flow more pressing than
her good sense. Stretched out on the shallow riverbed, she
fanned her arms and legs, gave herself up to the sun and the
narrow stretch of cool, wet earth fed by the far mountains.
That night and for two days following she was punished for
her midday audacity with a sun-stroke migraine. When she
emerged from the pain, she knew her foolishness and felt as
chastened as a silly girl. Even so, she was glad to have given
herself to water, one last time.

Heading away from the river, past her house, there was once
a path that took a long, straight route to the main road. She
has not walked that path for years and nor has anyone else.

'When I first came out here, I had visitors. My granddaugh-
ter, her son, a young cousin, an old friend, one or two lovers,
wondering if maybe, if still. I was not rude but nor was I
encouraging. Eventually they understood that while they were
not unwelcome, I did not need them. I learned this as they did.
I had never before known that I needed only myself. It was a
good lesson.'

She is bent over with arthritis, her left eye a milky cataract,
her white hair pulled back. As she speaks, she twists yarn
between gnarled fingers, over and around a crochet hook, the
blanket she is growing resting on her knees

'I don't miss much, maybe the ocean. I haven't seen the

sea in a long time. My people, long back, perfected the art of missing and surviving.'

My nod is a question.

She continues, 'My grandfather's people were slaves. We had both pride and deep pain in that knowledge, their fortitude, their capacity to survive. We wore it as a badge of reclaimed honour. Much later my daughter, an incessant digger, found that my great-grandmother's people were slave-owners.'

'That must have been a hard accommodation?'

She stares at me through her good eye, but it is the gaze of the clouded eye I feel, looking through me. 'No harder than growing up Black round here. Round most places, I expect.'

'Yes.'

'It was all, always, an accommodation. I grew as tired of that as anything else. I wanted to live alone, free of the gaze of others, determining me from outside.'

'Tell me more?'

And she does. Her burgeoning womanhood, the glorious body, a physical shape that enthralled and terrified her, attracting and enticing men and women and those in the many betweens: she revelled in her body, revealed it to herself and sometimes to them.

'I loved the curves of me, the way flesh took shape around my spirit. I welcomed that first change, at twelve, thirteen. Greeted the blood and the pain and the rage and the hard dark as a lost friend I had not known I was missing. Then the second change, my pregnancies, my babies, my miscarriages, the flesh that came of mine, living and dead. That change too, astonished me, fed me, bled me dry, and replenished me as each one weaned. I adored mothering. Even with the pain and the constant losses and the ever-present fear every minute of the day and worse at night, even so I loved it, flourished in it. Then they became adults and their ageing signalled mine. Mother turned to other and the third change. The end of bleeding, the start of old. I fought it, briefly. Held on to my middle stage with hair dye and potions, exercise and determination, and then, one late afternoon, I watched the sky commence a glorious sunset and I understood. I was now twilight, dusk. I was becoming night. And I have always loved the night. I embraced the cloak of invisibility that age grants us, wrapped it round me like a charm. When I left, no one saw me go.'

Her hands come to rest. The kettle has boiled. The pie that was cooling on the side is cut: we eat half each, no dainty slices for us, no saving for tomorrow. Tonight is all there is. We feed, we drink, we kiss, we stretch around each other, our old bodies, our crêpe-soft skin.

After we have made love, after the rolling and reaching, the holding, the sleeping, I shift myself out from under her. She wakes, notices my leaving, grunts a farewell and falls back into welcome rest. I place a log on the fire to keep her warm in the dark morning; I shrug off and settle a scale against the east window. When the sun rises, she will wake in sea green.

Leaving, I log what I have learned in the ledger of my gut – I could use my heart, but it sometimes skips a beat. I find my gut is a truer guide.

It is all, always, learning.

Hoga et al.'s 2015 study of menopause across North and South America, Europe, South East Asia, Oceania, and the Middle East showed that menopause is a transition associated with midlife and ageing, in which we experience emotional and physical changes. It looked at global studies in four different languages and found that resilience improves in the transition, which is profoundly affected by social and cultural expectations, by family and personal needs. It is complex and it is individual.

Each of us changes, differently, always. From conception forward we are mutating, growing, developing, dying.

Dragons shed our skin.

This is how I shed mine.

I was the one of whom they said, 'Here comes trouble,' as if it might have been a compliment. They were wrong. I was never a rule breaker. I was not intentionally naughty or misbehaved, rude or impolite. I did not wish to transgress, that was never my choice. And yet it seemed I was transgressive. By the sheer chance of my shape, my size, my look, my drive, I was too loud, too big, too much. Always too alive. I irritated them with my questions, I drove them wild with my uncertainties, my wanting to know why and how and who said and why should I? None of it was intended to annoy, yet annoy it did. They beat me, sent me off, tried every way to hush me, yet even in the enforced silence my questions grew. I did not mean to be other than a good girl, but in trying to be good, trying to be true, I was not able to be what they believed a girl was meant to be. And time passed and my girlhood slipped into woman-ing, and there again I was wrong. It was my fault when men desired me; it was my fault that they must offend; it was my fault I was too desirable.

I was thirteen. And yet somehow it was my fault.

And yet again, as a grown woman. However hard I tried to be good, I could not marry their good to my true. Eventually the trying wore me out. I came to the end of my tether and then I was tethered no more. When I opened my mouth, my voice won out. Rang out. And the truth was good.

It did not undo the hurt, but I no longer sought goodness and a culture that preferred good to true.

I weighed up the hurt against the scales of me, and piece by piece, loss by loss, I let them all go. I grew a new skin of green-gold scales that shift and shimmer as I move; they are easy on my body; they do not burden me. I am light. I illuminate. Tell me your tale and, in the telling, feel it all drop away. You are, and you are not, your story. Keep what serves you now, make space for new maybes.

The moon did not leave me, it dictates my rise and fall still, waning to rest, waxing for flight. I might visit and offer you the ride of your life. Listen out for my call: I am unlikely to reach for you more than once.

Feel for the green-gold. Catch it in you, make it yours.

Yes. There it is. There you go.

ABOUT THE AUTHORS

Margaret Atwood is the author of more than fifty books of fiction, poetry, and critical essays. Her novels include *Cat's Eye*, *The Robber Bride*, *Alias Grace*, *The Blind Assassin*, and the *Maddaddam* trilogy. Her 1985 classic, *The Handmaid's Tale*, was followed in 2019 by a sequel, *The Testaments*, which was a global number one bestseller and won the Booker Prize. Her latest work is a collection of short stories, *Old Babes in the Wood*. Atwood has won numerous awards, including the Arthur C. Clarke Award for Imagination in Service to Society, the Franz Kafka Prize, the Peace Prize of the German Book Trade and the PEN USA Lifetime Achievement Award. In 2019 she was made a member of the Order of the Companions of Honour for services to literature.

Susie Boyt, FRSL, is the author of seven acclaimed novels as well as the much-loved memoir *My Judy Garland Life*, which was serialised on Radio 4, shortlisted for the PEN Ackerley Prize and staged at Nottingham Playhouse. She writes columns and reviews for a wide range of publications and recently edited and introduced *The Turn of the Screw and Other Ghost Stories* by Henry James for Penguin Classics. In 2022 a play she co-wrote about T. S. Eliot and the music-hall artiste Marie Lloyd was staged at Wilton's Music Hall in London. Susie is also a director at the Hampstead Theatre. Her latest novel, *Loved and Missed*, was called 'a gentle masterpiece' in the *Observer* Books of the Year.

Eleanor Crewes is an illustrator and author of *The Times I Knew I Was Gay*, *Lilla the Accidental Witch* and *Ghosts in My House*. Her books have grown from zines and hand-stitched comics to internationally published graphic memoirs, MG fantasy and adult horror. She lives in North London with her partner.

Born in Dublin in 1969, Emma Donoghue is an award-winning writer living in Canada. Her latest novel, *Haven*, is about the monks who landed on Skellig Michael in the seventh century. She was nominated for an Academy Award for her adaptation of her Booker-shortlisted international bestseller *Room*, and recently co-wrote the Netflix film of her novel *The Wonder*. Some of her other books are *The Pull of the Stars*, *Akin*, *Frog Music*, *The Sealed Letter*, *Life Mask* and *Slammerkin*, and *The Lotterys* for young readers.

Stella Duffy is an award-winning writer of seventeen novels, more than seventy short stories and fourteen plays. In 2016 she received the OBE for services to the arts. Stella is also a psychotherapist working in private practice and for a low-cost community mental health service. She is currently completing her doctorate in existential psychotherapy, researching the embodied experience of postmenopause.

Her website is www.stelladuffy.blog

Linda Grant is author of four non-fiction books and nine novels. She won the Orange Prize for Fiction in 2000. *The Clothes on Their Backs* was shortlisted for the Man Booker Prize in 2008 and went on to win the South Bank Show Award. Her latest novel, *The Story of the Forest*, will be published in 2023. She is a Fellow of the Royal Society of Literature and holds honorary doctorates from the University of York and Liverpool John Moores University.

Annie Hodson is a queer writer and playwright from York, currently living in London. Her plays have been longlisted for the Bruntwood Prize, the Papatango Prize and the Theatre503 Award, and she currently has one in development with production company The Engine Room. She was previously selected for the Penguin WriteNow event and was part of the London Library Emerging Writers Programme cohort 2022–23. She is currently working on her first novel.

Claire Kohda's debut novel, *Woman, Eating*, was a book of the year for *Harper's Bazaar*, *The New Yorker*, *Glamour*, *HuffPost* and the BBC. She contributed an essay to the *East Side Voices* anthology, and her writing has also appeared in the *Guardian*, *TLS*, *FT* and *New York Times*. She is a violinist and has played with artists including Sigur Rós, The National and Max Richter, and on film soundtracks such as *The Two Popes* and *The Matrix Resurrections*.

CN Lester is a multi-genre musician, author of the critically acclaimed *Trans Like Me*, and founder and artistic director of the arts event *Transpose*. CN is a singer-songwriter, classical singer, deviser and composer. They hold an interdisciplinary performance/research PhD on composer Barbara Strozzi; academic research interests include performance and composition, gender and music, and the history of gender and sexuality. They work internationally as a trans/queer/feminist educator, writer, speaker and activist.

Kirsty Logan is a professional daydreamer and the author of novels, story collections, chapbooks, audio fiction, memoir and collaborative work with musicians and illustrators. 'Wench' is based on characters from her third novel, *Now She is Witch* (Harvill Secker, 2023). Her work has been optioned for TV, adapted for stage, broadcast on radio, exhibited in galleries and distributed from a vintage Wurlitzer cigarette machine. She lives in Glasgow with her wife, baby and rescue dog.

Caroline O'Donoghue is an author, podcaster and screenwriter. She has published two adult novels, *Promising Young Women* and *Scenes of a Graphic Nature*, and *The Rachel Incident* will be published in summer 2023. Her YA series *All Our Hidden Gifts* is a *New York Times* bestseller, and is published with Walker. Her podcast, *Sentimental Garbage*, covers 'the culture we love that society can sometimes make us feel ashamed of' and can be listened to anywhere.

Chibundu Onuzo is the author of three novels: *The Spider King's Daughter*, *Welcome to Lagos* and *Sankofa*, which was a Reese Witherspoon Book Club pick in 2021. In 2018 Chibundu was elected a Fellow of the Royal Society of Literature, as part of its 40 Under 40 initiative. Find her on Instagram @Chibundu.Onuzo.

Helen Oyeyemi is the author of ten books, including *Mr. Fox*, which won a 2012 Hurston/Wright Legacy Award. She was elected a fellow of the Royal Society of Literature in 2013, and was named one of *Granta*'s Best Young British Novelists the same year.

Rachel Seiffert has published four novels, *A Boy in Winter*, *The Dark Room*, *Afterwards* and *The Walk Home*, and one collection of short stories, *Field Study*. Her novels have been shortlisted for the Booker Prize and the Dublin/IMPAC Award, and longlisted three times for the Women's Prize for Fiction, most recently in 2018. If she isn't writing, then she's knitting, and if she has nothing to write or knit, then there will be trouble.

Kamila Shamsie is the author of eight novels including *Home Fire*, which won the Women's Prize for Fiction and was longlisted for the Man Booker Prize, *Burnt Shadows*, *A God in Every Stone* and *Best of Friends*. Her novels have been translated into more than thirty languages. She grew up in Karachi, and now lives in London.

Ali Smith was born in Inverness, and now lives in Cambridge. She has been shortlisted for the Man Booker Prize four times and twice for the Baileys Prize, which she won in 2015, for *How to be both*. That novel also won the Goldsmiths Prize and the Costa Novel Award. In 2022, she was awarded the Austrian State Prize for European Literature.

Sandi Toksvig was born in Denmark, brought up in Africa, then America and moved to the UK when she was fourteen. She has been on British stage, screen and radio for over forty years and was awarded an OBE for services to broadcasting. She is the mother of three children, married and lives deep in the woods.